Digging a Hole in the Sun

Digging a Hole in the Sun

Edward Staples

Writers Club Press
San Jose New York Lincoln Shanghai

Digging a Hole in the Sun

Writers Club Press
an imprint of iUniverse.com, Inc.

For information address:
iUniverse.com, Inc.
5220 S 16th, Ste. 200
Lincoln, NE 68512
www.iuniverse.com

ISBN: 0-595-16940-6

Printed in the United States of America

For Laura and John—did I ever thank you for saving my life?
And for Mom and Dad—nice work!

"May I live on until
I long for this time
In which I am so unhappy
And remember it fondly"

—Fujiwara No Kiyosuke

PART ONE

CHAPTER 1

The ferry even had a disco built into one of the decks, and after Forest and Kara went to bed the rest of us went there for a few drinks. I hardly knew the other students, so I felt brave enough to get up onto the floor and move around; I wouldn't really call what I do, "dancing." It was dim and crowded in the disco area, and the music was bad, and most of the other dancers were teenagers running amok while their parents were back at their cabins. Sometimes between songs we could feel the ferry rocking. Underneath the dance floor, under the bottom of the ship was the water, which went down and down like a dark nightmare. We were dancing on the surface of the ocean.

I got bored of tripping over the empty Heineken bottles that the pubescent Europeans dropped on the dance floor, so I joined the group at the table. Monique wasn't tired yet either, but the others were ready to find places to sleep. I knew two of the Americans from the campus gym, and I had pegged them as gay. They were pairing off with two of the girls from the university, so I had to reevaluate.

"Want to go for a walk on the deck?" Monique proposed.

"I'm game. It's going to be cold out there. Don't you want your jacket?"

"I won't need it. What about you?"

"I laugh at the cold. The cold will fear my might." I had on jeans and a tee shirt, and I didn't want to cover up, so that I could show off my muscles. Monique's feet were bare.

You would think that a wealthy girl from California with a pretty face and an exotic name would be a snob, but Monique was down to earth. At the bar after dinner our group had been playing truth or dare, and she always took the dare. Brad, one of the apparent heterosexuals from the gym, dared her to ask one of the crewmen, "How much is your room for the night?" and she did so without hesitation.

"Is that the best you can do?" she taunted when she returned. "Try me."

"I think that *sailor* wants to try you," I answered, and got a group laugh.

It was colder out on the deck than we had thought. We gravitated to the railing at the fore. When we leaned against it I touched shoulders with her, and I could smell her hair. She smelled clean, shampoo instead of perfume, and I could also smell the good salt wind from the ocean, and there was a little bit of the moon which Monique's bright face was turned up towards. We each threw a strange Dutch Gilder into the water for wishes.

"It's a beautiful night." The words eddied from her mouth between her perfect teeth. I told her my idea about dancing on the ocean, and then we were quiet for a while. It was about midnight, and we would dock in Rotterdam at half-five, Continent time. There was one other person on the deck, a forty-ish, American-looking man with a hat on, smoking a cigar. While we were quiet a number of possible remarks passed through my mind.

"Nice toes," I finally said. Her nails were painted one of those shades of purple that men never know the name of.

"Let's go somewhere else," she replied.

There were stairs behind us, which led to the highest level. Once we climbed them we were opposed by a chain with a sign hanging from it like a pendant, which demanded

No Trespassing!
Crew Members Only!
in English and French and something else. Dutch, probably. There was no question that the two of us were going to go over the chain. When we were at the top there were some machines, and the stacks, and there was a narrow walkway where one could get to the lifeboats. The lifeboats were suspended over the edge by massive ropes and tented with white tarps.

"Do you think you should be here?" a crewman surprised us with. He had that strange, Dutch accent which, as an American, I had trouble pinning down.

"We just want to sit in the life boat," Monique tried. He kept approaching us, daunting in his nautical slicker.

"Sorry. We didn't know," I answered.

"You shouldn't be here. You've got to go back inside now."

"We won't hurt anything," Monique continued.

"Come on. Let's not hassle the guy," I said to her.

"There's a sign telling you not to come up here."

"No, there wasn't," she lied. His face was a wordless question, and we returned down the stairs.

When we were inside she asked me to wait for her, and she went off to get a blanket. Alone, I considered having a cigarette. I'd overheard Monique earlier, telling someone that she didn't smoke. I watched the obsidian waves through the thick glass. A young couple walked by on the deck, hand in hand. She returned with the blanket.

"That guy didn't have to be such a jerk."

"Well, he probably has to deal with that every day. He probably has to deal with teenagers climbing in the lifeboats to make out all of the time."

"Let's wait until he leaves and try again."

In my best mockery of his accent, I said, "You don't think I'm going to let Hans stop us, do you?" It came out more like German. "Don't you want shoes?"

"No. I go everywhere barefoot," she said, facing me. "I don't like wearing shoes. I don't like wearing clothes. I wish people could just go around naked." If she knew what effect a statement like that had, she didn't show it. We saw Hans going down to patrol one of the lower decks once we were outside, so we hustled up the stairs and over the chain again. Monique offered me half of the blanket, and when I accepted she draped it over our shoulders. I put an arm around her.

Some girls like it better if you hold them around the waist, and some like it over the shoulder. I read Monique as one of the latter. She was tall, so she probably liked it when a guy was tall enough to hold her that way. We made it into the lifeboat without being detected. The bench was hard blue plastic, damp from sea-spray. We sat together facing the moon, and she covered us with the blanket again.

"I hope our friend Hans doesn't come back up here," she whispered, in on my joke now, and her voice and eyes were galvanized with the dangerous potential of the situation.

"This time he'll make us walk the plank." She thought it was funny. "He's just jealous that you asked that other sailor how much his room was for the night." I said a few more funny things, and she laughed at each one, but just a little. She kept not saying anything, and then we were quiet together for a little while, and the moment was upon us. I turned towards her. She was so close I could smell her breath.

"I bet that a girl like you must have a pretty nice boyfriend."

"What makes you say that?"

"Well, you've got the looks, you're funny, you're cool," and to be nice I added, "you're smart;" not that she wasn't, I just couldn't tell from the little I'd seen.

"No. I don't like English guys."

"Really? Oxford was a pretty poor choice for a university to come to on exchange." Oxford was south of my school.

"Call me shallow, but it's the accent. I can't stand it."

"Are you kidding? I think the English accent is the sexiest thing. It's one of the main reasons I came here. Sometimes I tell my girlfriend that it's the only reason I keep her around."

I extracted my pack of Marlboros from my pocket and offered them to her.

"No, I don't smoke," she said. She made a face that said the same thing more emphatically. I lit up using a wooden match since someone had stolen my Zippo off of the table earlier that night when I had gotten up to get a drink.

"Something is definitely wrong in the universe if a guy with my ugly mug has a girlfriend, but a gorgeous California girl like you doesn't have a boyfriend."

"I don't know about that." She didn't act flustered about the compliment or console me about picking on myself, so I worried that she was inferring an insult when I mentioned her not having a boyfriend.

We talked a little more, but it was one of those generic conversations that students have: "What's your major, where are you from, do you have any roommates?" I held the cigarette away from her and blew out the smoke in the other direction, but cigarette smoke naturally magnetized towards any non-smoker in a group. It was too cold to stay out for a long time for no reason, so we went back inside in search of a place to sleep.

We'd both taken the ferry without getting a cabin because it was cheaper. The ship was liberal about letting people sleep wherever they wanted to. There were passengers asleep on the couches and chairs on every level of the ship. We came across Brad and Runa, the Swede, bundled together on one of the long couches near a stairway. Runa advised us of a lounge on the third deck that was mostly empty.

Runa was a caricature of Swedish beauty, and I was impressed that Brad was with her. Some guys have a way about them that you just can't put a finger on. Brad had a black leather biker jacket with a bull's eye painted on the back. Pretty tough, like, "Go ahead, I *dare* you to shoot me," and even though I didn't read him as being that tough, he was cuddled up with Runa. I wouldn't have worn that jacket into another country. Some people don't like Americans just because they're Americans, and it isn't wise to be a punk about it.

Runa was right about the third level lounge, and we found a 'U' of unoccupied couches in front of the bandstand. Monique offered me the blanket, which I declined, and then she unzipped her jeans and pushed them down to her ankles. She wasn't base about it, but there was certainly no demur to it, and I suddenly knew that she was wearing white silk panties. Her sweatshirt fell into place to block that area of her from view. When she lay down on the couch she let her panties come into sight again before she made a correction with the sweatshirt.

"Sleep on this one," she told me, indicating the couch closest to hers, connected at a right angle. I took off my shoes and socks and lay down so our heads were near each other's. All of my luggage was in Forest and Kara's room, except for my money and passport, which were tucked into my jeans. I verified their existence frequently with a pat on my pocket. She had good legs, and I was very aware that they were naked a few feet away from me.

Monique rolled to face the back of the couch.

"If you wake up first, will you wake me up?" I asked.

"Mmm? Yeah, sure." She turned toward me a bit and then back again.

"Good night."

"Good night, Jake."

"I wish that I could turn the lights out."

"Mmm."

Then, in a little while, "What does your girlfriend think about you going on this trip?"

"Hmm? I don't know. She knows I had to go somewhere. I couldn't stay on campus."

"What's her name?"

"Her name is Tabi."

"That's pretty."

"She's a pretty girl."

"Why didn't you stay with her for spring break?"

"Well, we get three weeks for break, so I thought that might have been an imposition on her parents, seeing as I've never met them. Although they're pretty rich, and their house is so big that they might not even know I was there."

"Three weeks?"

"I know. It's crazy. It's too much time."

"How long have you been seeing each other?"

"We started seeing each other in January, but we sort of broke up for a while. We just got back together this week."

That seemed to satisfy her, because she turned her face back into the pillow her arm made and said, "I'll wake you up before I go to breakfast."

"Do you want me to wake you if I'm up first?"

"I'll be up first."

It was quiet on the ship. There was gambling somewhere, but it was on one of the other floors, and the noise didn't carry. If I concentrated very hard I could hear the ship making faint noises in response to the pitch of the ocean below. I met Tabi at the taxi stand in front of the university in January, after Christmas break. My mates were talking to one another, and I was sitting apart from them on the concrete steps and there was Tabi. I'd seen her around the dorms before, and you don't forget a girl like her. She had a heart attack of a body, and after that she had black hair, not dark brown but real black hair that flowed down her back like a waterfall on a moonless night. Her mother was Brazilian, so her skin was tan, and she had brown splashes of eyes, and flared nostrils; but her father was British, and out of her jelly lips flowed perfect cockney English.

But before how she looked there was who she was, hot-blooded and daring, interesting and interested, and she could drive me crazy better than anyone. She was the only one who could patch the hole Yvonne had torn in me.

I dumped Tabi for a girl who wanted to have sex with me. But mostly I dumped her because of how she drove me crazy, because she could tie me in a knot, everything I was made of, and I didn't think I could take it. When she was gone I found that nothing was as good without her, and when we got back together, we were so happy. The world was only correct if we were together. I loved her in the way that you would run into a burning building for someone for, that you would jump in front of the bullet for with total conviction.

Tabi.

A ship is good for sleeping, and I slept without dreams. Monique was right about getting up first. When she woke me she was already dressed, and she left me behind to find the others. My head was swampy with sleep, and I sat up blinking at the sun coming through the portholes. It's a surprise to come awake in a country other than the one you were in yesterday. While I put on my socks I smiled warmly at the people around me with the inherent intimacy of waking travelers.

CHAPTER 2

I walked to Forest and Kara's cabin through a kaleidoscope of people. There was some kind of grade school trip aboard, and sporadically throughout the voyage, packs of kids would come running by in the white tops, plaid ties, and plaid bottoms of their uniforms. The roughest looking passengers were the gamblers who'd been up all night at the casino. There were a lot of families on holiday, and a few clusters of college students like us. The night before I had encountered a few tough guys, the sort that roam in gangs of two or three, who won't make room for you when you pass in a hallway, no matter what. The kind who swear brashly and grab women's asses. The sort my father, who's a different kind of tough guy, would refer to as "cowboys."

Heads above all stood the cool Dutch crew in their short-sleeved uniforms. Every one of them, male or female, was taller than I am, and I'm about two meters tall. I felt huge in England, where the average height shorter than mine.

Forest and Kara were awake and almost ready when I knocked, so I waited outside of their cabin. She and Forest had been together for two years. Maybe it was just the way they looked in the morning, but they didn't seem happy together yet. They had appeared happy together the night before, but there was the excitement of the trip and of being in our group. I hardly knew Kara. She had flown over from the U.S. to spend break with him.

I led us to the dining room. The others were at a table that couldn't accommodate us. I noticed that Monique was sitting next to one of the English girls, and she seemed to be tolerating her accent. After breakfast I drank as much coffee as I could to try to correct what lack of sleep had done to me. I had been in good form the night before, introducing myself to everyone, telling jokes that went over well, and I was trying to come alive again.

"So Kara, how are you doing with jetlag?"

"You know, I didn't get it at all. Forest, knock it off," she said about his foot tapping and hand smacking on the table. He was a drummer.

"Almost done. Can you believe this weird money?" he said, and tossed a handful of Gilders and Pounds onto the tabletop. Some of them rolled off, and he leapt after them under a neighboring table, his braids flying.

"Really? Didn't get jetlag? Wow. It took me all of first semester to finally recover from it, and then I went home for Christmas break to see Yvonne, and it started over again."

"I just met some cool grannies when I was under that table," said Forest as he returned. He resumed the drum riff on the table.

"*Forest.*"

"You know, you can meet the coolest people underneath tables," I interjected. "I have. Mostly they're saying 'Sir, it's *closing* time, you have to leave.'"

They both laughed, even though Forest was still looking around, and I felt like I was good for them. Whenever I was with Forest I felt like he wasn't in the moment, that he was waiting for the *next* cool thing to happen. Forest was a friend of one of Yvonne's roommates back at our home university. Yvonne and I had a very serious relationship during the previous year and the first part of this school year. We had talked about moving in with each other when I got home.

The real bond between us was marijuana; not between Yvonne and I, between Forest and I. When I first met Forest he'd had me over to his room to get high with Kara and some of their friends. We'd talked about undercover narcotics agents on campus while we got high. Weed makes you paranoid in the first place, so undercover narcotics agents aren't a good topic when you're smoking.

A group walked past our breakfast table speaking German.

"Need to talk to those guys!" Forest announced, as though they had reminded him of something, and was up suddenly, following them to the bar.

"Forest? Oh, now what?"

"He'll be back."

"Yeah, but. Does he *know* those guys?"

"I don't think so." I tried laughing. "Don't worry about him. Hey, let's go play the blackjack machine. Do you want to?" She looked pensively towards Forest, who was entrenched in conversation with the Germans. "He'll find us. Come on, it'll be fun."

"I don't know how to play," she said, getting up from the table.

"Me either. Now I won't have to feel as stupid."

"So Jake, are you still going out with Yvonne?"

I looked at the scars on my hand. "No, we broke up during Christmas break."

"I'm sorry."

The machine was one of the many scattered throughout the boat. It was lit up like a carnival ride and covered in buttons labeled with cryptic functions. I pushed my money into the slot and we took turns losing. She laughed at my jokes after a while.

"You seem like you're in a better mood."

"I wasn't in a bad mood. Did you think that I was?"

"Maybe a little. Maybe you seemed a little tired."

"It's just, I flew to England, then took the train to your school, slept one night, then took the bus to the port, and now I'm on the ferry. You know?" And that she had flown half way around the world just to visit him and maintain their relationship, and he should be paying her some attention.

"I don't understand this button," she said. "'Nudge.' What does 'nudge' do?"

"Don't touch that. It's way too early in the morning to nudge. I never nudge before noon." I regretted the innuendo. Forest wasn't a great friend, but he was a friend, and I don't mess around with friends' girlfriends.

I spent fifty Gilders and won back ten. Blackjack was not a good investment. We reconvened with Forest, and then with the others, and waited close to the exit for debarkation. Customs coming into Rotterdam weren't stringent, which was to be expected, as the country had liberal laws regarding drugs. Brad and Chad led us to the train station. They were being looked to as leaders by the rest of the group. I was working hard to not resent their inferred leadership. We tagged after the bulls-eye on Brad's jacket into the train.

Matt, a guy in our group who hadn't made much of an impression on me, sat with me. Matt was from Georgia, on exchange to Oxford like Monique, although they didn't know each other. Matt was on his own. He didn't seem to want anything from me but my company. I wanted to leave Forest and Kara alone for a while. Forest was hard to read, but I thought that he was giving me a signal to back off a little.

We arrived at about two PM. The stops were announced over a bad speaker in Dutch, and I was nervous about missing the stop. The kid from Georgia was more nervous than I was. Every time the voice crackled over the speaker, I'd lean across the aisle to Forest and ask, "What did she say?" Then the Georgian would tap me on the shoulder to make sure I wasn't ignoring him and ask, "What did he say?"

Brad and Chad didn't realize that we had arrived until Forest made his move towards the door. I was amused that I had aligned myself with the savvier companion. It was wrong, but I allowed myself the amusement anyway.

We raced out of the dark train station up to the street level. Street hustlers sprang upon us pushing flyers that advertised youth hostels, and beyond them were steps leading down towards people walking in every direction, and statues, and trolleys, and a blistering chaos named Amsterdam.

CHAPTER 3

"Hey dude, have you gotten a place to stay yet?" pried a man of about thirty with a ponytail. He had a vague European accent, and by his use of "dude" I knew that he guessed that I was an American. He shook a flier from a stack into my hands. "I'll take you to the Aroma House. Nice people, lots of peace." He quoted the words off of the flyer, shoulder to shoulder with me, following along the writing with his finger. Forest and Kara had almost reached the tumultuous throng in the square.

"Thanks. My friends and I are going to check out a few places first."

"Bring them along." He kept describing his hostel. He spoke as though we knew each other. Forest and Kara entered the crowd. The other guy, the one from Georgia, waited for me a few paces behind them.

"We'll stop by," I interrupted. I began to walk.

"You're just saying that, aren't you?"

"Yes," I answered, still moving.

I caught up with the Georgia guy, whose name I'd already forgotten. The city was vast and threatening, and I was trying to think of how Dad would act in the same surroundings. I could picture Dad moving confidently through the strange cities of the vacations of my youth, but he hadn't taught these skills to me, he hadn't equipped me properly.

The Georgia guy stationed himself behind my left shoulder and maintained a friendly conversational buzz. Kara was stationed in a similar fashion at Forest's right. Forest had had the foresight to snag a city map from somewhere, as well as a **Let's Go to...Amsterdam** guidebook.

"*Konigsstraat.* Or something. That's what we need to find," Forest said, looking at the guidebook.

"Forest! Forest! Just wait a minute," pleaded Kara as he continued to trot.

"*Kon*igsstraat. Kor*nigs*straat?"

"Forest, wait a minute!"

"Hold up," I said. "What's the game plan?" Having the Georgia kid looking up to me lent me authority.

"Konigsstr*aat*. It sounds like a food preservative. I just saw it on the map."

"What's there, Forest? Where are we heading?"

"Forest!"

He brought both hands up to waist height in a pushing motion and looked fearsome for a second. One blonde braid hung over his left eye. "Everybody just relax, alright? I can't answer everybody at once."

We shut up, but when he opened his mouth, Kara jumped in: "Forest, will you please just—"

"Kara!"

"Wait," I said. "Kara, let me confer with Forest for a second," directing the words to her eyes. I was putting the small bond we had formed that morning to the test.

I lowered an arm around Forest and ushered him aside to face a canal. A water trolley full of people floated by. His features were taut and his fingers were spread wide. Forest had a deep voice and a mature face, each in opposition to his personality.

"I am going to ride on one of those things while we're here," he said of the water trolley. "Want to go?"

"Yeah, maybe. If I can afford it. You look like you're stressing out, Forest."

He bent at the waist, then snapped himself erect, lashing his blonde braids back out of his eyes. "This would go a lot smoother if I could just find this place alone. I have to find Konigsstraat, or something like that. I'm on a mission."

"I think you need a weed first."

"I think that weed should wait, Jake. We've got to have priorities. Maybe you can…no." He pulled at one of the straps on his backpack.

"Listen. Let's find a hash bar and get our bearings. You and I can leave our gear behind with Kara and what's-his-name and find this place you were looking for."

"His name is Matt. Actually, Jake, I think I'll find it quicker without you."

I sucked in air and said, "Okay, Forest. I have a poor sense of direction anyhow."

"I know," he said, looking at me sideways. "I mean, you can't even remember Matt's name, and you just met him yesterday, so forget about directions. Jake, Jake! You don't have to get all hurt, I was only kidding." His face was exorcised of tension.

"I'm cool. Let's station ourselves somewhere where we can sit down, and you can go scout out a place." Maybe I did look hurt, but I'd been insulted by Forest before, and I knew not to take it to heart. I was suddenly aware of his luggage. He wore one of those camping backpacks that had a tall aluminum frame, and it was made of shiny new fabric. When we walked he hooked his hands into the straps, and, except for the braids, he had the look of someone dressed up to make his mother proud. My own backpack was from an army surplus store, bought two days before I flew to England. It had cost me about as much as lunch, and it was some of the best money I'd ever spent. It was wide, had a lot of pockets, and would last forever.

That Zippo lighter stolen the previous night would have lasted me forever also. It was a gift from my father, and I was still nursing the loss of it. I lit up a Marlboro with a wooden match instead.

We shared the game plan with Kara and Matt, and walked out of the square. Beyond the square was a maze of narrow, cobbled streets, hedged in by low buildings. The first hash bar we happened upon was called Led Zeppelins, and we entered it at my insistence. It was decorated with the eponymous band as a theme, and their music was playing. We knew that it was a hash bar because of this amazing sign in the window. It said:

Café—Hash Bar

Hash Bar! It said it right out in the open, and I was starting to understand the type of city I was in.

Kurt, my English best mate, had tried to prep me for Amsterdam, but his second-hand information had holes in it. "When you go into a hash bar," he'd instructed, "you have to ask them to see the menu. If they just give you a list of drinks and whatnot, you have to say, 'No, can I see the *menu*.'"

Without having to ask in either inflection, the barkeep brought me a plastic-laminated menu that had weed prices on the left leaf and hash prices on the right one. I had smoked a fair amount of weed in my time, most of it in college, but I had only bought it on a few occasions. Marijuana is a social drug, so in any circle of weed friends, there was at least one person who bought enough to go around. All of the hash I'd bought in Europe up until Led Zeppelin's had been through Kurt, through a special credit arrangement I referred to as the Bank of Kurt.

Kurt had a dealer on campus, and he wanted me to buy in with him so that there'd be plenty on hand. After a few such purchases, I told him that I was thinking of cutting down. We were close enough as friends for me to share with him the reason for my hesitation: I was still waiting for the paperwork to be finalized on my third and final student loan.

"I tell you what," he'd offered. "I'm going to buy ten grams, and we'll split it up. I mean we always smoke together anyway, right? And when your money comes in I reckon you can just pay me back."

"I don't know, Kurt. I'm not sure that I feel comfortable borrowing money from a friend."

"Come on. You're not going to let a little thing like money come in the way of something important like weed, are you?" Kurt didn't have the appearance of a smoker. He was clean cut, and he wore clothes that had cost him or his parents some money. We were frequent lifting partners at the gym, and his body was lean, and huge at the shoulders.

I could hear Dad telling me, "If you don't have the money for something, don't buy it." Of course, that was the same Dad who advised me to get student loans in order to pay for school. It was my parents who had drilled the idea of going to college into me in the first place. I was certain that Kurt was not paying for school himself, nor were any of my close friends. Dad owned a car wash, and I thought that it was doing pretty well, and that he could have paid my way through, and that his logic seemed very situational, that it had convenient gaps in it.

The bartender at Led Zeppelin's was playing one of the ubiquitous gambling machines, milking it. Kara and the other kid, *Matt* was his name, didn't want to get any dope just yet, but they were watching me as I sauntered up to the bar. I was the entertainment.

I ordered five grams of Egyptian grass and the coffees that they had wanted. I chose Egyptian just because it sounded cool, but I tried to appear as though I knew what I was talking about when I ordered it. Back home when we bought weed it was just *weed*; we didn't care what country it came from.

I refused to let Kara and the guy from Georgia pay for their coffees in a magnanimous attempt to elevate the mood. Normally I am pretty good at rolling up a joint, but I rolled a crappy one for us, all fat in the middle and skinny at the ends. It was strange to roll one in a pubic establishment, shamelessly.

"Do you guys want to wait for Forest to get back before we spark this?"

The Georgia guy looked at me with an unwavering expression, which indicated that he would follow the majority. I'd forgotten his name again already; his name just wouldn't stick to stick to my mind.

"I'm ready to smoke some right now," said Kara.

"My kind of woman," I told her, and struck one of the wooden matches.

I passed the joint to that guy first, and it made its way around the table a few times. Kara bailed on it after two tokes, saying that she'd had enough. The other guy was choking on it a bit, but smoking his way through nobly.

"I bet you'd get pretty sick of Led Zeppelin if you worked here for a while," I suggested, loudly enough to illicit a smile from the bartender.

"Dude," said the Georgia kid, "You roll a really good joint. I am totally high right now."

"Thanks." No point in arguing the merits of my joint construction.

"I mean it. I am really high."

"That was some strong stuff," Kara said.

I analyzed the level of my own high. I got the impression that Kara had smoked a lot more than I had, if only because she was Forest's girl-friend. I would have been surprised if she was high already and I was not. There is a moment whenever you smoke pot when you discover that you are laughing uncontrollably about something that wouldn't ordinarily strike you as funny, or when you find yourself fixated on a riff of music or on some other detail of your surroundings. When the mundane blossoms into the profound.

It was just as Kara was saying the word "stuff" when the moment enveloped me, and I knew that I was high.

I noticed that I had been staring intently at our table for several seconds. A Led Zeppelin concert poster from 1970 had been shellacked to the surface. The band had made music so important that people actually shellacked their images to tables decades later. In my backpack was a sketchbook full of my own artwork, and I was proud of it, but was it a ticket to the same kind of immortality?

More: Led Zeppelin memorabilia was on the walls, the front of the bar, the bar top. A painting of the Hindenberg going down covered the back wall. The room was designed to saturate its patrons with the influence of the band, like being in a Led Zeppelin sauna. Every bar or restaurant has an atmosphere, but stoned, I was acutely aware of it. Stoned, my mind took apart the moment like it would read a recipe, noticing all of the little ingredients of the experience that would ordinarily be lost in the passage of events.

I was worried over forgetting the name of that guy at the table, too embarrassed to ask him to remind me. Kara sat next to me at my right, and I was tense about her presence, being the girlfriend of a friend. I noticed that I had instinctively molded my body into an expression of disinterest: leaning to the left, arms folded, crotch pointed away from her.

I evicted the tension from the back of my head. What was the use of the constant rejection of this woman? It was an apish social display, and I unfolded my arms and unleashed my smile.

"Dude, listen to this song," I said to the Georgia kid, paroling myself from the guilt of forgetting his name by picking up on his own use of "dude." In the song the band was playing with the stereo effect. The beat would alternate from the left speaker to the right one. I pointed to the pertinent speaker as it occurred in order to highlight the effect.

"Dude, this band is great!"

"You said it, Dude," I said, giving him credit. He had a face like vanilla and a haircut that would blend in anywhere. His army surplus jacket matched my backpack. Maybe this was what was cueing his fellowship towards me. I had been shunting his friendship because he was too eager to give it to me, yet someone like Forest, who always kept me at an arm's distance, I would spend my energy trying to win over. I resented Forest's rejection of me, so it was wrong for me to pass along the same treatment. I'm pretty ugly, so I'm used to immediate rejection by others, and I try to live my life without repeating that behavior.

More:

That raw spot on my shoulder, where the backpack strap dug in, the same raw spot I'd had when I first arrived in Europe and had more bags than this. Other little aches and quirks of my body that only I knew of: that chip of bone loose somewhere in my left forearm from a baseball collision, the testicle that hangs lower than the other, the skin across the knuckles of the first three fingers of my right hand, white with scar and numb. Each of these elements which occupied a space in the back of my mind were chaperoned forward by the pot to make a soliloquy. Each of them playing a role in my personality. Everyone has a set of such things, and we are all so different. What a miracle that we are able to communicate with one another at all.

Forest came back, and I noticed feeling a little disappointed.

"I found it. Jake, you are really stoned." My eyes must have been bright red. I responded by laughing. Dude and Kara laughed with me. "All of you? This is so very unfair."

"Let's check in and dump our stuff, and you can join us. I got a bag of Egyptian, and it's kicking my ass."

"Easy, killer. I've got to talk to Kara." Forest ushered her away from me into a corner. He put one hand on her back, and they discussed something in low voices as he caressed her. I felt banished, but they needed their space.

"Dude, you've got what my friend back home refers to as 'perma-grin.'"

Dude was smiling his face off. "So, are we going to check out hostels now?"

"I think so."

"I'm having a great time. I'm glad you thought of coming into this place."

"That weed really got you, didn't it?" He looked at me anxiously. "Me too. I'm out of my head."

"We should hang with each other while we're here. I think it would be a good idea if we stay in the same hostel, don't you? There's safety in numbers."

My mind went off tangentially on the concept of safety in numbers, but I reeled it back in. I realized that he was waiting for a response. "Of course, Dude. Don't worry about it."

"I'm glad. I don't think I'd know my way around otherwise. I don't think that your friend really likes me."

"Come on, now. You're not right about that."

"That he doesn't like me, or that he's your friend?" Then he smiled.

"Dude. That was pretty good."

He kept smiling and shrugged. Forest and Kara joined us again. They walked ahead of us, happy with each other, and we followed them out the door.

CHAPTER 4

I stole a *Let's Go to...Amsterdam* guidebook from the first hostel we looked at. The hostel was older than my country. Its stairs were ludicrously steep, almost vertical, and as I staggered my way up I kept bashing my shins and falling onto my hands.

"I see your friend has been to the hash bars already," the hostess joked to Kara.

"Because he's having trouble with the stairs?"

"You mean the ladder?" I grunted.

The hostel was too expensive for me. I was worried that Forest and Kara were going to take a room and leave Dude and I to find our own way, but Kara wanted to check out some other places before making a decision. While they were talking to the hostess I slipped the guidebook from a coffee table into my backpack. *I see your friend has been to the hash bars already*, huh, smart-ass?

The hostel we chose was right in the heart of things. Dude and I took beds in the communal room, and Forest and Kara split a single. The communal room had five sets of bunk beds and a row of lockers. The lockers were tall and narrow, too narrow for my gear. We had to be out of the room every day by eleven so the linens could be changed. There was no curfew.

I left Dude behind after we were settled to check up on Forest and Kara. I wanted to stash my backpack in their room. I brought along my new weed and my last rolling paper.

"This view is crazy!" Forest bragged. They had a shoebox of a room with a mattress on the floor. Kara was sitting on it, delicately picking through her luggage. She looked unhappy again. I moved to the window and looked down at the brown stones of the curved side street below. The windowsill was wide enough to roll a joint on. There was an old stone church down the block, not quite the size of the cathedral we had seen together in England, but impressive.

I agreed with Forest that the view was nice. I offered him the first toke of the joint. He turned it over in his fingers and looked at it.

"What the hell is with this tampon, Jake?" When you roll a joint, if there is extra paper at either end, you twist it shut. A "tampon" is when there is too much paper left over, all at one end, and when you twist it, it resembles the string on a tampon.

"From now on," he said to Kara, "Make sure that Jake doesn't try to roll any more joints." She cocked an eyebrow at it and went back to her luggage.

"Yeah, it's pretty bad. I'd re-roll it, but that was my last paper."

"Here. I have a pipe." He crumbled the weed into the pipe and we worked on it for a while.

"Forest, what's the name of that kid from Georgia?"

"Matt? Are you serious, you forgot it already? I just told you."

"I can't remember his name for some reason."

He chewed on the idea for a second and came out with, "Honey, is Jake to young to have Alzheimer's?"

"Are you going to pass that thing, Forest," she said of the pipe, "Or has it become surgically attached?"

"Yes dear. Jake buddy, you picked a good weed. Nice job. I was just kidding about the joint."

"It is decent weed. It's Egyptian."

"You looked like I hurt your feelings there, big Jake. It was a joke. I can't roll them any better."

"I know, Forest. I'm not made out of glass." Now I was getting annoyed, because I thought that I had taken his comments in stride. Forest had this way of complimenting after insulting, which made it even worse. It robbed the compliment of any potency it may have had.

"Are you two ready to check out the city?"

"Well, Kara and I were going to chill here for a while, maybe take a nap. Kara's kind of tired from all the travelling. You coming back?"

"I don't know yet. I've got to get some dinner in me so I can think better."

We said some other things, but they were lost in the rush of the weed as the high took hold. I went back to the communal room, and Dude was sitting there on his bunk, all alone. I collected him, and we went back out into Amsterdam to explore.

CHAPTER 5

My high was still escalating. At the corner of the street was an adult novelty shop. The window display was an array of rubber and plastic sex organs, some of them chromed and in leather sheaths, like weapons. There were also life-size, inflatable sex partners on display, in a variety of sizes, colors, and functions.

In order to get into the square we had to cross an amazing road. It consisted of a two-way pedestrian walkway, two bicycle paths, an automobile path, several sets of trolley tracks, another automobile path, and two more bicycle paths. I wasn't certain which way traffic would be coming from on any of the lanes. The first time we had crossed it to get to Led Zeppelin's I had followed Forest's lead, which was not such a good idea. I don't think that he saw so well.

One time during first semester I witnessed him look the wrong way to cross the street and walk into a bicyclist. He looked me square in the eye while he was getting hit, while he was still in mid-air, with a cartoon expression of surprise. With his arms, legs, and braids flying in all directions he looked like an asterisk with a face.

Dude seemed more like a man with a sense of his surroundings. I could imagine him hiking in the woods without a compass, finding his way by the sun. I hung back a step behind him as he traversed the road with ease.

I noticed a woman riding a large bicycle on one of the paths. On the back of the bicycle was a baby in a baby seat. I was terrified for them. She rode coolly down the road, so I figured that she was a native.

We reached the square with no specific destination in mind. Dude shifted back to follow me again. The crowd boiled around us. I looked up, and jutting out of the middle of the square was a ten-meter tall brick phallus.

"Dude, it's the Penis of the Gods," I told him, and pointed up at it.

"Where?"

"*Where?* Dude, right there! It's a thirty foot tall...penis." I looked and I looked at it, and my mind kept trying to reject what my eyes were giving it, but the thing continued to be an enormous erection.

"Dude, I can't believe that I missed that. I'm so glad that I'm stoned for this."

I led him across the square to some shops that looked interesting. We needed to eat, and I needed to get some more rolling papers. We went into a pipe and papers shop first.

The shop was in a very old, low ceilinged building. The walls were tilted from settling and shifting over the decades. The floor was creaky and uneven. The shelves were lined with rows of bongs and pipes, and there was a table that displayed about fifty different makes of rolling papers. I compulsively selected a package of them that looked like stained glass, and another kind that would roll up to resemble a regular cigarette, colored orange at one end to simulate a filter.

"Are pipes any good?" Dude asked.

"I find that pipe smoke is a little hot, but they're easier than having to roll a joint. Can you roll?"

"I've never tried to."

There were some ornate ones of carved wood, but the prices were imposing. I decided on a simple small one of carved black marble for myself. It was efficient and would last me forever with little maintenance.

When the clerk rang up my selections I had to count out my change three times in order to be sure of it. Dude lingered by the pipe display.

"Do you think I should get one?"

"Well, I tell you, the smoke out of one will be hotter than out of a bong, but they're easier to carry around."

He kept looking at me.

"Yes, you should get one."

He smiled at the answer he wanted and bought one of the carved wooden ones.

I took him to the first hash bar we happened upon to break in his pipe. The name of the place was Adam's Apple. We knew that it was a hash bar because the Adam, Eve, and Snake in the logo were each smoking joints. We ordered espressos and smoked a few buds from my bag. He wanted to order his own bag, so we studied the menu and decided upon an eighth of Iranian. He asked me if it would be any good, and I told him that I really didn't know, but we should try it for fun. There was some music playing in the bar, and I was consumed by it. I was still maintaining a conversation with Dude, but the majority of me was deep in the back of my mind, contemplative.

When I came back out of myself I found that we were in the company of Monique and her English friend from the boat, Jessica. I couldn't remember how we had connected with them. Was it that Dude knew where they were staying, or had Forest told me? Or did we just run into them?

We were very hungry by then. There was some walking, and then I found myself in a restaurant. I lit up a Marlboro and put it in the ashtray beside another one that I was already smoking. I couldn't remember what I had ordered, so I was looking forward to the waitress' return to find out. When she arrived, she placed a fat gyro in front of me. It thickened the air with the smell of charred garlic and meat, and I attacked it with gusto. My mind kept latching onto things like the music or the interactions of people at tables around us, and I would lose myself in thought for minutes at a time. When I came out of it, I had to work to pick up the conversation again. Mostly it was Monique and Jessica doing the talking.

"Are there any good places around here to get a drink?" Dude asked Jessica. I examined her reaction.

"Leave it to a lad. First priority is beer. We haven't been to any," she said in his direction.

"Do you want to go out for drinks with Jake and me?"

"Little early, don't you think?"

"Later? Do you want to go out for drinks later?" He looked at me after he said it, so I shaped my mouth into an expression of approval.

"Oh, well. Might be going to the Hard Rock Café with them lot."

"Can we go with you?"

"Don't really know when we're going. Why not just meet us there?" After she said it, she turned towards Monique. Monique was wearing a very expensive sweater from L. L. Bean, and she had a camera with her.

"Did Chad find that shop he was looking for?" she asked Jessica, and they began an exclusive conversation.

I had the *Let's Go...* with me, and I opened it between Dude and I. We wanted to check out the University of Amsterdam. I announced that that was where we were going. The girls looked at each other, something passing silently between them, and they shoulder-shrugged their consent.

When we left the city center, the streets were all made of old gray cobblestones. The girls started to drift away, lingering closer to the heart of the city. I caught a snippet of their conversation; Jessica saying, "Why did they bring us here?" to Monique, then Monique said "...(something something) follow us," but I couldn't hear the rest. Monique told us that they had decided to go back to their hostel to rest for a while. Dude offered to walk them back.

"Don't need any assistance," Jessica laughed at him.

I decided to see if Forest and Kara were ready to go out yet, so we headed back to our hostel.

"It looked like you working on Jessica, there, Dude."

"No, not really," but his face cracked apart with his smile.

"Duuuude...."

"No, dude. I mean, she's pretty, and I wouldn't mind spending some time with her, but." His focus went inside himself, then came back out. "I've got a fiancée back home."

"You mean *home*-home, or university-home?"

"Georgia-home."

"How long have you been together?"

"We've been going out for four years now."

"I used to have a long distance relationship with a girl from my home university. It's not easy. How is she taking it, you being away?"

"She's good with it. We've been together since high school, so it's kind of good that we're apart for a while."

"Are you faithful to her?"

He looked away. "Not exactly."

"Dude, you dog!" and I clapped him on the shoulder.

"I miss her, though." When he said it he looked sad. It was a sadness without complication.

"It's good to miss someone. It reminds you that you love them."

"So, what happened with your girlfriend?"

"My ex-?" It was time for a cigarette. "Well, Yvonne, that was her name, and I had a relationship for about a year. One of my friends had an off-campus apartment that he wasn't using over the summer. She drove up to school early, and she and I lived together there for the last two weeks before school. Those were the best two weeks of my life. We had talked about moving in with each other at the end of the school year," I rushed past that, "When I came to England, I'd call her every week, and I wrote her at least once a week, but she only sent me one letter in return. Then I went home for Christmas and she dropped the bomb on me. She told me she didn't love me anymore."

"Dude. I'm sorry. I shouldn't have asked you about it."

"No, that's okay. After it happened I kind of freaked out and put my fist through a window, but I'm good with it now. I didn't take flying all the way home just to get dumped too well, but I'm all right now."

He looked like he felt bad.

"It's okay, Dude. I don't mind talking about it. I'm the kind of guy, if I'd minded, I would have told you. There would be no mistake about it."

He remained quiet and attentive.

"What was strange, though," I thought out each word before I spoke it, "Was that she said her feelings for me were just *gone*. I mean, when you love someone, how does that happen? I know that she loved me." I hadn't talked about it too much to anyone, but when I did, whoever it was, I gave them a small piece of it, like a puzzle I was trying to get rid of.

After Yvonne had told me that she didn't love me anymore we talked for a while, and when I realized that there was nothing I could say to change the way she felt, I walked out of her room. I walked calmly out of the building and out to the parking lot. I found my car and patted all of my pockets for my keys, couldn't find them, patted them again, then punched my fist through the driver's-side window. The keys were in my jacket pocket after all, but first I had to walk to the infirmary to get ten stitches in my hand.

CHAPTER 6

We didn't see Monique or Jessica at the Hard Rock Café. We didn't see them in Amsterdam again at all. I saw Jessica back at the university a few times after Easter break, but that was the last of Monique. One part of me was disappointed that we lost them in Amsterdam, but a better, less primal part of me was happy that Monique was gone. If you let the moment pass without acting on it, things get stale. I liked Monique, but I could remember with total clarity what I felt like right before Tabi and I got back together, when I wasn't sure if she would have me back.

The day after, Dude and I went hash bar hopping with Forest and Kara. They took turns looking unhappy. At least one of us bought some type of weed in each bar.

There was a place called Elegantly Adam. It was well lit and had plush chairs at the tables. Reggae music came from wall-mounted speakers. While we were deciding what to order, I spotted a framed photo on the wall that matched the logo on the menu.

"Guys, did you realize that we're in a gay rasta hash bar?"

"A what?" said Forest.

"A gay rasta hash bar. Look," I said, and gestured to the photo on the wall. When they had all looked, I indicated the matching logo on the menu.

"Oh yeah," Kara agreed, nodding.

"I don't get it," Forest said, but the possibility of it was creeping into his voice.

The photo was of a large pink isosceles triangle pointed downwards. In the middle of the triangle was an athletically muscled, totally depilated man wearing nothing but spandex pants, and rings on his fingers, ears, and nipples. His arms were folded across his chest so that he was holding his shoulders, and pinched between the fore- and middle fingers of his right hand was a fat joint. The image of the man was in black and white except for his lips, which were colored the same pink as the triangle framing him. A ribbon of smoke drifted up out of his mouth.

The inverted pink triangle is an international symbol for homosexuality, which I explained to Forest.

"Plus the raggae music makes it rasta."

"A gay rasta hash bar."

"No. Not really," Dude said. "Really?"

"I think so," Kara voted.

When the waiter returned, Kara and I ordered for the other two. We all looked around the establishment with this new frame of reference, analyzing the customers.

"Well that makes perfect sense," Forest said when the waiter was out of earshot. "I mean after all, isn't this country famous for the little Dutch boy?" I knew what was coming next.

"What do you mean, Forest?" Kara asked.

"You know, he stuck his finger in the dyke?" "Dyke" was slang for a lesbian.

"That's pretty funny, Forest. I think my sister already told me that one. She's gay, so she hears them all first."

Dude stopped laughing. "Are you serious?" I was still looking at Forest, who knew I was serious by my face. I didn't make it too bad for him, though.

"Okay. But why 'Elegantly *Adams*?' That's the fifth place that I've seen with 'Adam' in the name. Is that a gay thing, too?"

"Forest," Kara chided, unnecessarily. Dude was quiet, neutral.

"I think it's A'dam, like Amsterdam abbreviated. Get it?"

It comes up every once in a while, this aspect of my sister. I don't have an attitude about the matter, but when faced with this situation, I have to make my point. In my guts I knew that, if not for my sister, I would have made the same jokes.

People expect it to bother me, but why should it? It's not like I was planning on having sex with her. I'm sure Dad wasn't planning on it either, but he didn't approve. I think Dad's opinion was that being gay was a choice, and that choosing to be so was wrong. I suppose that there was some choice involved for some individuals, though maybe not for my sister. In any event I found that I didn't love her any differently.

I suppose that the main reason one has children is to pass on the genetic line, and my sister's nature was not conducive to that end. The fact that Dad was so irked over the issue made me wonder if he thought I was unworthy to continue the family line. I couldn't think of a way to voice this to him, or to anyone, and not sound like a completely insecure idiot, but the feeling was real, so it sat deep inside me like a furnace of rejection. I was waiting for the day it would run out of fuel.

There were a lot of beggars in the streets during the day.

"Americans! You speak English!" this one yelled as he ran towards me. He'd heard me talking to Dude on our way to the Sex Museum. He was tall and lean and he moved too quickly. His face was taut, his eyes so wide that white showed all around the colored parts. His jeans were filthy like a garage mechanic's, but the dark stains weren't oil.

"Give me ten Gilders, man. Come on! I'm hungry! I'm hungry!" He clutched his stomach with one of his wide hands. He was close enough to grab me.

"No thanks." I sidestepped.

"Come on! You've got it! I need it! What can you give me?" He walked in front of me, his expression under the week of beard flickering between anger and hunger. I thought that he was going to reach into my pocket.

"Come on Jake," Forest called. I stepped to the side and walked past the dirty man. I was ready for him to try to stop me, but he didn't, and I was able to extract myself.

"You've got to learn how to avoid that, Jake," Forest said, shaking his head. Forest emanated beggar repulsion, which I figured was a result of being from New York City. They always managed to hook me by the eyes and get me to interact with them. I tried watching the way Forest avoided it. When they walked up to him he wouldn't veer from his course. He'd put up one hand, keep looking ahead, and say, "I'm all set." It was a concise and effective little statement. When he did this maneuver, in those moments, he seemed very adult, and I felt like I had a good idea of the kind of guy his father was.

I'd never seen a panhandler hit up my dad. Dad's intimidating.

The Sex Museum did not fulfil its promise. I didn't have specific expectations, but I wanted more than just an exhibit of dildos through the ages, some old tin prints of nudes, and a porn movie playing on a VCR. I kept the ticket stub as a souvenir; it would look as though I'd been somewhere interesting. I resented its keeping me away from the hash bars.

There was more smoking after, and at some point, I realized that Forest and Kara had left us. I had a hazy recollection of them bickering just before departing. Dude had taken a camera out of his pocket. I felt embarrassed that he would mark himself as a blatant tourist, and thus as a target. It made me feel protective for him in an avuncular way.

I remember being in a souvenir shop that sold all manner of wooden shoes. Some time after that we were back in the hostel. All of the other bunks were full with strange men. I knew that all my gear was locked up in Forest and Kara's room, so I only had to be careful of my passport and money. I got into my bed with my clothes on, figuring that if I had to get up in a hurry for some emergency, it was better to be dressed. I transferred my valuables to my underwear and lay on my stomach, and with all of that done, I felt all right to sleep.

Someone in the room snored. Once, I heard Dude talking, but it was somniloquy. I shifted onto my right side, which was better for me to sleep on. We were each provided with a small, hard pillow, which I pulled to my chest and held to me with one arm. When I first saw Tabi sitting on the steps in front of the university, I got that feeling that starts in your stomach and spreads through your body, making you feel stupid and clumsy and small-voiced. I'd only returned from Christmas break the week prior, from a Yvonne who no longer loved me and wasn't going to move in with me, and I'd never tried to pick up a strange woman before. I'd always had to have a woman trip over herself to let me know that she liked me.

And then there's my face. My nose is too big, and you'd swear that it had been broken. Like an hour ago. And the rest of my face was a real scrambled egg of eyes and lips. But I had put on some muscle when I was home on break, and I had new boots and my best Levi's, and a good haircut. I knew that if she rejected me, it would knock me down hard, but seeing her, I asked myself, "Can you do it?"

So I.

*No you fool, do not think of her right now. It's weeks until you see her again. Do not, do **not***

so I looked at her and said, "Would you like to share our taxi back to Ellison?" She turned and looked at me, and even though everything in me told me to avert my eyes against rejection, I smiled at her.

"How did you know that I lived at Ellison?"

"I've seen you around."

She liked that I had remembered seeing her around. She had already called for a taxi of her own. I tried to get her to neglect it and come with us, but she wouldn't. Not because she was shy, but because leaving her taxi driver in a lurch would be the wrong thing to do, and that's how I

knew that she was more than just looks *stop it*. She told me she liked my
lighter as she accepted a cigarette. I told her it was from my father. She
liked Americans. It would have been in character for me to introduce
myself and hope she did the same, but I said, "What's your name?" like
there was no chance she wouldn't answer, and she told me *stop it!*

"Tabi."

I had the hot, wet feeling in the back of my throat, but the hostel was
no place to exercise it, so I buried it. I put the pillow under my head
where it belonged and listened to the lullaby of the breathing men in the
room, and went to sleep with the Amsterdam night all around me.

"Let me borrow your lighter," she said; a test. I risked it. That first
time she came over to my room I was wearing the jeans I had on now,
my favorite blue tee shirt, and no socks. Returning the lighter was her
excuse to come over. She sat on the bed with her boots up on the blanket, and I sat in my chair across from her. I gave her a hard time about
the boots, so she put them on my pillow instead. I knew she was trying
to get a rise out of me with it because she felt like I had her at a disad-
vantage, so I didn't let it get to me. The night sounds of the hostel put
me to sleep, but they took their time doing it.

CHAPTER 7

Forest retrieved us the next morning. Dude and I followed him down to the hostel's lounge, where Kara was waiting. She and Forest had on blue jeans, and they both wore gray tops, and they each had a small backpack strapped to their backs. They were about the same height as well. He put an arm around her waist.

"Here's the plan," Forest announced. "We're going to the Van Gogh museum right when it opens. Then we can grab some lunch—"

"You know, they might have plans of their own, Forest," she interrupted.

He only missed one beat. Facing her, he said, "Those two? No, I think their only plan is to get fucked up and follow me around like the stoners they are." It hung there for a second, but he was still smiling. It wasn't an argument. He swiveled his body to make Dude and I part of the conversation.

I nodded. "That sounds about right. What do you think, Dude?" and he "Uh-huh"—ed his concordance. Forest kept his smile and led us into the city.

Leaving the hostel by the lounge exit brought us into a commercialized alleyway. On the other side was a bar called the Eagle. At first I thought that it might have been an American place, because the eagle is our national bird, but that idea had a short life span. "The Eagle" was spelled out in sharp, rusted steel letters above the doorway. The front of the place was covered with chains. The chains weren't used to lock up the bar when it was closed. They were those enormous chains that could carry a cruise ship's anchor, with links as thick as arms. The place had no windows. Its wooden door was lined with fat iron bolt heads, like nipples on a dog.

As we walked I noticed an adult novelty shop and a porn theater. There was a man standing by one of the lampposts that studded the center of the alleyway, throwing glances like darts at pedestrian targets as he worked on a cigarette. He was singing to himself. When we were near enough to him, he looked at each of us and changed the words of the song to "Cocaine? Speed? XTC? Acid?" Forest shook his head and pursed his lips, and I followed suit. I'd never been offered those drugs before. I was afraid of them, especially cocaine.

At the end of the alley was a woman who had to be a whore. She wore two clowns worth of makeup and a skirt so short that it could have been a belt. She kept bending over and adjusting elements of her costume, causing the neck of her shirt to hang open and expose her bra-less breasts. Under her eyes were the black gullies of her eye sockets; the eyes themselves were like scuffed plastic. Mostly it was the way she used those eyes to look at us with resigned hunger that made me assume she was a whore.

Prostitution was legal in Amsterdam, but the *Let's Go...*book had described something different than her.

We escaped the shade of the alley and encountered the Hell street. I aligned myself with Dude for the crossing.

When we were safely across, I looked back and saw Forest and Kara stopped in the middle of the road on one of the sets of trolley tracks. With their arms looped together, it was still a romantic pose.

"No, no, no," he said. "It would have been quicker to go the other way."

Kara put a hand over the open pages of his guidebook.

"Forest, it doesn't matter—"

"So we don't spend all day wandering aimlessly—" He braceleted her offending hand with his thumb and forefinger and lifted it away from the pages.

"—doesn't *matter*, Forest. We're on vacation."

"—like losers," he completed. "I know we're on vacation. It's my vacation too."

"Forest," I called. He raised an open hand to me without looking my way.

"Can you just try to enjoy yourself for one minute and get your face out of that map?" she said. Her tone wasn't quite a questioning one.

"Forest," I said.

"Someone has to be in charge, Kara, don't you think?" He said it forcefully. The words had the momentum of old arguments behind them.

"Forest, watch—"

"Jake, the last thing I need right now is your—"

She stepped backwards and yanked him by the arm. As he went, he looked her way with a knot of anger on his face. When he saw that she was looking off to his right, he followed her gaze to the trolley. It rolled towards the spot on the track where he had just been. He looked up at me with his face in emotional flux, and then the trolley sliced apart our eye contact.

I said something bad, but I did it quietly. A cigarette seemed obvious. The trolley was about as fast as a person walking, and about as loud. When the cigarette was planted between my lips, I reached for the lighter. Then I reached for the matches.

"Can you believe some asshole stole my Zippo lighter from me? It was a present from my dad," I said to the kid from Georgia.

"I'm sorry, dude."

When I had a satisfactory amount of smoke inside of me, I said, "It's okay. I know it wasn't your fault, Dude."

The trolley was only three cars long. When it passed, Forest and Kara crossed over the rest of the street. I started leading us in the direction we had been heading in.

"Do you smoke, Dude?"

"Cigarettes?"

"Yeah. Well, I already knew you smoke pot."

"I guess you do," he laughed. "No, I don't smoke."

"It's never too late to start, you know. You really should pick up the habit."

He genuinely thought that it was funny.

"You see the thing is, deep down, all you non-smokers know that we smokers are much cooler."

"What?" It's good when someone laughs at your jokes for real.

By this time we had made it to the Penis of the Gods, and I didn't know the way from there, so I waited for the other two.

"Jake, can I talk to you?" Forest's forehead was corrugated with stress. Kara was rifling through her purse a few paces back. I turned my hands over, palms up, in answer.

"Kara and I need some time alone. Will you be all right if we go to the museum without you, and then maybe you and Matt can go together later? And we can do something together sometime tonight, the four of us?"

All I did to answer him was shrug my shoulders.

"Do you mind? We just need some time…together, you know? Things are not going according to plan." He bumped his shoulder against mine. "It's nothing you did, Jake. Really."

"I know it's nothing I did. That's cool. We'll catch you later."

"Here, you guys can take my guidebook."

"Already got one."

"You do? I thought you didn't have one."

"Picked one up."

"I don't know about you, Jake," he smiled. He was trying to make a joke, and I let myself laugh a little bit.

"Listen, Forest, the only thing you should worry about is Kara. She's a good lady, and she flew all the way across an ocean just to see you. Matt and I will be fine. Why don't you take her out to a nice restaurant for lunch?" You're a real nice guy, Jake.

Forest looked over to Kara, who was putting her purse back in order, then to me. He moved a little closer to me.

"Jake, the thing is…" He looked at me for a second, chewing on the words. Then he remembered that I wasn't really one of his close friends. "How will we meet up with you guys?"

"We'll find each other back at the hostel. We'll check your room when we get back."

I went back to Dude and told him what was going on. He didn't seem to feel too badly about it. He didn't talk much when Forest was around. We walked in the opposite direction than the other two had gone off in.

"What do you want to do?" I asked him.

"Whatever, dude. How about you?"

"I'm kind of hungry. When's the last time we ate?"

He didn't know.

"Let's walk this way until we find someplace to eat."

We wove our way across the square and headed up a street we hadn't been on before. As we walked by a hash bar, he asked me, "I've been wondering, why do they call them 'hash bars?' Are hash and pot the same thing?"

I stopped short. "You've never tried hash before?"

"Nope."

"You need to come with me right away."

I took him into the very same hash bar that inspired the inquiry. Hash is made from marijuana that has been processed. I don't know the specifics of the process, but essentially the chemical that makes you high is taken out of the plant. The end product is a concentrated material the consistency of clay. It's bought in little bricks that resemble mud that got stuck in sneaker treads and dried up. For me a hash high is always a little more mellow and introspective than a weed high, but I'm sure it's different for everyone.

I ordered five grams of Jamaican. He used a little knife to chip pieces of it into his pipe, and we smoked it.

Except for the incident on my final evening there, that was the last of my clear, chronological memories of Amsterdam.

CHAPTER 8

Here are the stray moments prior to my last night in the city that I am able to recall:

Dude and I were in an affluent residential neighborhood. It was quiet, and there were potted flowers and potted trees out in front of the houses. They wouldn't have lasted five minutes in an American city, out in the open like that. There was hardly any litter or graffiti, and so few people about that I wondered if we had left the city limits.

Then I noticed the posts that lined the sidewalk. They were red, metal phalli about waist high, miniatures of the one in the city center, only these had cuffs a few centimeters below the round tips, just in case you didn't get it. They all had three raised letter Xs running down one side.

At the end of one block, a tree was growing out of the sidewalk. A little space around the tree was neatly manicured and bricked off, but before I could commit myself to thinking that it was a classy touch, I noticed the syringe lying in its topsoil. We followed the trail of relentless dicks back to the heart of the city. The city didn't want us to forget what she was.

I'm pretty sure it was the evening of that same day, when I found myself in a nightclub at a table full of people. My memory of the club was a random moment of lucidity, when I found myself wondering how

I'd gotten there, and how I'd become a part of that party. We were all listening to a girl who was a student at the University of Amsterdam.

I wasn't sure how I knew that the girl was a student. Dude was still with me, and something in the back of my mind told me that he had gotten us mixed up with that crowd. Brad and Chad were there as well, although I didn't remember when they had entered the scene.

The girl talking was dark skinned, but not in an African way, or an Asian way, or a Latin way like Tabi. The only thing I could figure was that she was an Eskimo. When I stopped listening to her for a moment, I noticed that she was very ugly. She commanded the attention of the whole table with an unwavering confidence that made her looks immaterial. I like to meet people like that.

The next thing I knew, a waitress was placing a fat piece of caramel cake in front of me. I must have ordered it. Everyone at the table was looking at me and making jokes about it. I tried to joke back, but the ideas in my head refused to coagulate into words. I realized that I hadn't said anything out loud for a very long time. I started eating the cake, which was too sweet to enjoy, and the moment of lucidity ended.

One time we were coming out of a sex toy shop, when I noticed the tightness in my belly and realized that the feeling had been there for quite a while. Once I acknowledged the hunger it became horrible. I ordered a gyro at a takeout booth and ate the whole thing while standing in front of the order window.

Once we'd eaten, I suggested having a little more of the hash. We went into a hash bar since one can't just smoke it out on the street. When I checked the bag, I found that we'd finished all five grams. Five grams is a lot for two people to smoke in one day. It's a lot to smoke even in two days, if that's how long it had been.

I'm pretty sure that this was dusk of the same day: we were walking by the canals. The streets were congested with foot traffic, so I figured that it was the weekend. We roamed the familiar radius around our hostel. Neither of us had said a sentence for hours that hadn't begun with "dude."

"Dude, do you know what I want to see?" he asked me. He struggled to maintain eye contact when he said it.

It was too late to go to the Van Gogh museum, and that was the last thing on our list. Suddenly I knew what he meant, even though we had never discussed the topic. "You want to see the brothels, don't you?" Something about the shape of his smile had clued me in.

"I was afraid to ask you. I didn't know if that's your kind of thing."

"Do you know how to get there?" I asked.

"Is it in the guidebook?" He was very excited.

"I don't have it with me. Come on. I can find it."

I have a special sense that allows me to find the red light district in any city. There are little hints that a city gives. I can't explain exactly how I do it; it's instinctive, and being high, I felt very in touch with that instinct. Once we were close to the nightclubs I started veering off down the darker, more discreet roads. There was a wide avenue we'd never been on before. There were no women walking about. Up ahead was the entrance to an alley, and men streamed in and out of it.

"Dude, this is the place."

We approached the entrance. The walls were brick. The men avoided eye contact with one another. Dude walked in ahead of me.

When we came around the corner I could see down the alley. It was just wide enough to accommodate the two streams of traffic. The alley was bent into odd angles, and along its length were illuminated glass doors. We joined the flow of the foot traffic. A few meters up on the left was the first glass door, and as I passed, I looked in.

There was a plastic woman on a wooden stool. She was the size of a real woman and incredibly lifelike, but her expression was too bold. Her brown hair was shoulder length, curled and puffed out to its maximum width. She was dressed in a gauzy blue teddy. The neck of it went down in a narrow V, all the way to her belly button. Brassy nipples showed through the cloth. As I walked by the door, her head seemed to turn and follow me. Her head was turning. She smiled at me. She said, "Hi, honey. Come on in." I couldn't look away. She shifted her legs; she was real.

Once past, I grabbed Dude by the shoulders as he did the same to me. His eyes were as wide open as mine felt.

"Dude, was she real, or was she a mannequin?" he practically shouted at me.

"Dude! I was going to say the same exact thing to you!" We gaped at one another as our faces bled our emotions.

"Let's go back."

"No, come this way. There's more."

Every few meters was another glass door, and behind each one sat a beautiful woman in lingerie looking at the men walking by. Many of them would beckon to us with their fingers and say things like, "Come on inside, honey. Come in, baby."

There were women of all races. One had cropped, bleached blonde hair, and she wore shiny, black plastic lingerie and a commanding look. There were two Asian women sharing a stool. Each had one hand on the hip of the other, and their smiles were wide, red promises. It went on and on until we came out the other side, to a street by a canal.

"Jake, when we saw that first woman, I really thought that she was fake."

"Dude, you just called me 'Jake.'"

I rewound the conversation in my mind and played it back, and he was right. It was my own voice calling him by my name.

"Sorry about that."

He shrugged. "I guess it really doesn't matter, does it?"

"Let's go back again."

We walked the way we'd come. When traffic bunched up, I would be extra careful of my passport. One traffic jam originated directly in front of us, when someone was let into one of the brothels. Further down the way some of the doors had curtains drawn behind them.

I felt that Dude was tempted to take a picture. When I turned to him, his hand was going into his jacket pocket. I broadcast with my mind that he shouldn't do so, and he stopped.

When we made it back to the opening of the alley I was out of breath, as though I was surfacing from a dive.

"Are you going to go into one of the rooms?" I asked.

"I considered it." His voice floated on ripples of laughter. "I don't think so." Then, "Would you?"

"No. I feel the temptation, but the whole thing is kind of depressing. Renting people."

"You're right. Me neither. I'd never go to one."

"How many days have we been here?"

He looked up and counted to himself, stopped, counted again, and laughed.

"I'm having such a good time I lost track."

"When's the last time we ate?"

He didn't know the answer to that one either. I could only recount three meals since we'd docked, including the caramel cake.

This was definitely on a different day: all four of us were walking somewhere, when that same beggar hit me up again.

"Can you give me some money?"

I raised an open hand and scowled in his general direction without stopping. I thought that I had gotten clear, but suddenly he was in my face.

"Hey! Say something! I know you can hear me! Talk to me! I'm here! I'm HERE!"

"No, I'm not going to give you any money!" I blurted.

"That's all you got to do," he instructed. "Don't ignore a guy. I'm *here*."

Transaction complete.

CHAPTER 9

Forest took me aside after my second meeting with the beggar.

"Kara and I are leaving on the next train."

"Are you two okay?"

"Probably not. I don't think we're going to last the trip."

I gave him a cigarette. He wasn't a real smoker, but this was the sort of thing that cigarettes were for. He puffed it like a cigar.

"The time alone will be good for you."

"We're going to take the train to Germany for a few days, then spend the rest of the time in Italy, I guess. I'd ask you to come along, but you know."

"Of course not." I was ready to be done with him.

"Are you and Matt going to be all right?"

"Don't lose any sleep over us."

"I love her, but something's changed."

"I know what you mean. Well, see what happens for the rest of the trip."

"I just think that I've matured in ways that she hasn't. I don't know how to tell her that. I feel bad that she flew all the way here." It was the type of thing I should stay out of.

"Don't give up. See what happens."

"I just wish she had done some travelling before this. Then maybe she wouldn't be so...I mean, she's not stupid."

"No, she's not. Anyone can see that. Why don't you try telling her what you're telling me?" The kind of thing I should stay out of. "It seems like men always talk to their male friends, and women to their female friends, when really they should be letting each other know what's on their minds. Tell her that being a traveler makes you different."

"Let's just drop it."

"Okay. It's none of my business, but I do have some knowledge of these things."

"You know what, Jake? You really have a gift for oversimplifying things."

Yes, I was really ready to be done with him.

"Well, good luck, Forest. I'll see you again after break."

It was a coincidence that Forest and I were on exchange to the same university. We had hung out a lot during first semester because we knew each other from home, because it was good to talk to another American sometimes, and because if one of us didn't have any weed, the other could probably find some. Forest had gotten me to join the Foreign Exchange Club with him; it was a cheesy, University-structured organization, aimed at "reinforcing the positive experience of our exchange students," but it sponsored some good trips.

We saw the Minster cathedral in York, England with the club, our first cathedral. It was a truly awesome sight, but all that day something had been bothering him. In the evening, while the club was at a pub waiting for the bus back, Forest left to take a walk by the river in the dark. I followed him out.

"What's on your mind, Forest?"

"I can't really talk about it." It was all over his face. He hopped up on the brick wall by the river and walked it tightrope style, and the expression was replaced by puckish concentration. It was important to me to be there for him.

Watching him walk on the ledge, I said, "You know what it is that we have in common? We're both independent. We dress a little differently, we don't follow the trends, we've both got what it takes to study abroad. We're not part of the flock. I think that's the heart of our friendship."

And then he looked me in the eye and said, "Jake, I hope this doesn't hurt your feelings, but you and I will never really be close friends."

I was trying to be there for him, so I told him that he hadn't hurt my feelings, and it was true when I said it. We returned to the pub and had a few drinks with the club until the bus arrived. It percolated inside of me during the bus ride, and by the time I got home I knew that he really had hurt my feelings, although I'd never tell him that.

Before he left Amsterdam, I retrieved my backpack from his room. I found that if I unpacked it partway, I could fit it into one of the lockers in the communal room. We shook hands before he left, and he said, "Jake? Do me a favor. You've got to stop saying 'dude' so much."

Dude left the next day. He had a Eurail ticket and was going to visit a few other countries before it expired. He asked me if I wanted to come along, but I couldn't afford my own ticket. We traded school and home addresses and promised to come visit one another. When we made the promise I really meant it, but after he'd gone, I knew that we wouldn't do it.

I wasn't sure if the others from the ferry were still in the city, or how to find them if they were. It was late afternoon, and I decided to get high at Led Zeppelin's again, but I couldn't find it. I settled for a place called the Student Bar, where I bought five grams of weed. I rolled a perfect joint using one of the pseudo-cigarette rolling papers, and I wanted to show it off to someone. It was too bad Kurt wasn't there.

After smoking it, I went walking. There were pornographic video stores all over the place, and I finally decided to check one out. Inside, a few men were milling about, looking at the merchandise. I kept my distance from them. I picked up a video box from one of the shelves, and read the title: "Farm Love," or something like that. On the back of it was a photo of a woman sitting bareback on a donkey, wearing nothing but panties. Underneath it was a picture of a woman and a German Shepherd, and they were doing something. I was a lot less shocked than I should have been. In Amsterdam it was just another thing.

I left the store and headed in the direction of the hostel. In order to avoid the Hell street I went around the back way. This brought me to the church that I had seen from Forest and Kara's room. It was fortified with red brick, but I could see areas where the original stone had been preserved, caked in dirt and moss. Even its moss looked old. Three Xs were carved out of stone above the doorway.

Across from the church was a row of brothels. The women behind the glass doors were at least twice as old as the ones I'd seen before. One of the women, wearing a bra and panties, had a gut that hung down in folds, and mottled thighs. She waved to me, just a little ripple across her fingertips, so I waved back.

In my stomach was the same shaky feeling I'd had on the first day of college and on the day I arrived in England. There was no one around who had any influence over me. I had never been so far away from my parents and friends before. My urges had a dangerous amount of power. It was only eight PM, but I went back to the hostel and got into bed. I was tired and low on cash, and being out would only cost me money.

Sleep only held me for about four hours. Two guys talking in an unfamiliar language woke me up. They were putting on sweaters. I listened to the rises and falls of their conversation, cresting into laughter a few times, and then they left. After a minute I went out again as well.

The beggars had been replaced by the pushers. I pinballed through them, and when they sang their medleys of wares at me, I shook my head and said, "I'm all set." I wandered aimlessly *no, you knew exactly where you were going, didn't you* and after some minutes I found the alley of the brothels.

It was busier than the last time. Most of the men were in groups of two or three. I watched a man haggle with one of the women, who held the door open a bit while they spoke. She was in her twenties and attractive, but she had the same baggy creases under her eyes that the rest of them had. The conversation was brief, and she let him into the room and slid the curtain shut.

When I came to an intersection, I turned left. The alley snaked its way along, and I snaked with it, until it dumped me out onto a street. I entered the maze again through another alley, trying to get my bearings.

One of the alleys dead-ended at the back door of a nightclub. I stood next to the enormous, dread-locked bouncer and looked inside. Half of it was a regular club, with a bar and a dance floor and disco lights, but on the other side was a room with four or five glass doors. Lingerie clad women danced behind them. You could go into the club and try to pick someone up, but failing that, there was the prostitution option. There was a loveless genius to it.

Going into a club meant spending more Gilders. "Oops. Sorry, I didn't know where I was," I offered to the bouncer.

"Dat's okay, buddy. Hey, buddy, Julie want to beer street?" or something like that, he rumbled at me in a friendly, thickly accented, bass voice. I smiled and nodded as though I'd understood and entered the line of people moving away from the club. He got into the line behind me, and I realized that he wasn't the bouncer after all, that he'd just been standing there.

"You going to see them girls, buddy?" He was a little shorter than I was, but his shoulders bulged under his black jacket with much more bulk than mine did.

"No, I'm just looking." I walked like I had someplace to go.

"Oh yeah. You with your friends, buddy?" We kept moving through the human traffic, he at my elbow between the wall and me. His hand accidentally brushed against my hand, which was tucked into the front pocket of my jeans.

I picked a sentence to end the conversation. "Yeah. Going to see my friends."

"What's your name?"

"It's John." I kept looking ahead.

"Hey buddy," he whispered, in that tone that says you are about to be offered something illicit. "Hey John, you want to buy some good hash it's very good, John."

"No, I'm all set," I said in a fuck-off tone.

"Hey John, hey listen to me," as his hand accidentally brushed the small of my back. "You come back with me to (something) street and we smoke some ungodly good hash, right? John?" His hand touched the nape of my neck, then between my shoulder blades, then the back right pocket of my jeans. We were coming to the end of the alley, which was getting very narrow, and the people and graffiti were swirling around me and I didn't know if he was alone.

I stopped abruptly and spun to face him, one hand opened in front of me, the other by my hip in a ready position. He was a lot wider than I was. "No hassles, man," I said, and gripped his eyes with mine.

"Hey, buddy, what you saying, buddy?" and then he dropped his voice to a whisper again and said, "Listen, John, listen to me." He said it like he was rocking a baby. I knew that I was smart not to have given him my real name, so he couldn't shake me with an illusion of familiarity. The line was backing up behind him. I pushed my way into the lane going in the other direction and walked away, and breathed out. I could hear his voice behind me, trying to explain, "My friend's acting so strange, I don't know why he's doing that."

I avoided going back to the club by turning right, down an unfamiliar alley. It was empty. I didn't hear him come up behind me, I felt the approach, and he said, "Hey buddy, you *better* listen to me," and now I was wide awake. "*Hey* buddy. *Hey* buddy." It was a threat.

When I felt that he was very close I lunged forward a step, sweeping my hands down and out to the sides at the ready. I was raised to full height with my shoulders spread wide, and my senses erupted: the hairs on the back of my neck touched the air for any disruption his movement would cause, my ears caught every rustle of cloth and scrape of shoe on tarmac. I did not turn to face him. It was a dare.

He didn't move. I took a slow step forward, careful not to appear like I was in flight. My senses were throbbing. I saw every shadow cast from behind me. I kept walking slowly towards the mouth of the alley.

When I came out of the alley, I turned right and started down a street at the edge of a canal, towards people. After a block of that, I stopped to light a cigarette and turned around and he was not following me. I couldn't remember his face, just his eyes with their strange gravity, hovering in the shadow of him.

It took me half an hour to find my way back to the hostel. My legs ached from the walking, and my lungs complained about the cigarettes, but that was no reason to stop smoking. The Eagle was open when I got there. A row of motorcycles glistened out front. Men in leather pants, vests, hats, and square-toed boots milled around in front of it, hitting on each other. One of them had chains running from his pierced ears to his pierced nose to his pierced nipples, then down into his leather pants. There was a fire truck at the end of the alley.

The woman at the hostel's front desk told me that there'd been a fire, so I'd have to wait downstairs for a while.

"Someone left a cigarette burning in a bed." I was glad I didn't have a cigarette in my hand when she told me.

"This fits right in with the rest of my night. Someone just tried to mug me."

"One of those damn Moroccans, I'll bet."

I wasn't sure what his nationality had been. She was so friendly to me that I agreed with her prejudice for the camaraderie of it.

"You won't have to wait long to go to bed, honey. Some of the other boys are in the lounge. Why don't you go talk to them?" Since she called me "honey" I did what she said.

A man sitting alone at a table invited me to play cards. We played five-card stud, and I destroyed him hand after hand. He smiled when he lost, but his eyes were meek, like he thought I was going to hit him.

"So, are you a student?" he asked me.

I told him that I was. I looked at him and judged him to be in his thirties. "Are you a student?" I asked just to reciprocate.

"Student of the world," he smiled. We were smoking my cigarettes. "Are you here with friends?"

I told him how they'd all left, and that I was sight seeing.

"Say, listen. I've got this plan. I'm going to leave this town and hitch my way around Europe. See Italy, France, Spain... Why don't you come along with me?"

"No offense, but I travel alone. It's just the kind of guy I am."

"Are you sure?"

"Thanks. No offense."

"Your loss." He didn't have the proper tone to carry such a statement. His jacket was a threadbare sports coat. His hair had almost evacuated his head. Despite his being older, he treated me as a superior. When I added him up and came to a total, I knew that he was never going to leave this place. The city had won. He was Amsterdamned.

Finally, they let us go back up to our rooms. It was three in the morning. The bed was redolent of smoke.

That was my last evening in Amsterdam.

CHAPTER 10

Somehow the Moroccan found me in my room in the morning, and he was shaking me awake. "Hey pal. Hey, are you awake?" His big fingertips were on my back and I came completely awake and spun to face him and I was afraid. It wasn't the Moroccan, though; it was just the man who changed the sheets for the hostel.

"I'm sorry to startle you. It's time to get up. I've got to change the room."

The housekeeper had a friendly smile in the middle of his beard, and he let me take my time. When I had everything inside of my army backpack, I donned it and went outside to find breakfast.

I'd let my hunger go for so long that the idea of food made me sick. I knew that my appetite would come back in a rush after the first bite, and I ordered a big meal at an Indian restaurant. There was something that I had to take care of, but there were too many eyes in the dining room, so I went into the men's room. In the stall I withdrew the money from my inside jacket pocket and counted it out. There wasn't a lot of it. I painfully removed a few bills and added them to my wallet, then went back out to eat.

After breakfast I meandered into the main square. In front of the train station I found a booth labeled as a travel agent's.

"What can I get you?"

"Just one moment." There was a map of destinations taped up against the glass. "How much is a ticket to Paris?"

It was as much as ten grams of weed. I bought it and stashed it in my inside pocket.

There was time to kill before the bus left. I went into the closest hash bar and spun a joint. The bar was on the second story of a building, and had lots of windows that overlooked the square. I hadn't done any drawing in a long time, so I slid my sketchbook out of the backpack and had a go at it. I deconstructed the old church on a few pages, and did a study of the fat prostitute who was its neighbor.

I was nervous about missing the bus, so I left early. The bartender who made me the coffee had been pleasant, so I said, "Here. A tip," and left him the rest of my weed. That would take care of getting through French customs.

I was anxious until other people started to wait along with me at the bus stop. The bus came on time, and I took a seat in the middle, away from the other passengers.

Once the bus was moving, one of the girls on board got up and knelt next to her friend, so that they could talk. She was eating cookies from a little package. When she turned to look at me, she offered them.

"Cookie for you?"

"Merci." I let my American accent permeate the word, so she'd know that I couldn't have a conversation in her language.

With my looks, I'm only attractive when I've had a shower and a shave and nice clothes on, so I didn't know why she'd flirt with me. The cookie was a thin biscuit with a thin layer of quality dark chocolate over orange jelly, and it was very good, and I wished that I spoke more French.

The bus started up and moved us through Amsterdam and the night, and I knew I'd made my escape.

What woke me was the movement of people around me. The bus had stopped, and everyone left was retrieving their luggage from the racks and from beneath their seats. I had been in a deep sleep, and the noises worked themselves into a dream until, gradually, the real world took over.

My body was soft with sleep, and my ears were tender, so that little sounds seemed loud. The driver was conversing with the passengers, and I avoided his eyes in order to avoid his words. Off the bus it was five in the morning.

Somewhere the sun was making an appearance, but it was very far away. In the darkness there was the beginning of rain. When the bus pulled away, I started walking in the opposite direction of the other passengers. There were no customs after all, and I had gotten rid of five grams of weed unnecessarily. There is no time in this life for regret.

There was no one about, so I sheltered myself in the doorway of a building and lit up my last cigarette. The rain was gentle and small and didn't make a sound when it reached the ground. I adjusted the backpack on my shoulders and began to walk towards the heart of the city, through the polite rain of Paris.

End of Part One.

PART TWO

CHAPTER II

The waiter in the brasserie wore a starched tuxedo shirt, a cummerbund, and a bow tie, and the way he moved gave the impression that being a waiter was a profession rather than just a job.

"*A coffee, please,*" I ordered in French. It takes three words in French to express what we say with the one word "please" in English. Using it filled out the handful of other things that I knew how to say in French, creating the illusion of a decent vocabulary.

"*And not any dessert? Why not? They are very good.*" He brought my attention to the confections in a glass case. I felt that I was at the cusp of his assessment, that I would earn his disapproval if I ordered nothing more than a coffee. I chose a piece of dark chocolate layer cake because it looked good, and because it was the only item out of the array that I knew the words for. My order had cost as much as I had intended to spend on food all day. The waiter was about forty years old, and I had let him intimidate me into it because my father had imbued me with respect for my elders.

I had $135 American worth of mixed currency in my wallet. I was figuring the return ticket to England at about $90 American, the same as the ticket over. The youth hostel I'd found was about $25 a day. There were two weeks left before I could return to the dorms. I didn't want to do it, but it was time to call Dad.

The floor of the brasserie was made of small, black-and-white tiles set in a diamond pattern. My chair was baroque wrought iron with a clean, firm cushion. The waiter presented my cake and was done with me. Melted chocolate had been drizzled onto its dark chocolate roof. Underneath was a layer of brown cake so moist as to be watery, followed by a sheet of caramel, a layer of a different kind of cake, and a basement of some type of granular, almond substance. I ate it as slowly as possible since I was killing time, but it was worth savoring.

When you order a coffee in France you get espresso. Coffee is very important to me. The English don't drink coffee, they drink tea, unless you run across an individual who does, in which case that person drinks instant coffee. Instant coffee is a sin. The espresso in the brasserie was served in a china demitasse, and when I picked it up, it clicked against the saucer and made a crisp china note. Asking my father for money was serious business, so I didn't add milk, but I did add sugar, which came in cubes wrapped in stiff paper. The coffee was strong and rich and was the best coffee that I'd ever had. I was in France.

Before coming to England I'd never been abroad, unless you count going to Canada, which most Americans don't. Dad had told me that I'd end up calling him for money when I proposed the year on exchange. I had told him that he was wrong. I mentally rehearsed the phone call I was about to make to him to be prepared for every direction the conversation might take.

When my waiter's disdainful scrutiny got to be too much, I settled the bill and left. At the corner was a newspaper and tobacco shop. I bought a pouch of Drum loose tobacco, which was a lot cheaper than pre-rolled cigarettes. Perhaps my frugality would count in my karmic favor when I called.

It was still too early, so I walked off the rest of the time and wound up in a business district. The buildings had much more presentation about them than the ones in America. American buildings were all glass and steel and rectangular and anonymous; the Parisian buildings were arches and flares, and stone carved into leaves and angels. The American Express building spread itself out over a corner of a boulevard, as grand as a court house. Small European cars of unfamiliar makes and motorbikes passed by, filling the air with three-or four-cylinder corkscrews of noise. People hurried about in suits, ties, and hard black shoes, in spite of my vacation. I found a public telephone and rolled a long cigarette on it, then tucked the cigarette behind my ear. It was eight AM where my father was, and he would have been at the office for an hour by then.

"Feather-Touch Car Care, good morning."

"Tell me, do feathers *really* touch the cars in your car wash?" Heavily recycled joke.

"Yes, down feathers plucked by the hands of vestal virgins. Is that my son, the bench-press champion of England?" My bench-press weight was a source of my pride. Dad was always happier to hear from me when I'd been gone for a long time.

"Hi Dad. How are you? Is everything well?"

"My son Jake, calling me. Hold on a minute, let me get my checkbook out."

I tried laughing the reality out of it. "How's Mom?"

It's important to him that I ask about Mom right away. My sister was "still a lesbian" he informed me, but it was a good day to leave their battle between the two of them.

"How's the car wash?"

"Big news, Jake. You're not going to believe it."

"Okay, I already doubt you."

"I bought out Peter."

"What? Really?" Peter had been Dad's business partner.

"And I'm negotiating on a second location."

"Really?" I scrambled to find the response he wanted. None of this was expected. "Dad, that's fantastic. Well, congratulations to you."

"Yes, have a drink to me. Oh, maybe you've already had a few. You can claim that they were in my honor. What the hell, you're old enough; have another one on me."

"Um, it's only three in the afternoon here, Dad."

Dad shielded his business strategies from me, and it made me feel like I was five years old again once he finally revealed them. I was still holding it together.

"Well, I know the only reason you called was to hear about my business. I'll tell your mother you love her. Goodbye son," he said too quickly. He knew that there was more and was forcing my hand.

"So Dad, do you remember that last student loan that I've been waiting on?"

"Yes."

"Well, I'm kind of in a spot where I'll be needing it. Pretty immediately."

"I thought it would be a good idea to get out my checkbook."

"No, Dad, I just need to know if that loan is ready yet. Or if not, if you can advance me a little against it until it is." I was still holding it together.

"Jake, you should forget about that loan."

"What do you mean, Dad?"

"You're not going to get that loan."

"Why not?"

"The only way you were going to get that loan was with a co-signer, Jake. I can't sign for a loan with you right now because of what's going on with the car wash."

The cigarette was still tucked behind my ear. Something about the presence of my father made me swallow the news and get on to the next step.

"I was really counting on that loan, Dad. I'm in Paris, and I'm almost out of money. I won't be able to get back to England."

"*Paris*? What are you doing in Paris?"

"I'm on spring break. I couldn't stay in the dorms—"

"Well, you're already there, right?" There was a big sigh. He didn't say, "I told you this would happen." I should have saved more money over the summer. I had bought a car instead, so that I could get out of the house. My parents could have paid for the car. He had told me not to get it, but he always discouraged me when I displayed independence, and I had no way of sorting out what was good advice. He never equipped me to handle the paperwork on the school loans. I should have figured them out before I left, should have made him show me. Should have worked out the money before I went on vacation to Paris, but all my friends were able to do things like this.

"What do you propose I do, son?"

"Could you wire me some money?"

"*Wire* you some money?"

"Dad…"

Testy sigh. I held my ground. "Call me back in an hour."

"Dad, these phone calls cost me ten dollars. Is there any way you can give me an answer now?"

"Son—" Something hard was behind it, but he didn't let it out. "How much do you need?"

I minimized it rapidly. "Five hundred?"

"Five hundred. How am I supposed to get this five hundred to you?"

"There's an American Express office right here. I'm looking right at it."

"How will I know that you got the money?"

"I can call you?"

"I'll advance you pay so when you come home, you can work it off."

"I will, Dad."

There was the sound of breath through teeth.

"I really appreciate it, Dad."

"I can do two hundred."

"Whatever you can manage, Dad. I really do appreciate it."

"I bet Paris is nice this time of year. Wouldn't I like to be there. Oh well."

It was mandatory that I endured that. We worked out the rest of the details of the wire, deciding that I would only call him if there were a problem receiving it. After hanging up, I turned away from the telephone towards the buildings and removed the cigarette. I shook a match from the box and lit the cigarette with it, taking two drags while I withdrew myself from the phone call and became part of my surroundings again. The sky was the color of a banker's suit. Sometimes drops would blow off of the roofs, and sometimes it would be real rain. I walked the way the streets wanted to take me, and ended up by the Seine, the river.

There was a black iron fence running the length of the riverbank, and along the fence were vendors' carts. The vendors sat on folding chairs, watching tourists finger the books and postcards on display. Below the bank was a concrete path that ran close to the river's edge. I leaned against the fence and watched the river for a while, then turned right and followed the water.

Bridges arched to the other half of the city at every block or so. Far ahead in the middle of the river was what I knew must have been the *ile de la Cite*. A shape I guessed was a cathedral sat waiting on the isle, gathering sky with its stone fingers. Somewhere in the city, a police siren *hee-hoo hee-hoo hee-hoo*ed its two note alert, then *hoo-haw hoo-haw hoo-haw*ed as it Dopplered away. I moved from the river and back into the net of streets.

Along the boulevard were cafés and restaurants with patios, although it was still too cold to sit outside. On a corner at a *boulangerie*, fresh baguettes filled the air with aroma that seemed to curl down into my stomach. Behind the counter were baskets of the bread sticks in an array of lengths and widths.

Down the rain slick sidewalk I saw a woman in the midst of a flock of pigeons. There must have been a hundred birds in a red-footed, turbulent mass in front of her, and more were landing to be in her vicinity. She was a robust woman of about fifty, wearing a great, hooded cape that enveloped all but her face. She took a handful of crumbs from a plastic bag and scattered them into the cooing congregation. Four of them launched themselves from the sidewalk to perch, after a corrective flutter, on her arms. Finally, one kept post on the top of her head.

I stared at her for many minutes, stopped in the middle of the sidewalk. She never said a word. On her face wasn't a smile so much as it was the shape left over from a lifetime of smiling. She was concentrating very hard on what she was doing.

Usually when I saw something like that, some beautiful *event*, I would try to fit it into my sense of values, try to figure out what it meant in my world, which direction it tipped the balance in favor of. I was starting to learn that it didn't mean anything; it was a beautiful thing and totally random. And perhaps my father was like he was towards me because, in his grand scheme of things, he was trying to toughen me up, to force me to be as independent as he was. Or maybe not, but it didn't really matter: they both added up to the same answer, that I was in Paris without enough money for food and lodging. The lady was dressed all in black, and it would be poetic to think that she resembled her birds, or a nun, or some other symbol, but she did not. She was a woman whose values included feeding the pigeons until they climbed all over her, and that was exactly what she was. My cigarette had gone out, but only because of the rain. I headed back in the direction of the American Express office to check on my wire, and then I would go to the hostel to retrieve my bag. Afterwards, I would return to the Seine and check under the bridges, because I had it in my mind that that's where bums slept.

Dad had wired me $250 American, less than needed but more than promised, a number by which he'd managed to color disappointment with generosity. It felt nice to have a fat stack of bills, but I didn't allow the feeling to infect my actions. I still needed money for the remainder of the semester after break was over. I'd have to worry about that when the time came. I couldn't afford to think that far ahead. I pictured Dad's oval face, the remains of his brown hair, his almost-smile; then put the picture away again in my mind.

I took the stairs down into a Metro station, the Parisian subway. A display yielded a free map, my first equipment procurement. I emerged onto the street, reoriented myself, and walked downhill towards the Seine. A stone stairway led down to the concrete bank at the water's edge. The river reflected the cloud soaked sky, and was the same concrete color.

I was the only one walking so close to the river. Passing under the first bridge, my conjecture was verified; tucked into the osculation between the bridge and the bank were a few men. One of them was wrapped in blankets, sitting up, rifling through a plastic bag. He looked at what his stubby, grimy fingers were doing, but I could tell that he was tracking me in his peripheral vision. I could see how his blankets were a commodity. It was still that part of spring when snow wouldn't be a surprise. I could sleep in many layers of clothing to stay warm, or perhaps I'd manage to get a blanket. Somehow.

As I passed from under the bridge, I looked back and saw a young couple leaning against the railing above, touching foreheads as they hummed French to each other. Maybe there was another option. Didn't churches allow the poor to sleep there? Had I read that in some history class, or in my British literature class?

Just before the *Ile*, I climbed stairs to the top of a bridge. I followed the roads until one brought me onto the *Ile*. People were rushing towards its center as though they were heading towards a concert or a game. Their current washed me into a cobblestone square. At the far end of it, droves of tourists swarmed in front of pair of gargantuan wooden doors. The doors stood in the center of a stone arch that was taller than a house, and soaring on and on above it was the rest of a cathedral.

A belt of statues spanned the center of the structure. Each three meter tall statue was of a different character, dressed in flowing robes and crowns, some holding staves. Above them was an ornate circular web of stone filled in with stained glass. When I reached the bushes in front of the cathedral I noticed two more arched doorways on either side of the main entrance. Each of the arches was lined with more carved figures, stacked all the way to the peak. Every place I looked, my eyes were met with more and more detail. Everything was frosted with painstakingly carved stone: saints, Jesus, Mary, angels, and other things I wasn't familiar with.

I considered how long it must have taken to carve even one of these stone details, and when I saw so many put together, it filled my lungs and throat with an ache. I hadn't believed in God for a long time, but someone did. Thousands of people had, and had given decades of art and labor to prove it. Just for that moment, even in the midst of my doubt, I thought, *God is great.*

There was a procession into the right-hand set of doors, and I added myself to it. A girl working the door would only let a few people in at a time. I checked the map and learned that I had found the Notre Dame. I felt certain that this was not the type of church that the poor were allowed to sleep in, but I wanted to see what was inside. I was hot from the adrenaline.

Just inside the doors was a dark, wood foyer. The others who had entered with me were milling about at a rack of fliers. I stepped past them around the corner. There was no way to avoid looking up. The cathedral leapt higher and higher to a vaulted stone ceiling that held an impossibly large piece of the sky. My breath pushed itself out of me. All around were carvings of Biblical stories set into the walls, and paintings, and frescos, and higher up were more stained glass windows and columns. Some of the pillars went all the way from the ground to the ceiling, and they were almost too much to look at. People walked slowly about the perimeter, observing the cathedral's features. No one spoke more loudly than in a whisper. In the back of my throat was suspended that hot, wet feeling, not exactly the one that comes before crying.

At the fore of the church were simple wooden pews. A young couple sat smiling with their arms around each other. It felt inappropriate. An old woman sat in the first pew, her bowed head almost touching her clasped hands, her eyes squeezed tightly. She had short gray hair. She wore a wedding ring on her right hand, European style, and she was alone.

I placed myself a few rows behind her and slid to the center of the pew. I began to meditate the way I'd learned in karate class, releasing the tension from every part of my body, my conscience rolling its way up my body piece by piece, letting go, then clearing my mind of all the thoughts it was working on.

I breathed that way for a while, then let my thoughts back in.

I would make it through the rest of break. If I thought I was so smart, then I should be able to find a way. And damn me for trying to keep Forest's pace. Forest and the thousands of dollars that he'd saved up over the summer, wearing the clothes that his parents had bought him. Forest and his parentally funded education. Why was it always so important for me to be able to do everything my friends did? I'd been through this lesson before; when was I going to learn from it? What was it that really mattered to me?

The third time she came over to my room, I finally asked her where she was from. She started on this discourse about how her mother was from Brazil but her father was from England, and I cut her off and said, "I guess if I wanted your family tree I would have asked for it. I meant where do you live when you're not at school?" She called me a bastard but in a cute way. I figured that the British assumed she was a foreigner because of how she looked. I looked her all over and it was time to kiss her so I did, and I wished I had something smooth to say when I kissed her but I didn't, she asked "What are you doing?" and I said, "This," and I was thinking "Oh that was smooth you idiot," but those lips, they those lips on mine she was shaking I made her feel that way her breath was hot cinnamon and she oh.

Then came the times when she'd go to the pub with her friends and I'd go with mine, and she'd stop by my table for a cig, or I'd cruise by hers and buy a few drinks. Both of us pretending it was nothing, but that high voltage tension flowed between us, our own specific lightning.

The first time we walked to the pub together, she wanted to hold hands, and I wondered what the English would think about us, the white American and the Latina. Maybe they'd think that the foreigner was trying to pollute their purebred ways with his American interracial ideas. And from somewhere inside of me came the solid steel feeling that it would be a fool's suicide to say something bad about the two of us, or even to give me the wrong look; she was my woman. I didn't know that I had had such mettle inside me, and it was mined to my surface because of Tabi.

It had been a Thursday night, crowded, and when we entered the Ellison pub, everyone stared at us. She was so beautiful, and men looked at her with desire and their eyes would flicker to our clasped hands and she was mine. When I was with her I was ten feet tall and indestructible, and there was heat in the eyes of the women around me.

Then weeks later when everyone knew, she whispered to me at the bar one night, "Let's get out of here, it's time," and I was no fool. She wanted to stop at her room first, and she told me to go ahead and wait for her. "You'd better be there when I come over," as if even if the place were on fire I wouldn't be there. In the room I brushed, changed my underwear, lit my candle, and waited forever, lying on the bed, wondering if maybe she wouldn't show. And she didn't even knock; she rushed into the room and dropped her bag on the ground, walked straight to the sliding glass door and said, "It's hot in here," slid the door open, and turned back to me. It was a show. She had changed into those jeans with the tear just beneath her left buttock, and a top that showed all the smooth skin above her hard breasts. And right then is a moment I have engraved in my mind: when she climbed on top of me with her fresh perfume and smoke, and her lips were swollen, and she felt like a fever, I can remember exactly the width of her hips in my hands, and she was shaking, but she gave me that look that would burn a stone, those pools of brown eyes under half closed lids caught mine and I pulled her to me hard and kissed her.

And on until three and there was biting and the sheet came loose, and these were memories I could still have in a church because we didn't, the two of us didn't quite

but she stayed with me. She stayed. In bed until noon and she was there in my arms and I knew that for her, for Tabi, as long as it took, I could wait.

Then in a few days I was walking with her after dinner and she said she had something to tell me. She said it the bad way. She said she'd lied to me about something and my stomach just disappeared but I said it's okay, and she told me.

And I said, "Really? That's it?"

And she asked if I was mad at her, and I said, "Really? Never? Not even with," and she said no but was I mad? "But why did you lie?" and she said she was afraid that if she hadn't that I wouldn't like her, and didn't guys want women who had, and I said I'm not mad, but please, just please don't lie to me, don't make me into the fool.

When I opened my eyes, the old woman who had been praying in the pew up front was gone. A new mix of worshippers had settled in. I realized that a choir was singing, and had been singing the whole time I was there. The song echoed its way up and around the pillars and joined thousands of older songs in the stones. Church would be a pretty good place, I decided, if only you could smoke there.

CHAPTER 12

I crossed back over to the West Bank in search of a more modest church. I wondered how it would be to sleep on a pew. The rain had stopped. A Van Gogh book in a bookstore window caught my eye. He was my favorite painter, and I was mad at myself for not seeing that museum when I had had the chance. The window of the bookstore was so old that the glass was thicker on the bottom.

There was something strange about the books lined up in the window. I read one title after another until I figured out what it was; I *could* read them. They were all in English. An American couple nearby pulled cheap, used, paperback romance novels from a wooden shelf on the sidewalk and laughed at the cheesy back-cover synopses.

I stepped away from the window and looked for the name of the store, and there it was in wooden letters:

Shakespeare and Co.

A memory I'd never used before rustled to life, on a shelf so far back in my mind I hadn't known it was there. A session of my American Writers class on Hemingway, just a few sentences from my professor about Paris and Sylvia Beach, before moving on to bull fighting. The memory swam dolphin-swift through my desperation. I hurried to the well-used door and entered the shop before reality chased this bizarre coincidence away.

The shop was dim, and customers were standing or sitting all about, reading. It smelled of old wood and old pages and fresh coffee. Books were shelved from floor to ceiling, and there were stacks in front of the desk, behind the desk, and under the windows; anywhere they would fit. I watched a plush bodied girl in a flowered skirt find a volume for an older couple. The three of them spoke in British accents. She led them to the front of the shop and excused herself past me to take her station behind the desk.

"*Bon jour.* Can I help you?"

"*Bon jour!* Thank you. They were here first. I can wait." My father always told me that you get more miles out of a horse with sugar than with the whip. She thanked me and picked up her conversation with the customers again. I liked her Shetland sweater. Hanging between her untethered breasts on a piece of blue yarn was an ankh, the Egyptian symbol of eternal life.

When she finished with the couple she turned to me.

"Nice ankh."

"Thanks."

"And I'm guessing that you're from…not northern England, but not quite Wales. Manchester?"

"Pretty close. Just outside." That's the way you show an Englander that you know your way around England. "How can I help you?"

I hoped that I'd won her over enough. "This is kind of a strange question, so if I sound like I'm crazy, just let me know." She didn't look put off. "I was told in one of my college literature courses that if a writer wound up in Paris with no money, he might find a place to stay at Shakespeare and Company in exchange for work."

Maybe a look of acknowledgement on her features. "What was the class?"

"American Writers."

"I see."

"Is this the place, or do I sound crazy after all?"

"You don't sound crazy. That's my situation as well."

"Really? Well I'm here on break from college, and I've found myself in a bit of a fix, and I was wondering…might I be able to stay here? In exchange for work?"

"We might be full up now. Hold on, you'll have to talk to George."

She stepped away from the desk and headed towards the back of the store. I heard her run up some stairs. I smoothed my hair a bit with my hands. I needed a shave and a shower, but this would add to my destitute appearance. I should have said something about the sweater.

When she returned, I had a copy of **Hamlet** in hand as a prop, and I wore the respectful Nice Young Man look on my face. Trailing her was a man in his sixties with a voice like a parrot's. They were at the tail end of a conversation about how well a line of art books were moving. His hair was a spaghetti of grays and dying browns that looked like it had been through three windstorms going in different directions. His shirt was a neon orange oxford with a party of orange paisleys on it. The material looked expensive, but it was wrinkled like his brown wool trousers, and the width of the collar put it at about fifteen years old. At the end of his spindly arm was a ball peen hammer. His focus on the girl when she spoke was so total it was almost amorous.

"Is this the boy you mentioned?" he asked her.

"Yes, but I can't recall his name."

"Jacob, sir. A pleasure to meet you." I extended my right hand. He looked at it like it was something that dropped out of a dog. "You must be George?"

"Do you know how to use a hammer?"

I straightened my spine. "Yes sir."

"Make me a set of shelves, here, here, and here," he chirped. He stabbed the hammer at an empty space behind the counter. There were some old used boards leaning against the wall, a bag of nails, and a stack of books. He put the hammer in my hand. I got the impression that his outfit wasn't a colorblind accident, but rather it was the intentional

expression of his style. His moustache was white. He had the first Van
Dyke beard I'd ever seen.

"What are you waiting for, the armistice?"

I cut through my fog of duh and started measuring the space on the
wall. When I looked around again he was gone, and the girl was back at
the desk.

"I'm sorry, I didn't catch your name."

"It's Camille."

"Can I borrow a pencil, Camille?"

She dug around the chaos of the desk for one.

"What do you think? Is he going to let me stay?"

"It's possible."

I hoped her indeterminate answer was just her way of toying with
me. It would have been pretty crappy of George to put me to work and
not let me stay.

Customers strolled about the store choosing volumes and sitting
wherever they felt. There was a woman sitting on a couch in the back for
a very long time, smiling at her book. Camille wrote in a spiral bound
notebook in cursive while I worked.

When I was done, I lined the books up on my shelves, facing some
of the covers out. George inspected my work and said, "Do you call
these shelves? You're the worst carpenter I've ever seen!" He yanked at
the wood to test its anchorage, then slashed at the books so they flew
to the floor.

"I—"

"You may sleep downstairs with the other boys. Be back by eight
o'clock because the door will be locked after," he said sweetly.

"Do you want me to do anything—"

"Go on, boy, you're in Paris! Go enjoy yourself."

He was smiling. His hands brushed me away. Camille was red in the
cheeks with stifled laughter.

"Thank you, George. Thank you very much. I really appreciate this." He wouldn't look at me. "I just can't thank you enough."

He started talking to Camille as though I wasn't there. I walked delicately out the door and into a fresh breeze. It felt like I'd hit my first homerun, and I was standing at home plate staring at the bat.

It was dusk, but I figured I had enough time to go see something I'd always wanted to see. My new map showed me how to reach it. I went left down the sidewalk. There was a telephone booth on the corner that I noted as my first landmark. Tabi was wreaking havoc in me. I wanted her to know of the coup I had just pulled off. I fantasized that she was holding my hand as I crossed the busy *Rue Monteparnasse,* and I was telling her about it.

I cut through the Latin Quarter, a nest of one-lane cobbled streets congested with people, mostly couples. There were the sounds of a fight up ahead. When I got closer I saw a man wearing a good suit, shouting in Greek. He had a stack of plates in his left hand, and he took one off the top and smashed it onto the tiled floor of the doorway.

A couple in their thirties wearing black leather jackets and black Levi's jeans watched the spectacle. The man had on an expensive pair of rectangular framed glasses. He said something to his companion in French. She had fantastic hair, a multitude of tight curls like the bubbles in boiling water. She widened her eyes and said something back. He laughed a little laugh and put his arm around her waist. She smiled, and she looked like she felt the kind of happy that you want to make a woman feel, and they went into the restaurant. The plate thrower commended them on their choice and punctuated it by tossing two more dishes to the ground.

At the end of the block was another *boulangerie,* where I bought a baguette. It was warm and came wrapped in a slice of brown paper, and I thanked the woman at the counter very much, "*Merci beaucoup.*" The crust was the right color yellow. I bit the end off of it. It was just chewy enough, and it tasted even better than it smelled. I walked more quickly, bearing left up a main street, cutting across the city.

The rain was beginning again. There were a lot of people out, going into the restaurants and movie theatres. Umbrellas popped open along the sidewalk. I was full of bread, and it would feel nice when I got back to the store and was dry and warm.

Strange how it feels as you accomplish a lifetime goal, how all of the little elements of the experience balloon in their importance: a wrapper from a crepe that made me notice how free the streets were of litter otherwise; the smile I was given by a girl too young for me as she caught up with her friends; the way her smile made me look down and into a puddle too big to jump, big enough to hold the entire reflection of the Eiffel Tower, and I looked up and saw it for real.

It was made out of naked girders, but it looked nothing like an unfinished building. I wasn't certain what her designer was trying to say, but I could feel that there was some idea being expressed in her shape, some archetype to her architecture. I passed underneath it and looked up at the huge bolts, and at the four legs curving upwards in sweet and specific degrees. I got into queue for the elevator.

In front of me was a pack of rich looking teenage boys; behind me was a cluster of teenage girls. Some lovers holding hands walked past, but none got into line. As we moved forwards, one of the boys would say something to one of the girls, or say something loudly enough to his mates for it to carry over. French is a beautiful language to hear, especially in a young voice. I thought of all the things I would do differently if I was their age again, if I knew then what I'd learned since.

When we got to the head of the line, I paid for a ticket and got into the elevator. It stopped at the middle level, and I took the stairs to the top. They were narrow and metal, and they made *tank tank tank* noises with the fall of shoes. When I finished the stairs, I moved to the railing and looked through the fence, over the bridge, down to the Louvre, and on past it to the misty tops of skyscrapers, and beyond to the vague field of buildings. Breeze fingered my hair across my forehead and reddened my knuckles, but I could take it.

I walked to another side of the tower and looked down at the bridges dissecting the grammar of the river like commas. Cars were so far away that they were ladybug small; people were so small that they weren't there. Much closer were twin buildings that seemed to be apartments. They made me think about living in the city, and I decided, *yes, I would like it here.* I could learn the rest of the language and get a good job to afford such a place, and she and I...

I went to another side of the tower and looked out over a strip of lawns long enough to land a plane on. Lamps lit up the grass, highlighting the metal statues along the sides. Deep into Paris was an American sized skyscraper, but it was too dark to make out much else.

I went to the final side where there was no one else and leaned against the railing. In the shelter of my arms I rolled a Drum cigarette. The glistening crown of a building caught my eye. It stood taller than everything around it, topped by a gold dome. A sign on the railing identified it as the *Palais Royal.* Just above my stomach it felt like someone had taken a shovel and removed part of me. Okay, so I was going to miss her now. Well okay then, so miss her properly. Yeah, that's right, don't just masturbate with the idea, really miss her. Ache so that she can feel it all the way in London.

I saw you a few times, on campus or at the dorms, in the few weeks we'd been split up, after things were over with the other girl. Every time I saw you, the feeling was just as strong. By the night we went to the Olympia, the nightclub everyone from the university went to on Thursday nights, I knew I was going to try again. Nothing was as good without you.

I went with my best mate, Kurt, and his girlfriend, Rachael, and the rest of them from Kurt's hall. When Albert found us he passed on the message that you wanted me to sit with you, and I knew you were still interested. You were with all your friends, whom I figured hated me

by then, and we each tried to out-blasé the other. Then you went off
to get cigarettes.

It went on like that all evening; you'd go for a smoke, or to see someone, or you had to dance to that song, and I couldn't suss you out. I cor-
nered you at the bar and asked if you wanted to go somewhere and talk,
and you suggested having a cigarette outside. We sat on the steps and
talked about nothing for a while.

"I got a haircut," I babbled.

"Did you get it for Camilla?"

I stupidly wondered where to begin and couldn't find anyplace, and
we went back inside, you to your friends, me to mine.

"We need to talk," I told Kurt. He and I went upstairs, and I told him
the situation. "I don't know if she knows that Camilla and I broke up."

"You want me to tell her for you?"

"Hey, would you?" I hadn't thought of it, and it was a really good
idea. He started to head off to find you.

"Wait, man. Punch it." "Punching it" was a ritual of Kurt's invention.
I thought it was cheesy, and I had never initiated until then. We did it,
and I felt strong, felt confident again.

I waited nearby while he did his work, then made that casual entrance.

"So did Kurt tell you?" I asked, but I could see that he had. The
moment was there, and we kissed. "I missed you," I whispered, and you
said, "Then don't ever do that again, you bastard." We hugged and
everything before that moment disappeared, and my body remembered
yours and the world was right.

You and I went back outside again and did it right that time.

I was missing her properly by then. I smoked my cigarette and
watched a cloud slide by the white hint of moon. Maybe she was looking up at the moon too. At least we had the same moon to look at. At
least we were under the same sky. People were moving down the rail
closer to me, and I wasn't in the mood to interact with them. I took out

my best pen, the black fine-tip that I preferred for sketching, and I wrote on the railing, "I miss you Tabi."

Going into the elevator, I passed those teenagers. And if I had my life to do over again, knowing what I know now, I would still make the same mistakes as long as they would still lead me to you.

The elevator took me back down to the ground, where there was a tremendous line. My cigarette was still going, but my body was telling me it needed something else. Orange juice perhaps. There were some cravings that nicotine just wouldn't substitute for. On my way across the city I found a market that sold little juices kept cold in a bucket of ice. I paid a ridiculous, tourist price for one, but it was something that I needed.

I walked so far that I began to wonder if I'd passed it, until I sighted the Notre Dame. The store was across the river from it, just a block further up. It was dark inside the shop. My watch told me it was eight thirty. The door was closed and locked. My bag was still inside.

CHAPTER 13

Just in case, I tried rapping on the window at the front of the store. The carts with the cheap paperbacks had been wheeled inside. I was the only one or thing on the sidewalk out front. It was a cold night, and I thought about the bridges.

Something moved inside, and as it approached it became a Chinese lad, about my age.

"We're closed," he said in English.

I clasped my hands together. "George said I could stay here."

"The store is closed, brother," he said, a little more loudly.

I spoke up as well. "George said I," pointing at myself, "Could stay here," pointing into the store. Understanding blossomed on his face, and he reached for the door and turned a latch.

"You're lucky we were awake," he told me. Other half of "we" was short, pale, young man with long, straight, black hair and squinty eyes, sitting on a blanket near the back. He was holding a hand of cards. The one who had let me in held another.

"Thank you so much. George told me to be in by eight, but I got lost on my way back from the Eiffel Tower."

I was braced for them to question my right to be there. I recovered my backpack from underneath the front desk.

"We were wondering whose that was. Come on back with us."

They had spread thin foam pads and blankets on the floor. I sat with them and took out my tobacco pouch.

"Have you guys been staying here long?"

"We've been here for about a week. We're teachers in London, but we're on Easter break. My name is Lu Tang." He extended his hand, which I shook. He was all smiles. The pale one appeared to be about my age physically, but his expression was much younger. He was watching how Lu Tang dealt with me.

"This is Vladimir," Lu Tang introduced. I extended my hand.

"Pleased to meet you." Vladimir's greeting was robed in an unfamiliar accent.

"I'm so relieved you heard me knocking. I was getting ready to find a bridge to sleep under." They both laughed at it. When I finished rolling, I offered up the tobacco to Lu Tang, who accepted it and passed it along to Vladimir. Heavy footsteps came down the stairs behind me.

"Oh, not him," Vladimir hissed. In his accent, it came out, "Oh, not *heem.*"

It was a blonde guy, older than we were, in a white tank top, jeans, and cowboy boots. It was too cold for the tank top, but he was showing off his arms. His hair was tied back into a fat ponytail. He plunged the boots down onto each stair, so that they made him sound bigger than he was.

"You guys not smoking down here, are you?" German accent. "You know George don't like smoking." He was standing a few stairs up, looking down on us.

"All right, Sigmund. Just relax," Lu Tang replied.

"You guys know that it's not smoking in here. There was a fire in here, you know."

Just as loudly, and in his same accent, I said, "Sorry. It was my fault. I'm new here and I didn't know. I'm the one smoking. I'll out put it right away."

He squinted at me. "You German?"

"No, I'm American," I continued in the accent. "All my fault. I will out put it right away."

It stopped him up for a second. "Well out put it then." He stomped back up the stairs.

"He said he would," Vladimir muttered.

When he was gone, I said, "Sorry if I got you in trouble."

"It's okay," Lu Tang answered, and Vladimir nodded in tandem. "He's nobody. He's moving out tomorrow. Come on, let's go smoke outside. We'll leave the door unlocked."

"*Hees* an asshole," Vladimir agreed.

I let them walk past me as I stood zipping up my coat. They waited until I was finished to go further, so I knew that they wanted me to be part of their group.

There was a low stone wall in front of the store, and the three of us sat on it and re-lit the cigarettes. Vladimir had rolled a real tampon. I got them talking about themselves. Lu Tang was from Hong Kong, hence his English accent. Vladimir was from Romania. They taught art at an English private school for boys whose parents were fabulously rich.

Lu Tang asked me where I was coming from, and I told them Amsterdam.

"I hear there's a lot of weed there," Lu Tang told me.

I decided to take a risk and reveal, "There's a lot less now that I've been there."

"Got any on you?" Vladimir piped up, and I knew the risk had paid off. I told them about the bag I'd needlessly left at the bar, and they both groaned in vicarious regret.

"Brother, you never, ever do that," Lu Tang lamented.

"We should tell *heem* about tomorrow," Vladimir said to Lu Tang. Lu Tang flashed a look at him. I pretended I hadn't caught it. "Breakfast," Vladimir continued.

"Good thinking," Lu Tang consented, though I felt he had thought differently the moment before. "Are you interested in free breakfast, Jake?" he asked softly.

"My favorite words are 'free' and 'food,' especially when they're in the same sentence."

"We're going with Elias for free breakfast tomorrow. Have you met him?"

"I've only met you all, and Camille. And Sigmund."

We went back into the store and locked the door again.

"Would you like a mat?" Vladimir asked me in his little voice.

"That's okay."

"It's for you. It's extra sleeping stuff. Here's an extra blanket, too." He looked down when he spoke, in the way of one who is speaking his second language and is uncertain he's making sense. I thanked him for the bedding and settled myself on the floor around the corner from them. There was a lot to think about, and I fell asleep quickly.

That was how I managed to keep a roof over my head in Paris.

The dreams just before I woke up all had books in them. Someone had to step over me in the morning to get by, and I pretended I was still asleep, and soon I really was again. In a minute I heard Vladimir's voice telling Lu Tang, "Let *heem* sleep a little longer."

"I'm awake," I said, and sat up. My watch told me it was 7:00. There was plenty of light out already because of the encroaching spring. Vladimir had hauled a mop bucket to the front of the store, and Lu Tang was moving things out of his way. I laced up my boots and joined them.

"This is the job George gave us to do every morning," Vladimir sang as he stabbed at the corners with a string mop.

I helped Lu Tang move the book carts out to the sidewalk, then we both assisted Vladimir with mopping and dusting the shop. Camille came downstairs when we were through and turned on the lights. She looked good in the morning, but I didn't say much to her. I was too grouchy. Hunger was in me like a nursery of screaming babies.

There were footfalls on the stairs. A giant man, about five inches taller than I, marched from the back of the store to where we were.

"Hi Elias. Are you nipping off for breakfast?" Camille asked him.

He angled his face at her. "Yep. I'm going to *Chez Universite*. Do you need anything while I'm out?" His voice was big and deep, like his lungs were kettledrums. He wore a black beret and a black leather jacket, and he had cheekbones like razorblades under three days of whiskers.

"Thank you, no." I looked at her face when she spoke to him, and I decided, *She is in love with him.*

"Come on." He just barely glanced at Lu Tang when he said it. He didn't look at Vladimir and me. We followed him out the door. There was a park and a church on the first block over, and we walked past them up a hill.

"So Elias, have you been at the store long?" I asked to his back.

He kept walking. His strides were tremendous, and it was hard work to keep up with him. My shins felt like knitting needles were being jabbed into them.

"So Elias, have you—"

"I heard you the first time. About a month."

Lu Tang took two steps for every one of Elias'. Vladimir did a silly little jog to keep pace, with his hands stuffed into the pockets of his pants. He wore a black cape over his clothes, and it flapped behind him. Lu Tang wore a bright blue marching band uniform, complete with epaulets and big, brass buttons.

"Where in the states are you from?" I asked Elias.

"Texas."

"Oh yeah? I'm from Massachusetts."

That was the end of our conversation during the walk. There were hardly any cars on the road at that time of day. In ten minutes we were in sight of *l'Universite Politechnique*.

"Listen. The food is free, as long as they think you're a student. If you start talking in English, they're going to know that you're not." His eyes landed on mine for the first time, for the smallest moment, then flew off again. We queued up with the students and moved with them in silence.

At the front of the cafeteria was a long row of wooden tables. The first couple of tables had baskets of fresh baguettes on them.

On the next table were stacks of deep ceramic bowls and an industrial-sized coffee maker. Further down was a huge saucepot full of hot milk. I'd never had that before, but it smelled good, so I ladled my bowl full of it. There was a dish of chocolate powder on the same table, and I spooned some into my milk and stirred it around.

At the end of the tables were a pot of raspberry jam and a loaf of butter. I sliced my warm baguette in half down its length. Since it was fresh it was easy to cut open the crust, but I had to finesse the knife through its soft interior. I rubbed pats of butter onto the bottom half, smeared the top with globs of jam, and pressed it back together. The hunger threw a furious tantrum inside me. I followed Elias to an unoccupied table and sat across from him on a stool. Lu Tang sat next to me, across from Vladimir, and we spread napkins out under our meals.

When I bit into the loaf, the simple flavors of warm bread, butter, and raspberry jam sang to my tongue. My body told me that I was giving it exactly what it required. At the tables around us, clumps of freshly washed students in costly clothes and polished shoes conversed in French. Since we couldn't speak, we concentrated on our eating.

Elias didn't look at the rest of us. He ignored us with the cool confidence of one who is used to being stared at for his good looks. I resent people like that, and made a point of looking at him as little as possible.

The students lifted the big bowls to their lips, tipped them up, and drank. I followed suit with my chocolate milk. It was so warm going down my throat, it felt like I was spilling it onto the front of my chest.

Most of the students were skinny men, a lot of whom wore glasses and had crops of pens sprouting from their shirt pockets.

In my lowest voice I said, "It's a geek festival in here."

In just as low a voice Elias replied, "It's a polytechnic school," which was sufficient explanation.

We were all covered in crust crumbs. Some of the students went up for seconds. I brought my bowl up and filled it with coffee. The workers were starting to put things away, so I figured it closed at eight. When I sat back down Elias stood to leave.

"Meeting Joe," he said in Lu Tang's direction. Lu Tang nodded.

The coffee finished waking me up. Many of the students were starting to leave. I turned to Lu Tang and raised my eyebrows for his attention, glanced around at the exodus, and made as if to get up myself. He raised his chin and eyebrows slowly, *Ahhh,* then made a similar series of gestures to Vladimir, who sharply nodded his assent. Vladimir tucked half of his loaf into his sleeve. I wished that I had thought to do the same.

It was a little warmer outside.

"What did you think?" Lu Tang asked me.

"That hit the spot. It was a simple meal, but it was perfect."

"It's so good to have a full stomach," he amended.

That was how I managed breakfast while I was in Paris.

CHAPTER 14

We crossed a bridge to the other side of the river, strolling, not really going anyplace. Sometimes I'd sense Vladimir trying to formulate a question but miss the beat while struggling for the words. Eventually he came up with, "You are a student?"

"I'm a student from an American university on exchange at the University of Harlan, England." He squinted at the word "exchange." "I pay to go to a school in America, but I spend the year in England. A student at Harlan University did just the reverse." I wasn't certain that he got it. "I finally figured out what your accent sounds like. Have you ever seen old American vampire movies?"

He and Lu Tang smiled at one another.

"Transylvania is in Romania. I am from a town just near it."

"Show him your fangs," Lu Tang urged. Vladimir put his face closer to mine and grinned widely. His bicuspids were very pointy. Lu Tang was laughing.

"Why does everyone think that's so strange?"

"'Why does everyone think that's so strange?' asked Vladimir the Transylvanian of his vampire teeth," I said. He echoed Lu Tang's laughter. I tried leaving room in my assessment of him for the question to have been intentionally ironic, but I finally decided it hadn't. Lu Tang was in on the joke; Vladimir was merely aware that a joke was there.

I told them that I wished I could find a gym so that I could take a shower. Lu Tang said he knew of just such a place and led us to it.

We were there in a couple of blocks. *"Municipal Doucher"* a sign confirmed, *Public Shower*. It resembled an American YMCA.

I remembered, "I don't have a towel."

"You can rent one," Vladimir reassured.

"Your English is pretty good. How long have you been taking it?"

"See? What did I tell you?" Lu Tang added.

"Maybe twelve years. We take it even young in Romania. Teaching in English has helped a lot."

When I had decided study abroad, it was a choice between England and Australia. The challenge of communicating in a foreign language compounded with the rest of the challenges of studying abroad was too imposing. My only knowledge of a second language was the anorexic remnant of my college French.

I hadn't known that England's English *is* a foreign language to an American. I learned this the first weekend at the University of Harlan. I had been out with my hall-mates on a bus, heading for a bar in town. It was that getting-to-know-you part of the school year. We occupied the rear half of the top of a double-decker bus, flirting and trading witticisms, defining our roles in the group. I saw a chance to tell a funny story, so I jumped into the conversation with it.

"That reminds me of something that happened to me at home. One time my friend Jamie and I were drunk off our asses, wandering around campus—"

"Is that like being rat-arsed?" This girl Angela who lives across the hall from me cut me right off.

"Don't you have those enormous fucking cars in the States?" asked Devlin, another hall mate. He had a thick Manchester accent, and it sounded like *"Doont* you have *thoos* enormous *fakking* cars in the States?"

"An American car could eat one of our cars," someone else chimed.

"It makes for more spectacular car chase scenes on telly," said Alex, the ringleader of our hall. "Everything's on telly in the States."

Everyone laughed at it, so I started up again.

"Right, anyway, my friend Jamie, a total madman, and I were just rocked on cheap beer—"

"Which one of you had the gun?" asked Alex.

"Gun?"

"You Yanks have always got guns on you. Come on, which one of you was packing?"

"Oy, careful Alex, he's probably armed right now," Angela added, and got a laugh from the rest, and the conversation moved on. I never got the whole story out. That was about the last thing I said that night.

It took me most of the first month there to develop the ability to participate in a conversation. With observation I realized that in addition to the accents and shibboleths that separated the two Englishes, there was a different set of rules to conversation.

American conversation involves a lot of story telling. In America one person could keep the floor for many minutes at a time if their tale was interesting enough. Others interject to spice it up, but the flow is controlled by one person.

English conversation was more like tennis. One person serves up a comment. The first person to react starts up a volley. If the return was poor, someone else could jump in. It would go back and forth like that until someone finally scored a point, usually in the form of saying something clever.

Due to this difference, I didn't feel like most of the people at school had really met me. In America I was much funnier. I knew some pretty good stories. I empathized with the struggle Vladimir was facing.

When we reached the end of the line at the *Municipal Doucher*, Lu Tang tried to gesture what we wanted to the woman in the booth. I figured he didn't speak any French, so I spoke over his head to her.

"*Three for showers, please. Do you have towels?*"

"And three towels?"

"Please."

She gave me a total, and we paid it. She gave us locker keys and little bars of soap along with the towels. I'm not awake until I've had my morning shower, and I hadn't had one in three days. I stripped and locked my things in my locker, then picked a shower cabin. It was a stall with a frosted glass door. I let the water run for a while before getting in. Inside, the hot water was endless. The cabin filled with steam. After I soaped up with the little bar, I stood under the water for a very long time. It melted some of the stiffness in my neck. The pressure was so high it felt like hot fingernails scratching my scalp.

There was something I wanted to take care of, and I realized that, living in the bookstore, this was the only privacy I would have, so I went ahead with it. No one could see through the shower door. Once it was done, the hot water carried it down the drain.

I let the shower thaw me out for a while longer, then toweled off. Lu Tang was shaving at the sink.

"Vladimir's still in the shower. He takes about a half an hour."

I joined him at the mirror. He had an extra disposable razor, which he gave me, and I seared my cheeks with hot water to prepare them for a shave without cream. I had about ten times as many whiskers as Lu Tang had.

"I'd better go to the bathroom," Lu Tang told me.

"In here?" I asked and made a face.

"Let me give you some advice. If you have a chance to go somewhere other than in the store, do so."

"No bathroom?"

His turn to make a face. "It's Turkish style."

"Oh," I said as he left, as though I understood.

We met Vladimir in the locker room afterwards and got dressed.

That was how I managed bathing in Paris.

It was just barely the type of weather outside to keep my jacket zipped up. The streets paved with gray stones locked together in rows, or sometimes set in concentric circles like ripples in a cobblestone pond. Buildings were flush with one another. The windows were skirted with decorative, wrought iron grates. They spoke to me of warm weather, sitting on the sill and leaning out over the traffic, cigarette in one hand, cup of coffee in another.

"Do you guys think we should go back to see if there's any work to do?" I wanted to cement my place at the store. Lu Tang breathed in through his teeth while he thought about it. When I changed my glance over to Vladimir, he turned to look at Lu Tang.

"He gave us the floors to do. We should be fine." Lu Tang used the same voice as when they invited me to breakfast: quiet, monotone, not punctuating any of the syllables.

"You helped us," Vladimir added.

"I just don't want to get in trouble with George. I'm screwed if I can't stay at the store."

Lu Tang produced his pouch of tobacco from one of is uniform pockets. "You'll be okay. We can check back at the store later if you want. It's good to stay out of his way in the morning."

Now Vladimir's hands were in his pockets, and he was looking at the ground. They'd been good to me so far; they had let me in on breakfast.

"What are you guys going to do?"

"We had the Louvre in mind for later. Just going to look around for now."

I produced my own tobacco pouch and extracted what I needed for a cigarette. I offered the pouch to Vladimir, who accepted.

"I'll check in at the store after lunch to make some points with George. Since I'm new. Mind if I hang with you till then?"

"By all means," Lu Tang said.

"Thank you," Vladimir said, handing the pouch back. Lu Tang lit us with his lighter, and we continued our walk.

"You should make sure you go to the Louvre," Lu Tang urged. "I've wanted to go all my life. It's supposed to be one of the greatest museums in the world."

We explored some shops. They weren't simply hat stores, or shoe stores, or bookstores. They were personality stores, eclectic showcases where proprietors displayed whatever they were interested in. Being in one was like witnessing a fight between an attic and a yard sale.

Vladimir ogled a display of virgate lengths of wood and metal, encrusted with crystals and semi-precious stones.

"Magic wands. Look at how much," he lamented. I wondered what a reasonable price was for a magic wand.

"Just take it," Lu Tang whispered.

"*Bon jour!*" the shopkeeper said.

We each *bon jour*ed him back in our full house of accents. He rattled off a couple of sentences to us.

"*No thank you. Just...to look,*" I tried. He didn't just frown at us; his entire face turned into a frown. We only stayed a minute more.

"Did you get it?" Lu Tang asked out on the street.

Vladimir smiled and pulled it out of his sleeve.

"I thought he saw me."

"So did I."

They laughed, and we were still walking, and there was a little bit of silence, which I realized belonged to me.

"That cape must come in handy," I said. "I don't think he was onto us. I think he was just being rude."

After a few hours, the guilt of not checking in with George had reached a critical mass. Lu Tang and Vladimir walked me back.

"Hey, there's Joe and Elias," Lu Tang said, pointing. We were crossing a bridge back to the West Bank. Lu Tang was pointing to the lower bank, where Elias shared a bench with another man.

"Who's Joe? Is he from the store?"

"Elias! Joe!" Vladimir shouted to them and waved.

"No, he's this street person that Elias hangs around with. He's at the store all the time," Lu Tang answered. There was no tone in his description.

"Let's go say hi," Vladimir implored.

The upper bank was much higher than the water at that part of the river. We walked down a long flight of stone steps and approached the other two.

"Hey guys, what's going on?" Elias effused, smiling at us.

"We're going to the Louvre," Vladimir gushed.

"Really? That's great. You've been to the Louvre, haven't you, Joe?"

"Overrated," Joe pronounced in an American accent. "The museum to go to in this city is the Rodin statuary. Just one man's opinion, happens to be mine." Elias laughed.

Joe wore a fedora above a wedge-shaped face with Italian overtones. His trench coat would have been fancy and beautiful ten years ago when it was new, when it wasn't ragged at the elbows and stained at the bottom, if it was the right size, and if one epaulet wasn't lolling off to the side, buttonless. I made him at around thirty-five to forty years old. He was tuning a six-string guitar. He was a bum.

Lu Tang looked to him respectfully. "The Rodin? We'll have to go there next, Vlad. We just want to see the Louvre because it's supposed to be the thing to do."

"Joe and I are going to the Mazet later on to hear some music. Now *that's* the thing to do, right Joe?" Elias laughed. Joe finished with the string he was working on, then answered Elias by jutting out his lower lip, raising his eyebrows, and lifting his chin. Everyone waited for him to speak.

"We're going to learn a thing or two about jazz music tonight."

I don't have much of a stomach for bums, thanks to my experiences at the car wash. Every summer we'd get our share of them moping around the car vacuums, picking through the trash for returnable bottles and change and other salvageables. Dad didn't trust them, and coached me that they'd steal out of the cars if we didn't keep an eye on them. For my part I had a little sympathy, and I wondered how they got through the winters, but there was also the fact that they were filthy, and a lot of them were drunk, and I usually got the job of telling them to take a hike when necessary.

The conversation continued, and when Elias mentioned that he was moving out of the store, I figured out my exit line.

"When are you moving?"

"Two more days." His tone was a compromise between the syco-phancy he had for Joe and the disdain he'd shown me that morning, but at least he looked me in the eye. "I'm moving in with Kandra," he said to Joe.

This won a smile. "The supermodel?"

"Speaking of moving, I've got to move back to the store. Anyway, my name is Jacob. Pleasure to be introduced to you." I stuck out my hand at Joe, but said it half to Elias. My mates stumbled over little apologies, and Joe summoned his hand, which was actually clean.

"Oh, sorry, I didn't realize this was a formal affair. I left my tux at home."

Joe gave a good handshake. Elias laughed; it was the kind of laugh that was supposed to let me know that this was a joke. "What tux?"

"What *home*?" Joe finished. That was actually pretty funny. I made my way back up the stairs.

CHAPTER 15

Lu Tang's opinion on things changed with the tides of his audience. He had been good with me so far, but I made an internal shift to be cautious with him. People like Lu Tang were dangerous.

Rather, people like Lu Tang were dangerous to me. I keep the fragile things inside, but I expose a lot to people whom I think are my friends. I've been hurt before by people who use one face to listen and a different one to talk.

Shakespeare and Company was full of customers. Camille was working the front desk. George was charming a woman in her thirties as she filled her arms with books. He was dressed in a dark gray suit with the sleeves rolled up to his knobby elbows. A black and white cat clutched tight-footedly to his left shoulder, and as George and the woman spoke, they shared the electric humor of pretending it wasn't there.

When he decided that I deserved his attention, he assigned me to make sure that the science fiction section was in alphabetical order. He explained how to do so in a tone of voice that told me I was born yesterday, but I'd caught the look of surprise on his face when I asked for work, the good kind of surprise. I figured that his rough manner of speaking to me was what it took to get his old body going, like the way you warm up a car by revving the engine. He was the kind of old that bore wattles and other assorted wrinkles of loose skin on his hands and at every joint, which the flesh beneath would never again fill.

It was warm in the store, and the customers looked content with their books. The science fiction section was in complete disarray. As I reorganized it, my list of got-to-reads grew geometrically. When I was finished George had nothing else for me to do, so I picked up Philip K. Dick's *Do Androids Dream of Electric Sheep.*

"George prefers you do your reading in the library while the store is open," Camille roused me with. I'd been gone inside the book for at least an hour.

"The library," I said, not quite a question, not quite an acknowledgement. I was playing with her.

"Right. We like that the residents are reading, but it should be done in the library."

"Library." I blinked at her rapidly.

"You don't know where it is? Upstairs. Here, I'll show you."

I followed the jiggling sway of her ballet-slippered walk up the stairs Sigmund had descended the night before. A string of tiny bells hugged her pale, unshaven, right ankle. The walls on either side of the stairs were clogged with hard covers. At the head of the stairs a sign read:

You are entering

THE SYLVIA BEACH LIBRARY

Noon to Midnight

Open exclusively for study

TUMBLEWEED HOTEL

Midnight to Noon

Fraternization Authorized

I assumed that the "Tumbleweed Hotel" referred to the manner in which I and my fellow denizens of the shop resided.

The library wasn't just full of books; it was a twenty-car pileup of books. It was a dozen forests worth of books. Every flat surface—the railings, the table at the center of the room, unused chairs, was covered with books that covered other books. A hallway was flanked by stacks of books piled to the ceiling like pillars. Walls didn't just have bookcases up against them; the walls *were* bookcases, floor to ceiling and corner to corner. After a few seconds of grabbing some of the titles with my eyes, my brain surrendered and refused to try. It just registered the onslaught as a wallpaper of bindings.

The tomes were mostly old hardcovers without dust jackets. The room was toned in the husky burgundies and hunter greens and cobalts of covers built to last for decades. A pair of girls who sounded European sat whispering at a square table; another sat on the floor in a corner, reading. Camille left me to them without an introduction. I squeezed myself into a corner neutrally equidistant from the others and got down to the job of reading by the light of the raw bulbs on the electric chandelier. My concern about my funds made me forgo lunch, but it was a very good book. In a while I fell asleep without dreaming of sheep, electric or otherwise.

Another dream of books, with a soundtrack of chatter between the girls at the table. There was a new voice in the mix, speaking as I woke, hot-faced and sticky mouthed from the nap. I remembered hearing the *cot cot cot* of high heeled shoes coming proudly up the stairs in the seconds before opening my eyes, too real a sound to work its way into my dream, pulling me back out of sleep. My eyes focussed as easily as if someone was trying to throw them into the sockets from across the room. When I had them properly tuned I saw a woman so hardcore beautiful she should have needed a license.

She was two meters tall; tall enough so that in order to look at her, I had to angle my neck farther back than a guy my height was used to. Her body was so long and lean and even that she could have been sculpted. A wide black scarf was wrapped around her swan neck. Her face was very French and just the slightest bit tanned, like the color of dinner rolls just before they're done, and her wide eyes were angry ocean blue. Her long hair was the red and yellow of your best summer. She was the kind of beautiful that you keep looking for flaws in and keep coming up with an empty net.

"Maybe he knows," she said of me, and my throat went dry. "Do you know where Elias is?" and I thought, *it figures*.

"Last time I saw him was a few hours ago. He was down by the river." A guy his height was one of a minority who could make her feel small and delicate. Plus there were his good looks.

He didn't possess leadership abilities, though. He had all of us in his potential command this morning, but he opted to fawn over Joe instead. Not leadership, but a *way*. He had a way.

The sculpted woman was disappointed that Elias was absent and soon took her leave back down the stairs. When she was gone, I said in the direction of the girls at the table, "That must be Kandra."

"No, that's Lissette. Kandra's *really* beautiful."

I wanted to indicate that Lissette wasn't exactly an emetic, but I didn't know these women. Instead I asked where the bathroom was.

The one who'd rated Lissette second place, a Pole by her accent, pointed to the hallway across from the head of the stairway, first and only door on the left. The hallway was a little mouthful of space between the library and the room at the front of the building. There was a doorway blocked by a ceiling-to-floor cloth curtain, like a shower curtain, hanging from a wooden rod.

I cleared my throat to alert anyone that might be inside and slid the curtain open. It looked like it was a shower with a cement floor painted mud brown, that thick sort of paint that comes from a bucket. There was a thin chain with a metal "O" hanging from some plumbing near the ceiling. In the middle of the floor was a hole a little wider than a fist.

At either side of the hole were grooved, concrete footpads.

"Um, hi, excuse me," I said as I reentered the library, interrupting their conversation. "Is that it behind the curtain?"

"Yes," said the Pole. "It's just right over there." She pointed to the curtain.

"Okay. Just double-checking. Be kind of embarrassing to go to the bathroom in the storage closet or something." I thought I was being funny. She didn't. I went back to the room, closed the curtain behind me, put my feet on the pads, and hoped that nobody decided to open the curtain. This was what Lu Tang had warned me about.

Turkish style.

I didn't think I would be able to get used to it. When I was done I pulled the chain, inspiring a swirl of water to churn in the hole in the floor.

It wasn't long before Lu Tang and Vlad returned from the Louvre. Vlad was very excited, and followed Lu Tang like a son coming home from the circus with his father.

"When do you guys want to eat dinner?" I asked. "I'm getting to that point where I'm so hungry, I'm starting to get cranky."

"That sounds like a plan," Lu Tang agreed. "There's a student refectory that's really cheap, but it's closed today. There's some kind of a holiday."

"That's nerve. Having a holiday when I'm hungry."

"What is 'cranky?'" asked Vlad. "It doesn't sound good."

I told him. "Let's walk until we find something cheap," I suggested. They acceded to my suggestion and followed me out the store. We passed a small grocery shop on the road behind the bookstore, then crossed over the *Rue Montparnasse* into the Latin Quarter. My landmark phone booth was down the block.

Plate smashers were going into overdrive on either side of the narrow alleyways. Shoulder to shoulder with the restaurants were pastry shops. Each one had a rotating tower of cookies, pastries, and other sweets I'd never seen before. We lost Vlad to one for a moment as he stood transfixed in front of the window.

"What is this?" He stabbed his finger on the window as the confection rotated by.

"Baklava," I answered. On one of the lower tiers was a bright pink thing in the shape of a pretzel, covered in thick glaze. I bet it was just pure sugar.

"Come on guys. I've got to eat."

"That looked so good. I'm going to eat one of those before we leave," Vlad promised.

"I've reached that point of hunger where I could kill my own meal," I told them.

"Did I keep you for too long? I am sorry." Vlad looked very serious. I patted his shoulder.

"It's okay. I've just got to eat soon."

We reached the end of the Latin Quarter without any luck. We cut back down to a road closer to the river and headed back. Up ahead of us, a pair of men was entertaining a small crowd by playing a flute and a set of drums. They had spread a Mexican blanket out in front of themselves, on which coins were accumulating. While Lu Tang and Vlad paused to listen, I spied a vendor selling whole roasted chickens from a cart. The scent had attracted me.

"How much is a chicken?"

He told me. I divided the figure by three, then multiplied by the exchange rate for American, and it wasn't bad at all. I brought the other two around to show them, and they agreed without thinking.

"We'll take one, please."

"This one, this one, this one," Vlad chanted, pointing out a good one. The red arrow of the tip of his tongue slid across his pale upper lip.

"Your friend, he likes this one?" the vendor asked me.

"I wonder how you know?"

Instead of laughing he fired off a reply too quickly for me to follow. I wasn't sure if my joke really carried. The chickens were slowly spinning on skewers on the metal cart, under a glass roof. The vendor slid the one Vlad had chosen off of the skewer and placed it in a plastic tray, to which he fastened a plastic lid. Lu Tang paid him since he only had large bills, and the vendor handed him the package. I imagined it was nice and warm holding it. Vlad and I settled with Lu Tang.

"We could eat it outside somewhere. Maybe by the river."

"The river," Vlad agreed.

"We should get some wine to go with it," Lu Tang suggested. We followed him to the grocery shop behind Shakespeare and Company. While the other two were looking at the wine, I went to buy some bread. It was at the end of an aisle that had packages of cookies, packages of crackers, pots of jam, and some other things. I didn't recognize any of the brands of the packaged foods. The girl at the bread counter handed me the fat baguette that I chose, and I met the others and paid at the front desk.

The bald man who took our money was in his fifties, and I made him to be the owner or the manager. When you're in a family that owns a business you get a sense for determining who holds such a role in other businesses. He had nasty eyes, and I worried that he thought that I had stolen from him. He didn't say as much, but he didn't say anything to me at all, not even a return *"Bon soir"* as I left.

We sat down by the water a couple of blocks away from the store. The lower bank was only about three meters below the upper bank at that part of the river.

"The best way to do this," Lu Tang said, "Is to just take the meat off with our fingers."

"And I have a knife," Vlad added, and he unsheathed a long, shocking, shiny implement of death from under his cape and placed it by the bird. I laid the bread on top of its wax paper next to the knife. Then I unbuttoned the sleeve of my jacket and freed the pot of jam that I had trapped there.

"We can put this on the bread for dessert."

"I didn't see you buy that," Lu Tang said as he tore off a drumstick.

"I didn't." I showed them how I had unbuttoned my sleeve, put my arm down over the pot, and rebuttoned the sleeve, capturing the jam inside.

"That's a good idea," he commended.

That pretty much settled where I stood with the other two. Lu Tang unscrewed the plastic lid from the top of the seven-franc burgundy, and we each took a drink from the bottle.

The chicken was so good, because I was so hungry, that eating it was almost an emotional experience. It was still warm and quite juicy. The bread was fresh, the crust, chewy. We demolished the chicken with devout concentration.

The good thing that comes with not knowing anything about wine was that I could enjoy a seven-franc plastic magnum. We took turns drinking straight from the bottle. It was a good sign of friendship. The night was a little warmer than the last; it was almost the kind of weather that you could go out without wearing a coat.

When the meat was done we scooped jam from the jar with chunks of bread. It was strawberry, and there were large slabs of fruit in it, which were cool and sweet and slippery. I heard a cracking noise and saw Vlad breaking open the larger chicken bones with his little white teeth to suck out the marrow. I told him that that was disgusting, but he countered by telling me that he'd gone hungry before, and some nights, even bone marrow would have been a blessing.

When we were done eating, we threw the bones into the river and smoked.

CHAPTER 16

Many people were walking along the bank above us in search of a night out, but we were alone on the lower bank. Every ten minutes or so a long boat would ease by. The boats were floating dining rooms. The walls of the decks were glass, and inside, tourists in formal wear were being served dinner by tuxedoed waiters. Classical music seeped out. The boats had spotlights on them aimed at the banks. We waved to the tourists as they floated by, separated from us by water and glass and hundreds of francs.

"They paid all that money for a meal on that boat, and we just spent forty francs and had a wonderful meal—"

"And cheap wine," amended Vlad; we were still drinking it,

"-on the Seine. To the Parisians, we're the tourists, but to those tourists, we're genuine Parisians."

"Look at those Parisian bums, darling," Lu Tang said in an affected woman's voice. "Look at them drinking on the Seine. Isn't that *charming?*" He mispronounced Seine to sound like "See-en." "Oh look at them waving!"

"They wave so charmingly," Vlad continued.

"I'll drink to that," and we all did.

Sometimes the tourists would wave, and some of them took pictures of us. We'd wave back and raise the bottle to toast the prettiest girls. If they waved we'd blow kisses, and if they blew them back, we'd blow more back.

"Wouldn't it be funny if one of us jumped onto one of the boats? Then went into the dining room and kissed the hand of the prettiest girl? *Bon soir, mon ami.*"

"It's a pretty big jump," Vlad warned. It was a pretty big jump. It would have to have been quite a girl. I pictured myself making the leap. I wondered if I would look handsome doing that.

I needed to pee, and we all drank to the occasion. I walked fairly steadily under the closest bridge to get rid of some of the wine I'd drunk. Having myself in my hand I considered sex. My most recent vivid sexual memory was the box cover of that bestiality video in Amsterdam. I wished that I'd had sex more recently, if only to supplant that memory. I was glad that I was being faithful to Tabi, though.

When I returned, we passed the bottle around for another drink.

"You picked out a good wine," Vladimir commended. He was the drunkest of us.

"I told the shopkeeper to give me his finest seven-franc wine in a plastic bottle," Lu Tang said.

Vlad took out his stolen magic wand and ceremoniously blessed it.

"The wine is almost gone," Vladimir announced. "What will be your last toast?"

He handed me the magnum. "To Tabi," I toasted, and took a long drink. I handed it back to Vlad.

"To Annette," and he took a deep drink from the bottle. He was smiling, but I read off of Lu Tang that he had said something serious. Lu Tang got the bottle next.

"To our newfound brotherhood."

"To our newfound brotherhood!" Vlad and I chorused, and when Lu Tang finished the bottle, he tossed it into the Seine. We put our arms around each other and professed our true friendship until the next boat came by, at which point we switched to professing our love to "*Nous ami*" in the blue sleeveless dress, who blew us kisses. Those two were my inseparable friends for the next week. Eating, getting money, reading, seeing the sites, visiting the museums, walking about; doing nothing was our everything.

It was getting late, so we mounted the stairs and made our way back to Shakespeare and Company. The store wasn't closed yet, so we paused out front for one last cigarette.

"So who's Annette?" I pried. I plowed past the concern on Lu Tang's face. If I offended Vlad it wouldn't matter by morning, because of the wine.

"She used to be my girlfriend. I cheated, and she left me."

"That's not quite it," Lu Tang said. "She never found out about it, Vlad."

Vladimir shook his head. "That's why she left me. It was my fate. When you do bad, bad comes to you."

"We have a saying, 'What goes around comes around.' I don't believe in it, Vlad."

"Even if you do not believe, it is so," he persisted.

"But you've seen plenty of jerks who have everything, who get away with being jerks without ever being paid back for it." I was old enough to know that he must have experienced people like that. Everyone does.

"I agree with Vladimir," Lu Tang supported. "Sooner or later it all evens out. For some people it just takes a long time."

It was a pretty thing to believe. The lights started to go out in the store, so we went back inside and got ready for sleep.

CHAPTER 17

So every morning during our week together at Shakespeare and Company we'd mop the floor and put the bookcases out on the sidewalk, then run the store until Camille came down. Occasionally George would have us unpack and shelve shipments of books for him.

There was other work for us, like the morning when he marched us up a hill to transfer books from another bookstore. The three of us loaded the transfer into burlap sacks while George talked to the owner of the other store, then we slung the sacks over our shoulders and trudged back down the hill like elves who'd lost a bet to Santa. It was warm enough so that we couldn't see our breath, even that early in the day.

The extra work meant missing breakfast at the *Polytechnique*. On those occasions we'd buy something from the grocery store with stolen money and eat it in the little park next to the store. There were benches to sit on under a great pine tree just inside the black, wrought iron gate. The money we used was "liberated" from the till at the store by Lu Tang while he ran the desk. There wasn't a cash register to track sales, only a notebook for writing them down and a drawer with a cigar box in it for the cash. He would neglect to record one or two early sales and pocket the money. Since I was in on the secret and kept watch for them, I benefited as well.

It bothered me that we were stealing from the man who had given us a place to live. Lu Tang justified it by saying that George made us work for him without paying us, which was slavery. His logic ignored the roof over our heads. I didn't point this out, but I did eat the food we bought. Especially good were these yogurt shakes that the grocery store carried.

Once Sigmund and Elias left the store, we were moved up to the library. The women who had been sleeping there moved into the writer's studio, the room down the hall from the library at the front of the building. Camille explained to me that sometimes writers passing through the city would be invited to stay in the studio, but there weren't any writers in residence at the moment. Camille herself was allotted a spare bedroom in George's apartment on one of the floors above. She was so privileged because she worked for George full time.

When we traveled across the city it was by the Metro, but we hardly ever paid the fare. Lu Tang and Vlad had discovered a broken exit turn-stile at the Metro stop closest to Shakespeare's, a block down from my phone booth. We'd wait until a train was just arriving, then dash through the exit and board before we could be caught. The only times we ended up paying were when we rode back. We walked back quite a bit, though, because it was getting nicer out.

By this method we traveled to most of the museums in the city. Their teaching certificates got them in for free. Vladimir had an extra one, which he lent to me. None of the museums' employees noticed that there were two Vladimir Bramstokoznys in our party.

Joe was right about the Rodin statue museum being very good, although I didn't have the Louvre to compare it to. Many of the statues at the Rodin museum were outside, some of them around a duck pond behind the museum building. By then it was warm enough to go out-side without a jacket.

In the evenings we'd walk around the city and watch the people who could afford to go out, and sometimes we'd find a spot to have a cheap beer. George had another full-timer to run the shop at night, so I invited Camille to go out with us a few times. There was a funny energy between her and Lu Tang; they didn't like each other for reasons they kept to themselves. She had lunch with us in the park a couple of times.

I was alone in the library reading one afternoon when Vlad ran upstairs to get me. He had a couple of hamburgers in hand, the fast food kind, wrapped in logo-printed wax paper.

"Joe's got hamburgers! Hurry!"

"For me too?"

"He's giving them away. Hurry!"

So far my interactions with Joe had been meager, but I was hungry enough to try. Hunger was becoming an imposing monument in my personal landscape. I was trying to save money by eating as little as possible for lunch. The hunger made it hard to go to sleep at night, and harder to get up in the morning.

Joe was sitting on a low wall out in front of the store talking to Camille. He had on an oxford shirt with the sleeves rolled up, blue trousers, and his snappy looking fedora.

"What do ya want, burger? Fish sandwich? Got chicken..."

"For real?"

"I wouldn't have asked if I couldn't produce. Burger? Fish? I got salad..."

"A burger would be great." Since I'd seen Vlad with his, I'd had the taste in my mouth. "Where'd you get them?"

He rolled his eye up at me wolfishly from where he sat. The eye tracked all over my face. "Does it matter? Do you want a burger or don't you?" It wasn't a threat, but it was a serious tone. I was affronting him.

"Yes please. Thank you very much, Joe."

Joe piled some burgers into the arms of Camille to distribute to the others who were staying at the store. Lu Tang wasn't around, so he missed out. I didn't have the gumption to ask Joe for another one.

Elias had already moved out, so I didn't know what kept bringing Joe to the store. George was annoyed by him. Was he trying to work something with Camille? I smothered the thought; I didn't even want to *think* something negative about a man offering me food, lest he sense the sentiment.

The wrapper said "Le Quick." I assumed it was some type of French ersatz McDonalds. The burger wasn't enough to make me full, but it gave my stomach some satisfaction, a specific kind of American fast food satisfaction, and I thanked Joe again a number of times. When I was done I felt like I owed it to him to at least talk to him for a while, but he slung the sack over his shoulder and kept moving away like he had somewhere else to go.

CHAPTER 18

Camille had never been to the Eiffel Tower, so I invited her to come along with us. It was the last thing Lu Tang and Vladimir wanted to see before going back to England.

"You've lived in Paris, what, four months," I asked her, "And you haven't been to the top of the Eiffel Tower yet? Shame on you."

"I'm the one working full time, aren't I?"

"I don't want to hear your lame excuses." I'd found that if I kidded around roughly with her she responded well. Maybe she had brothers.

I moved away from the rest and lowered myself onto a bench. "You guys go on up. I've already seen it."

"You're not going with us?" Camille asked.

"No. I've already paid to do it once. You go on, I'll wait down here."

"Oh come on then," she said.

"No, I've got to save money." I'd only had a stick of bread for lunch that day.

Lu Tang turned and led Vladimir towards the line without waiting for Camille, and she ran to catch up to them. Again with that animosity between them. Lu Tang could be nasty to her like that sometimes. It was getting to the point when I would have said something about it to him if it wasn't for the fact that he was leaving that day. I have principles, but sometimes there's no point in stating them.

When they were out of sight I concentrated on constructing a cigarette for myself. The pouch of Drum had lasted me a good long time. Only then, when I was nearing the end of it, was it starting to dry up. When the cigarette was built, I watched the afternoon crowds. A thirty-ish woman in a very short skirt was being chatted up by an office-worker type in front of me. Their French was too rapid for me, but I understood that they didn't know each other. When the woman started to turn her body away from him, the office guy took a step in the other direction, as if to comfort himself to her departure with his own. He said something to be funny which she laughed at as he started away, and I watched the space between them grow, and right when I thought he would he threw a final glance over his shoulder at her. I added the scene to the rest of my experience, and I knew then what the Eiffel Tower was: the official pick-up spot of Paris.

I wondered how far my friends had gotten. I wondered if they'd reached the top level, and the railing with my graffiti. Maybe they were being decent to Camille; Vladimir usually was, more or less. What the hell did I care, anyway? She wasn't my girlfriend. My girl-friend was in London.

The memory of the worst thing I'd ever done to her broke free. Her little knock on my door the night I'd dumped her.

"Can I come in?"

Panic, trying to remember if I'd locked it. I hadn't. "No."

"Are you with someone in there?" A naked, post-coital Camilla next to me.

"Yes." Tabi's feet running back down the stairs. Crying. I am a bastard.

My mind summoned the best memories of us in self-defense: the week after she took me back, spending every night together. Not our game of control, not she provoking me, and I seeing how mean I could be to her. Just she pursuing me, and I showing her again and again that I liked her a lot, that she was good.

I fantasized that she was walking by me right then on a spontaneous vacation alone. I took her by the hand and walked her to the elevator and she said, "Where are we going?" and I answered, "It's a surprise. I've got something to show you." We got to the top level without running into my friends, and I led her to the railing and said, "See? I've been thinking about you." Then I tried to imagine the look on her face, the one I got from her very rarely when I've done something that really makes her happy, the one where I break through her shell, right clear down to the heart of her, and I imagined her kiss. I was still sitting there alone on the bench, smoking.

When the other three came back downstairs I was quiet, but I didn't try to tell them why. Maybe they thought I was mad at them for leaving me behind, even though I'd insisted, or maybe they just weren't sure. We walked together back to Shakespeare and Company.

Lu Tang and Vladimir got their gear ready so they could leave. They weren't departing right at that moment, but I said a preliminary good-bye. We traded addresses.

"Do you guys need anything?"

"We're all set," Lu Tang responded. "We liberated a little money this morning." He made sure Camille wasn't within earshot when he said it. It dawned on me that it was convenient for him to dislike her, since he was stealing from the drawer that was her responsibility. When George had gotten us up that morning he had been particularly viperous in his repartee.

"What the hell am I going to do about these floors when you boys are gone? What the hell are you doing to me?"

"I'll—" I started, but he had no brakes.

"You don't care. No, you just go on. Where's the bucket, is it full yet?"

There was a terrible squealing; the cat had gotten under Lu Tang's foot as he came down the stairs with the bucket.

"Watch your damn feet! You stepped on my cat!"

Maybe this was what made it easy for Lu Tang.

Here was my analysis of George's manner: it was George's way of saying goodbye. He must have seen hundreds pass under his roof. Except for Camille, everyone who had been living there when I had arrived would be gone once Vlad and Lu Tang got on the bus. George couldn't afford a sloppy emotional goodbye for every one of us. Maybe he couldn't afford to absorb the gratitude of each departing tumbleweed, so he was nasty towards us at the end to ward it off.

This was the way George made sense to me.

I walked them to the Metro stop when they were ready, shook hands goodbye, and watched them go down the stairs leaving Paris all to me. I had the second best sleeping spot in the store then, the couch in the library.

I woke up the next morning from a dream of Yvonne. In it we were looking at each other, our faces close. Her hair was short like it had been last summer. I saw the freckle that I'd forgotten about on the right side of her chin. Her eyes were wide and bright like a doe's but wise. Her forehead glistened with a thin sweat she'd suddenly broken into, and the dream was so sharp I could smell her. She told me she'd made her decision, and she wanted me back. We moved our heads closer and our lips were coming together, our mouths were open, I felt her breath in my mouth as her top lip came down onto my lower lip, the way we used to kiss, and I woke up and oh. And oh.

I sat there on the couch, awake, and thought *What are you doing here, Yvonne? Aren't you done with me yet?* I had forgotten what it felt like to kiss her, but the dream had opened a door to a room in me I hadn't known existed, and there was her kiss.

It was still dark out. I got to work filling the bucket with a tap next to the Turkish bathroom. I had gotten comfortable enough to use the bathroom even if there were people right outside. The things one can get used to. I carried the bucket down the stairs and started on the floor.

The floor was a patchwork of materials: a portion of it was marble, a portion was made of flat rocks glued together with concrete, a corner was covered in little raised square ceramic tiles, and the rest of it was alternating black and white squares of linoleum. I didn't usually remember my dreams, but this one remained with me.

It was as though I'd been in a state of shock about being dumped so hard, and so I'd put the ordeal away in my subconscious to deal with a bit at a time. The dream was a little piece of it. I still didn't know why she'd dumped me; if it was because of something that had happened inside of her or because of something I'd done, or maybe just because of the person I was. How long would it be, Yvonne, until I could answer that question, or at least until I could ask it without it hurting so much?

Camille came down before I was done with the morning routine and helped me move the book shelves out onto the sidewalk. I hiked my way up the hill to the *Universite,* had breakfast alone, and smuggled half a stick of bread out in the sleeve of my shirt.

With Lu Tang and Vladimir gone I felt disconnected. Maybe it was due to inadequate sleep, or to a lack of something in my diet, iron or something, but I couldn't focus my thoughts. All the paints of my life were mixed together, but I couldn't make them into one color. I went to the Notre Dame.

I found an empty pew and sat with my head down. I wondered if Tabi and I would still work out when I got back to school, or if she would lose her spark for me as well. Maybe I would worry about it so much that I would lose my cool and ruin things. Wouldn't that be ironic, wouldn't that be fucking hilarious.

Nice thoughts, Jake. Nice thoughts for church. Still, it was a real concern. I had been a wreck when I first left America, calling Yvonne all the time and crying. My need must have been crushing. After a while she must have dreaded hearing the phone ring. Oh boo hoo, Yvonne, how am I going to make it.

I missed Tabi. I was picturing how she would look in the morning, all grouchy until I brought in some coffee; or how she looked when I woke up in the middle of the night, and in the moonlight I could see her mouth open and her little fingers and all that hair. My missing Tabi was warmth, not desperation.

I got up from the pew and left the Notre Dame. I wanted to hear her voice. It was an hour earlier in Paris than in London, and I didn't think I should call her house before, say, 10 o'clock her time. Yeah fool, you should call her. It worked so well with Yvonne. I'm surprised she didn't send you a bill for all those collect calls.

Along the upper bank all of the vendors were out selling old books and old photographs and naughty postcards. Many of the drawings utilized the Eiffel Tower as a phallic joke. No, I wasn't going to let Yvonne get away with changing me. I wouldn't give her a piece of Tabi. I would call.

But wasn't this defiance a mistake? Maybe my neediness was the death of the other relationship, and I was just being stubborn. Would Kurt…but Kurt was different than I was. Kurt and Rachael had a different kind of relationship. Would my hallmate Alex call her? No, Alex wouldn't call her, but Alex was a lady-killer. Alex could get away with never calling and still have the women chasing after him. "Treat them mean and keep them keen," was his maxim.

I could picture Elias calling Kandra, but he would be smooth about it, not desperate. He would cup the phone in his big hand and say all the right things in his deep voice. Anyway, it was still too early to think about calling her.

I walked to a good café I knew of for a coffee. There was a high counter at the front of the café that customers would lean against while they stood drinking. I struggled through a conversation with the man behind the counter regarding the weather. It was good coffee, and I had a second cup, trying to put my head back in order.

I went to a nearby tobacconist and bought a new pouch of Drum. The plate smashers weren't doing their thing that early in the day. Waiters were sweeping up the dish fragments, getting ready for another onslaught of ceramic fireworks that evening.

I emerged from the tight road that intersected with the *Rue Montparnasse* and turned right. There was a cheesy little tourist shop that sold little Eiffel Tower keychains and bookmarks and snow orbs, and replicas of the Tower and the Arc de Triomphe in metal or china. There were tee shirts and baseball caps with Parisian images. They sold long distance phone cards as well, and I bought one. I felt a twinge as the money left my hands. The shop was right in front of my phone booth. There were two girls taking turns talking on the phone. When they were done with the call I picked up the phone, read the instructions on the phone card, and dialed her number.

"Sharpe residence," a woman answered. It sounded like her.

"Tabi?" I could hear the faint echo of myself over the receiver after speaking.

"Yes?" Her voice was taut.

"Tabi, it's Jacob."

"I knew that!" Half a pause. "Where are you?"

"I'm in Paris."

"You are? I'm so jealous!" Pause. I should have asked, "Is Tabi there?" instead of just assuming it was her; I hated it when people did that to me. I waited too long to speak.

"Are you with Forest?"

"No, he and Kara took off in Amsterdam. How's your break going? What have you been up to?"

"Haven't been doing a thing."

"Good girl," I interjected.

"My parents were supposed to take me to Barbados, but then Daddy had to go on a business trip instead." Daddy. Then in a rush, "Are you cheating on me?"

I answered with our old joke. "Not unless you count wanking off. I have to a lot you know, because I'm an American."

She laughed. It felt good. She reeled her voice back out of the laugh and said, "I mean it. You're not cheating on me, are you?" There was a need in her voice that I couldn't identify.

"No, Tabi."

I had my eyes closed, her face in my mind. There was a long pause. I remembered the way I had been the night I met her, when I approached her at the taxi stand, completely myself and impervious to rejection. "I'm living in a bookstore. The owner lets me sleep there in exchange for a little work. It's right across from the Notre Dame. Have you ever been in the Notre Dame? It's beautiful."

"How did you end up in a bookstore?"

"I heard about it in one of my English classes. There're people from all over the world living there. I've been hanging out with a guy from Hong Kong and a guy from Transylvania."

"Any girls staying there?"

"Well, yeah."

"You're not sleeping with any of them, are you?"

"I told you no." Then I stopped being an idiot and figured out that she needed to hear the words. "I'm not cheating on you Tabi." Well, I couldn't blame her for asking. "So I'm eating at the University of Paris. We just queue up with the students and help ourselves. You can get away with anything if you act like you know what you're doing." I brought out another old joke. "Everyone here wears white socks just like me. I fit right in. See how stylish I am?"

"No they don't. Stop it, you're making me cry."

"What'd I do?"

"You know what you're doing. Stop it."

I knew enough to shut up.

"You'd better not have any fun without me."

"I won't. I promise. I will experience nothing but misery until I see you again." It made her change what she was doing into a laugh. "No fun for you either. I forbid it." And then I told her, "I miss you. It's no good without you."

"I miss you too. Cut it out," she scolded. You tell her you miss her because you have to. And if only you can leave it at that then you can keep her.

A recorded voice cut in over us in French. I recognized some numbers in the words. "That's the operator. I'm not sure how much time is left. I'm on a calling card. So listen, if it hangs up suddenly, it wasn't me, okay? I don't want you going off like, 'That bastard, he hung up on me!'"

"Okay. So where else have you been? How could you go to Paris without me? Wanker." She was more herself again.

"I'd rather have stayed at your house for three weeks. You should have invited me, you brat."

"My parents would have loved that. Stupid American."

"So you didn't answer me. Have you talked to anyone from school?"

"I did so! Pay attention. I talked to Christine, and Kay, and…oh, do you have Ray's phone number? I've been meaning to call him."

"Ha ha."

The recorded voice cut in again.

"Can you still hear me?"

"Yes. Hello?"

"Listen," I said over the recording, "It's going to hang up. Tabi? I love you."

"Can't hear you. What'd you say?"

"I love you, Tabi."

"Oh-I love you too."

"Look, it's going to cut us off, so—"

Silence. I closed my eyes and kept my breath inside and held onto the phone call until the city around me crept back and became my reality again. She fell for the guy at the taxi stand, and that was still me. The constellations still held their places.

The two girls who had been using the phone before me hadn't left. One of them held a franc piece in her hand. I avoided their eyes.

I couldn't think of anything to do in the city, so I went back to the store. George was dressed in one of his suits and looked very happy. He was surrounded by Camille and two new girls who were staying at the Tumbleweed Hotel. He was always happiest when he was talking to women. He didn't have any work for me.

I offered to bring Camille a cup of coffee, and she said she preferred tea. I asked her how George took his. She thanked me very much when I refused her money. When I returned with the paper cups, Camille told me that George had come up with some work, and that I should go upstairs to the library. I left George's coffee with her and went up. The new girls were sorting the books that he been singed during a fire. If they were worth keeping they washed the ash off of them with a sponge and soapy water. I added myself to the task.

George came in from the writer's studio to check on our progress. He was critical of our choices, which was in character for him, but there wasn't a lot of venom in his criticism. I noticed that he was drinking the coffee I'd brought him. He didn't thank me for it, but I didn't really want him to. It felt good just to see him drinking it.

CHAPTER 19

In the evening I walked alone to the student refectory for dinner. It was cafeteria dining, very cheap and not very good, but I was so hungry by the end of the day that I ate everything I was served. I kept myself company with a copy of Shakespeare's Coriolanus, which I'd smuggled out of the store. I was a couple of plays behind in my Shakespeare course, and this way I might catch up a bit.

Just beyond the refectory was the star shaped intersection of some interesting avenues. I took the broadest one in the direction away from the river. I'd found that if I kept the position of the river in mind, I could go exploring and still find my way back to Shakespeare and Company.

There were some dim, expensive looking restaurants along the street. I paused in front of the glass face of one and looked up at the diners. Every candle-lit table sat two. I continued walking down the avenue until it became a residential neighborhood, then turned and retraced my steps. Another restaurant I glanced into also primarily catered to deuces. A waiter sat a couple in their fifties by the window. The woman held a bunch of roses; a first date, or an apology, or an anniversary, or perhaps spontaneity. Behind them a man in a sports coat fed a fork full of his pasta across the table to the woman he was with. It was a tough street to be alone on.

It was just turning dark. Passing the refectory I followed a different arm of the intersection in the direction of the river and crossed it at an unfamiliar bridge. It brought me to the part of the city that set off my red light district radar. There was a prominent pornographic movie shop that offered private viewing cabins, in case you couldn't wait until you were home to watch. This wasn't what I was looking for either.

I walked into an arcade for some cheap entertainment. The video games were a couple years out of date. There was a fighting game I used to be pretty good at down one of the aisles. I pumped franc coins into it and unloaded aggression on the animated opponents. A couple of rounds into it, a guy came up to me and demanded, "*Give me a franc.*" I glanced over to size him up without releasing the game. He was younger than I was, but a good-sized kid. He wasn't as big as the Moroccan from Amsterdam, but he was with a friend. I was annoyed because I was in the middle of a game, but there was danger implicit in his action, and in the time of night it was, and in the fact that I was alone in a dead-end aisle.

Looking at the game I said, "*Why would I do that?*" in a pretty good accent.

He advanced a step, bumping me, and repeated, "*Give me a franc,*" more insistently. I did something stupid and lost the game. The count-down started on the screen to warn me to put in more money to continue, and I wanted to because it was good. My passport was safe in my inside breast pocket; my money was safe there as well.

"*Do you want to play the game with me?*" I asked him. He looked at me with frustration, maybe thinking I didn't understand his demand.

"*Do you want to play this game with me?*" I asked again, this time more vigorously, as though I didn't think he had understood me either. I acted like I thought he was just being friendly. I fished some francs out of my front pants pocket and said, "*I'll play with you here if you want. We can play this game together at the same time. But I'm not going to **give** you any money.*" I kept looking in his eyes when I said it.

"No, I want to play this game over here," he said, pointing behind him, but it was in a hopeless tone, a child's tone.

"This game is better," I let him know. *"Come on, let's play two player."* I knew how to say "two player" because it was written on the machine. I put the coins in the slot. The countdown was already over. After recognizing my money the machine waited for my decision, one player or two?

"No I don't want to play that." He made a gesture like he was batting away a fly, his hand coming close to my head. Something he did to keep face in front of his friend, I figured. I'd lost interest in the game since I had to start from the beginning. I played out my money's worth, and when I was done, the boys were gone. It was getting close to eight by then, so I walked back home along the Seine. I was hungry again. My hunger wasn't stopped by the dinner. My hunger was a constant companion, like a loyal dog.

The next day, after breakfast, I decided to do some sketching in front of the Notre Dame. Crossing the street I heard a car horn beep and someone shouting my name. I couldn't think of anyone I knew in Paris with a car, but I looked. Elias was waving ebulliently from the passenger seat of a Mercedes Benz. The driver was probably Kandra. He'd probably made her beep the horn to show her and the car off to me. I preferred Tabi to Kandra by a mile, I decided. It was a cheap little victory, but I'd take it.

I found an unoccupied stone bench in the courtyard in front of the Notre Dame and tried to draw, but it wouldn't happen. What I really wanted was Tabi, but she wasn't there. And I wanted a hamburger and a salad, but I couldn't afford them. My foreseeable future did not hold any hamburgers or salads.

I could afford to buy myself some French fries at one of the Greek fast food places in the Quarter, but that would involve walking past the expensive restaurants with their Olympic sized prices, and the rotating spits of meat being sliced off into gyros that were just past my wallet's reach. If I took the money I had reserved for food, subtracted a portion of it to save for the end of the semester, divided the remainder days I had left in the city...

While I worked on rolling up a Drum, a woman sat on an opposing bench, took out a pack of French cigarettes, Galois, and slid one out. I took a quick look at the neat, pre-made, paper tube as I measured out tobacco into my pretty, Amsterdam rolling paper, cupping it against the breeze. The woman looked at me, took a second look, and on the third look walked over towards me.

"*Would you like one of mine?*" She took one out and held it in front of me.

"*Thank you very much.*" I let my American accent pollute my words. She lit me with a pink plastic lighter and returned to her bench. I wanted to tell her, "*These are a lot less work than rolling my own,*" but I didn't know the words to express rolling, or how to change the verb "to work" into its noun form. She was dressed like she was on break from an office. I could have asked her where she worked, but I probably wouldn't have understood the response.

She was reading a paperback book with a French title. I could have asked if it was a good book, but then what would I say to her? "*Good day. How are you? Me, I am Jacob, a student at the university. I study English. Do you want to play a two player game?*" I just didn't have enough words to be nice to her.

I smoked the cigarette too fast, embarrassed by my apparent misanthropy, and told the woman goodbye and thank you very much. What the hell. I mean just what the hell.

Out in front of the store the newer residents were sitting on the low stone wall, talking to Joe. I said hello to them all. The other residents were wary of me; they were uncertain as to how much authority I carried at the store.

"Hey kid," Joe called out to me. "How goes the battle?"

"It's going. I've decided that it's time for me to return to England."

"Ah. Is break over already?"

"No, not until Monday. I just have to get out of this town."

He squeezed one corner of his mouth and pricked up the eyebrow on the same side of his face. "What's the matter, kid?"

"I'm just not happy here, Joe. This is no town to be without money in. I can't do anything, I can't go anywhere, I can't buy anything. I've had enough."

"Hey, hey, ho, ho," Joe soothed. "Let's go for a walk. Come on." It wasn't a question. "Hey Beata," he called over his shoulder at the Polish girl, "Don't forget our discussion about morality, all right?"

"I won't, Joe."

"And remember." He stared at her meaningfully.

"What?"

"Just remember. Everything. In general."

Her cheeks blossomed blush as her laughter demolished her composure.

Joe marched into the tightly packed streets of the Quarter with his hands tucked into his pockets and his elbows out wide. I'd thought that he was as tall as I was, but walking abreast of him I noticed that he was about three inches shorter. I had to work hard to keep pace with his big strides.

"Why would you ever want to leave Paris?" He left just enough room for me to answer, but when I tried to he said, "Everything you need is right here. Look, you like French-fries? Right here are the cheapest fries in the city." He raised his head bullishly towards a narrow little take-out joint that I had overlooked. The sign showed that the fries were half as much as I'd been paying. "See? You aren't so broke that you can't afford that, are you?"

"Ptomaine at that price," I wisecracked, but it was ignored. Right on the cusp of my words, he said,

"Here, I'll show you where you can find produce. Man needs his vegetables." He moved through the multitude as adroitly as a squirrel leaping between branches. He addressed people in his path with a syllable or a word, or even by putting a hand on their shoulders to negotiate passage around them. Joe acted nothing like the hesitant, anti-social bums of my experience. His method moved him so quickly that I had to assume the same tactic in order to keep his pace.

There was a tear in his shirt, and his pants were too wide and too short, but you couldn't tell that he lived on the street just by looking at him. He really made the fedora his own. He hooked around a corner and up into an open-air market I had never been in before.

"I like your hat."

"Got your vegetables for you right here," he said over my insignificant comment. He was focussed beyond me like he was taking measure of something happening around us. "What time you got?"

"About eleven."

He stopped and stood amongst some empty crates at the side of a vegetable seller's table. I came around to stand facing him. I felt like he had steered me into this position. I replayed the moment in my mind, and noticed how he had danced a dance of subtle body language that urged me into that position, then smiled strobe swiftly when I was where he wanted me to be. He hadn't touched me, but it was as effective as if he'd grabbed me by the shoulders and pushed me there.

"This is about the time when they start throwing out their bruised merchandise. Now and at three o'clock." From his vantage point he could eyeball the man who ran that particular table, as well as the empty boxes around us. "Not as much as there usually is." He stepped towards me and tapped me aside with one finger on my shoulder, then squatted very slowly in front of one of the crates on the ground. The vendor was busy with a customer, but he was watching Joe peripherally. I felt like he was going to yell at us to go away, but Joe squatted inexorably towards the crate.

"They don't mind if you take the discards, as long as you don't hang around all day," Joe instructed. I peered into the crate, which contained some brown lettuce leaves and other vegetable refuse. Out of it Joe produced two enormous, red apples. He deliberately raised his head and hands towards the vendor, theatrically presenting the apples. The vendor added just the sharpest little nod to his movements in speaking to the customer, and Joe rose.

"You like apples?"

"Sure." He handed me one. It was the size of a softball. It had a flat brown bruise on one side of it. I turned it and snapped a bite out of it, and my body sang with satisfaction. It was exactly the food I had needed.

"Here, I'll show you where you can get a beer for five francs." He was eating his apple but still moving. We charged through the open market. A couple of times he checked behind him to make sure I was keeping up. He turned down a residential street and brought us into a curved alleyway sloping down a hill.

"Here you go. Not much for atmosphere, but what do you want at five francs a brew?"

I read the hand painted sign over the doorway: *Chez Chien.*

"The Doghouse," I translated.

"Yeah, well, we all end up there every once in a while. Thirsty?"

I checked my watch. "Um. Well I—"

"Okay. Come on, then. I've got to go to work."

I wondered if he was trying to shake me off already. He advanced out of the twisted alley a few steps, stopped, and looked back at me. Joe's shoulders were still angled ahead, but his brows were raised and his mouth opened into a questioning rictus, *Coming?* So far he'd been giving to me without asking for anything back. I jogged to catch up.

"So come on, kid. Out with it. What would you ever want to leave Paris for? You got no money here, so what, you got money back in England?"

"No, it's not that. I've just had enough."

"Uh huh. She must be quite a girl."

We pulled around a corner, Joe always at least a step ahead of me.

"Yeah. She's quite the girl. Worth jumping across a river for. Even if I went back now, I still wouldn't see her until Monday when she gets back to school."

He processed the information without responding. We were behind the Pompideau Center. A cluster of tables from an outdoor café was in our path, and he slowed his pace to one more leisurely and led me into its midst. He stopped and steered me into a different position. He had that look on his face again like he was assessing our surroundings for a purpose. I tried to guess it.

"Hold this, will you?" he told me, handing me his fedora.

"Okay."

"Pass it around for me."

"What?"

"Ladies and gentlemen, I have today for your enjoyment a medley of tunes from the classic American musical *West Side Story*." His voice was at a theatrical volume, and he smiled at each table as he spoke. "And so, without further ado," and then he sang. "Maria! I just met a girl named Maria!"

Just then the waiter came rushing out from the interior of the café, shaking his head and saying *"Non non non non."*

"What do you do with a girl like Maria? Marry her off, kid get busy with the hat!" Joe sang. He turned away from the rapidly closing waiter and serenaded another row of tables. I worked in his wake, shaking the overturned hat at the seated patrons.

"Merci. Merci beaucoup, monsieur." A man with a date poured change into the hat. I knew he would to keep from losing face. I moved to a table that seated a family. The husband dropped some money into the hat. His blonde daughter kept looking at me. I boldly offered her the hat, and she deposited a bill. A concerned look crossed her mother's features, which I deflected by gallantly bowing to the girl and moving on to the next table.

"I want to live in America! That's the way kid in America!" Joe sang. I leapt to the table he'd just been at and offered the hat. There were four very old ladies sitting there, and they giggled at my attempt, impervious. I moved on to the next table so I wouldn't lose the momentum. The waiter put his hand on my chest.

"*No. You cannot* (something something)."

"*Pardon me. Excuse me,*" I apologized, backing off. When he turned to chastise Joe, I resumed where I had left off. Some of the crowd was laughing at the antics. I located the tables where the laughter emanated from and quickly allowed them access to the hat.

When the singing stopped I looked over to Joe, who was being vigorously scolded by the red-faced waiter.

"Ah, don't get your knickers in a twist already," Joe retorted in English, but he stepped back. Some of the patrons began to applaud him. Joe found me and met me at the edge of the café, past where it was roped off. I handed him the hat, and he began counting out the take.

"This city just isn't what it used to be." He forced some of the money into my hands. "Used to be they would welcome live entertainment in the cafes. It's part of the soul of the city."

"You sing pretty well, Joe."

"Ah, I was a little out of voice today."

We were walking back into the Quarter, away from the Pompideau Center. Maybe he'd have made more if he'd had his guitar.

"Hey, where is your guitar?"

"At home."

"Where do you live, by the way?"

"Got a little corner all to myself. I'll show you sometime."

"Hey Joe, see this?" I stepped into the doorway of a restaurant and motioned to a pile of broken plates. "Have you seen those guys that stand there and smash them?"

"Yeah. The Greeks."

"Why do they do that?"

"It's a gimmick to attract customers."

"That's it?"

"I could make something better up if you'd like, but that's it."

So that ended the great plate smashing mystery.

"Look, I've got some things to take care of," he said in a way that told me that I wasn't included. "You know how to get back?"

"Sure. No problem. Thanks for showing me all your tricks. I really appreciate it."

"Kid," he smirked, "Those aren't all of my tricks. You never show all your tricks." He stepped away from me, half turning, then turned back. "You want a taste of some jazz later on?"

"Yeah."

"Real jazz. I don't mean amateur crap, I'm talking real music here. Are you serious that you want to hear some?"

"I'd love to. What time, though? I have to be back in the store before it closes."

"Cami'll let you back in. Just tell her you're going out and ask her if she'll let you back in." I took it he meant Camille. "Oh, say, don't tell her where you're going. I don't want to bring her along this time. I already took her once. I don't want her to get the wrong idea. It'd be too easy for her to fall in love with me." He smirked.

"I won't tell—"

"Tell her you're going to…nah. Well, you're a smart kid. You know what to say." He snatched a glance at his watch.

"Do you want me to meet you there, or—"

"I'll come get you," he stated firmly. "Nine o'clock. If you can't make it, don't beat yourself up. I understand."

"I'll be there Joe.

"And kid, listen."

"Yeah?"

"Just listen. In general. To everything." He walked backwards a few steps, getting my reaction, before he turned back around.

I took Cami with me to the refectory that night and paid her way in. "You don't have to do that."

"Joe and I made some money today. You'll never believe it." I told her about our adventure.

"Hey, I was going to go out with some friends tonight, but they might be out later than eight. Is there any chance someone will be awake to let me back in?"

"No. Have to sleep out on the sidewalk, won't you?"

"Brat. It's obvious that you weren't spanked enough as a child. It's never too late to make up for that, you know," but I didn't touch her.

"Tell you what. Going to move you into the writer's studio tonight. You can sleep in there until you leave. Don't have much longer, do you? Hope not."

"The less time around you the better. I'm not sure how much longer I'll be in the city. No longer than Sunday, though. That was nice of George, putting me in the studio."

"I'm giving you the studio!" she asserted indignantly. "George is off visiting his daughter. Left this morning. Does that sometimes, no warning when he's coming back. So just come in the apartment entrance and I'll leave the side door to the studio unlocked."

"All right. Thanks, Cami. That's nice, George seeing his daughter. Does she work outside of the city?"

"She's seven." She was amused at the shock she must have predicted I'd display. "So you're out late. Must be a lass."

"No, just going out with the lads." Seemed like everyone thought I had a girl lately.

CHAPTER 20

Joe showed up early, but I was already waiting for him. It was a ten block walk to the Mazet. Along the way he stopped me and ducked into the thin mouth of a dark alley. He reached down next to some plastic garbage bags and pulled up a new shoebox sitting in its own lid, housing an old pair of shoes. Someone must have bought a new pair and thrown out his old ones. Joe examined them, black dress oxfords, and determined, "Too small. It's getting to be time to find some shoes. Mine are starting to take on water." He deliberately placed the box on top of the garbage bags. "Someone will want them."

"You're pretty observant, huh?"

"You got to keep your eyes open, kid," he answered in his typical fashion of deflecting my flattery. I wasn't winning him over with that, so why was he taking time with me?

There was a lot for me to learn. It's good when you find that you have more to learn.

"That's the place," Joe indicated, slowing his pace to a cordial one. "I'm going to introduce you to Riverboat Pete. He's been leading jazz bands in Paris for twenty years. He should be warming up soon."

Sitting at an abbreviated table with his back to the brightly lit Mazet was a wide, white man reading a newspaper. He wore a salty, black mariner's cap. Above his lips was a blasted looking mustache of pubic looking hair. It was about the only whiskering his face was capable of.

"Pete, how come you're not set up yet? Are you taking a day off or what?"

Pete jutted out his lower lip and slowly looked up at Joe without fully removing his attention from the newspaper.

"So you're my manager now? Are you trying to tell me that I'm doing my job wrong, is that it?" Pete spoke like an American who had been away from home for a long time. He looked back down at his paper and shook his head disapprovingly. I kept an eye on him, sticking to my role as back-up muscle to Joe.

"It's getting kind of late, Pete."

"It's early," Pete said without looking up.

"I mean if you can't hack it tonight, I'd be happy to run the show for you. I know that you're old and all, so this might be kind of late for you."

Pete went through the motions of opening up the paper and turning the page as an excuse to look up to where Joe was standing. He laughed derisively, kind of a "Hoo hoo hoo," noise, and said, "Boy, I can run **circles** around your sorry ass. Can do now, will be able to do when I'm eighty, you **bet**."

Joe patted him on the shoulder. "It's all right old man. You had your day. You done with the sports section?"

"When did you learn to read?"

"Pete, I can read *War and Peace* in the time it takes you to read that newspaper."

"You can have it when I'm **done** with it."

Joe stepped in closer. "Come on, Pete. I'll be done with it before you know it. I just want to check out the horses."

"You want it so bad, you go out and buy your own paper."

"Pete, you're sweating me over a section of the newspaper, after all I done for you? Give me a break."

"All you **done** for me?" Joe made a grab for the sports section. "Hey! Hands off my paper," Pete barked, holding it away. He looked angry, but Joe was laughing it off.

"Come on!"

When Joe finally stepped back, Pete carefully withdrew the coveted section and handed it over. He turned and looked me in the eye unexpectedly and said, "You enjoying watching me get taken by this **bum**?"

"Jake, this is Riverboat Pete, one of the finest bandleaders in all of Europe. Pete, this is Jake. Jake's just come over from England where he's a student at the university." He said it as if it were obvious which university it was.

He offered me his heavy hand. "Staying for the show, Jake?"

"I can't wait, Pete. Joe's been telling me you're the best."

"Is **that** so?" He hooked a glance up over his shoulder at Joe, who was leaning against the window of the bar reading his sports, smiling and nodding without looking. "You watch yourself around this bum, Jake. You keep one eye on him at all times, hear?"

"He's been pretty good to me so far."

I had taken what he'd said too seriously. Pete nodded and turned away from me. I didn't know how to joke like they did. I was a little embarrassed that I couldn't keep the pace.

"How'd you meet a kid from England, Joe? They wouldn't let your **bum** ass in the country."

"If I was in England, I'd be on my knees in front of the queen within a week. I'm a legend."

Pete started to get his musicians together. There was a woman on a twelve-string guitar, a man on saxophone, and another man on percussion. Pete himself was plucking a thin rope tied between the top of a broomstick and a wide metal washtub that the broomstick stood on. It made notes like a brutal bass.

A crowd had been coagulating around Pete's band. When he decided it was time, Pete reeled in the warm-up sounds of his musicians with a steady bass beat. The percussionist was the first to pick it up, using a set of bongo drums. The woman spiced it up with an opposing rhythm on her guitar, and finally the sax player joined the scene. When he got in on things, everyone knew it was really a song.

"Stay here, kid," Joe told me and slid his way around the circle of audience to the other side. I did as he said. People kept adding themselves to the crowd. The kid on the sax blew a happy, energetic solo that made me start tapping my foot and snapping my fingers and not caring who saw it. Damn, that kid could knock some notes out of that horn.

They jumped out of that song and into something thick and bluesy. Pete was singing this time, in the kind of fat, smoky, gravely voice you'd think he had by looking at him. He and the saxophone took turns dancing with the tune. Pete would sing what the saxophone had just played but give it something more. The sax took it back, plus Pete's riposte, and stacked it with something else. They were kicking my musical ass.

They really had it going by the third song. Then suddenly someone shouted something from a window a few stories up; I didn't recognize the words, but there was no mistaking the intent; and they threw something at Pete. Something wet. The band kept playing, but Pete looked really angry. He looked up in the direction the projectile had come from and, still keeping the tune, sang, "**Fuck** you, you mother **f**—"

"Hey, hey, ho, ho, easy," Joe cut him off with. Just then I realized that Joe had joined the band, taking over guitar duties from the girl, who was leaning against him, back to back. She had a tambourine that she shook while she smiled. She wasn't flashy looking: average height with an average build, dressed in jeans, a blouse, and a scarf, but she was captivating in the way she moved. The way she smiled with her eyes half closed, not looking to see if anyone was staring at her, which made everyone stare. I knew that if I turned to the man next to me, he'd be staring at her, too.

Pete took a minute to wipe himself off after the song was done. He checked to make sure none of the instruments were damaged. Joe talked him down.

"Now, ladies and gentlemen," Pete announced, taking center stage. "Those of you who **do** appreciate good music. It is my pleasure to present to you, all the way from the state of Montana in the United States of America, the lovely and talented…Magrite."

The girl took Pete's place at the center of the circle and swayed back and forth as Joe and Pete dug a slow groove for her. Then she sang.

Magrite had a voice like a lot of lonely nights all strung together. She played with all the low notes in a voice that could never reach the high notes but had learned to get along without them. When she came to the refrain, Joe's voice joined hers in harmony: "But Baby, a whole entire me died when your love left."

When she looked my way with those half-closed eyes I tried to look back at her like I was the only one there. The song ended and the audience went crazy. Pete and Joe started working the crowd for money on the merit of Pete's promise that there was more of the show to come. When Pete came my way, he pulled his collection box away from my money.

"No, kid," he told me. "You're with us."

I pocketed the money discretely so as not to interrupt his momentum of collecting. Joe joined me again after the collection to watch the rest of the show.

"That girl can really sing, huh?"

"That's my girl," he said, looking sideways at me while clapping. He didn't say it in a paternal way.

"You mean, she's your girlfriend?"

"It's an off again, on again sort of relationship. She's a woman who's fickle with her moods, know?"

When the show was over, Joe drifted over toward the band.

"Listen, kid, you're on your own, okay? I've got to make a little time with my lady. You gonna be all right?"

I didn't want him to feel like I was being a burden even for a moment, so I played it cool. "Yeah, I've got to get to bed anyhow. Hey, thanks for taking me to the show."

"You going to be at the store tomorrow?"

"It's about the only thing I can afford to do."

"Catch you there, all right?"

"Hey Joe, I have to thank you."

"Why is that?"

"I'm not going to leave Paris yet. You were right. Everything I need is right here. I wouldn't have known that if it weren't for you."

"You made the right decision, kid." He was next to Magrite now, and all of his focus went to her.

Joe and Magrite. I watched them for a few seconds before heading back for the store.

The apartment entrance was an anonymous looking, street level doorway between the main entrance of Shakespeare and Company and George's one-room antiquarian book shop. I took the dark stairs to the second floor landing where the side door to the writer's studio was. It was unlocked, as Cami had promised.

I took off my boots, leaving the rest of my clothes on, and got into the single bed. I wondered if the relationship between Joe and Magrite was all in Joe's head. I didn't see anything between the two of them. What would he do if she wanted to go home with him? Where did he live? Come on back to my bridge, baby? Maybe she lived on the street too. She didn't look it, but I was learning to keep my mind open to all sorts of options. I would have missed my best night in Paris if I had given up on it.

Someone knocked on the door, and I didn't have a clue as to who it would be.

"Coming," I announced in a loud whisper. It was Cami. Her room was on the floor above. "Sorry. Did I wake you coming home?"

"I was up. Just wanted to make sure you got in all right." She was in pajama bottoms and a tee shirt that exposed her stomach. It wasn't the best stomach in the world, but she seemed happy showing it off. She didn't have a bra on, as usual. Cami took half a step away from me. "You want to go back to sleep. I'll stop being a bother."

I'd had a snarky expression on my face; one I'd worn as armor in case some stranger from another of the apartments had been the one knocking. "You're never a bother, Cami. I got in fine. Thanks again for letting me use the studio. It's like the Ritz compared to the floor downstairs. What are you doing awake? Isn't it past your bedtime?"

"Couldn't sleep." She hunched her shoulders and put her hands together in front of her, shivering and chattering her teeth. "Cold," she whispered, looking up at me. She took a barefooted step closer.

I put my arms around her shoulders and hugged her, rubbing my hands up and down on her back to warm her up. This happened because she was so close to me and shivering. I felt wrong about it, so I let go of her and stepped back away.

"You wouldn't be cold if your weren't running around half naked. You'd better get back to bed and warm yourself up."

"Have you any more cigarettes?"

"When did you start smoking?"

"Always have. Don't tell George, or he'll kill me."

"You just gave me the best reason *for* telling him."

She laughed.

"Yeah, a cigarette's a good idea."

I rolled one on the desk and gave it to her, then rolled one for myself. I opened the window at the front of the room, and we leaned out over the railing, blowing the smoke out into the dark. I finished mine first and got under the covers of the bed. Instead of taking the hint, she stayed sitting on the edge of the bed talking, confiding her opinions of the other residents to me.

"Okay, now get the hell out of here. I need my sleep," is what I finally resorted to. She laughed when I said it, though.

CHAPTER 21

At half-five AM there was a car crash. I heard the noise outside and suddenly I was exactly awake, exiled from dreams without a souvenir. I opened the window and leaned out over the ledge, looking to the left. There had been a head-on collision in front of my phone booth. Both of the drivers were out of their cars talking. There wasn't anyone else around that early, nor any other cars. I'd never seen the city so naked of people. The sky was an hour less than black.

I smoked. I was careful to hold the cigarette out the window so that the room wouldn't smell of it. We all knew how much George hated smoking. He hated it the way only an ex-smoker can. The flashing lights on a tow truck brought me out of a stupor. I leaned out the window to watch that for a while, until the accident was cleared and the sky was gray and a few more cars passed by. Men began the morning sidewalk ablution, hosing away the dirt and litter so that a fat brown stream burbled in front of the curb.

Then it began to rain. I knew that if I tried going back to sleep I'd wake up more tired later, so I took care of my morning chores. It rained during the walk to the *Universite Polytechnique*, and when I was done with breakfast it rained on the walk back. I went up to the library and removed my copy of **Coriolanus** from where I'd stashed it behind some other books. New books weren't supposed to be brought into the library.

Beata and Anje, the German resident, talked to me for a while when they were awake. Cami had told me that she was annoyed at these two because they didn't do much work in the store. Now they were being friendly to me, perhaps seeking an ally. After they left I went into the studio and finished reading the play. It was half-eleven.

It wasn't raining out anymore. I had seen the city before the rain, when the rain began, and when it stopped. I had seen a car crash on a street where traffic now flowed unaware of what had occurred there in the dark. Only those of us who worked the city very early in the morning knew it in this way. I felt like I'd crossed over from tourist to resident of Paris. It was almost time for lunch. I decided to have a cigarette out in front of the store before I sought out some food. There on the low wall, sitting between Beata and Anje, was Joe.

"Kid, I was just coming in to see you. Got anything going on?"

"I was just going to find some lunch."

"Come on, we'll go for a walk. Hey Anje, do me a favor."

"What?" she smiled.

"I don't know. Any favor. You'll come up with something."

"Oh *Joe!*" she admonished, but he got the blush. He jammed his hands into his pants pockets and started us down the block.

"I was worried about you, Joe. What do you do when it rains?"

"Really? That's touching, kid," he said in a tone which would have sounded sincere if I hadn't known him. "I stayed on Pete's houseboat last night with the band."

"Why you don't ask George if you can stay at the store? I think he'd offer you a place to sleep." We were crossing a bridge.

"Me and George, we don't exactly get along. He doesn't trust bums."

"You're not a bum, Joe."

"Let's just say he's not fond of my bohemian lifestyle. I ever show you my home?" He jumped from the first sentence to the second so quickly that I knew to leave the subject of George alone. "I'll give you the nickel tour after lunch. What're you in the mood to eat?"

"I'm thinking burgers."

"Don't waste your money on a burger. I can get you a burger. Can you hold off until tonight?"

"Sure. I've got to get some bread or something, though. I can't concentrate when I get too hungry." I'd probably lost fifteen pounds over break.

"You learn to live with it. I know a place along the way."

Without rehearsal I asked him, "Will you show me how you get all those burgers?"

A look that I hadn't seen before settled into his features. "Tell you what," he whispered. "I will show you. I'll just ask one thing of you: don't go yapping to everyone at the store how we do it, okay? I'm only going to show you because I trust you not to misuse the information. I don't go telling this to just anyone. Deal?"

I promised him what he wanted of me and thanked him the best I could. We stopped at a *boulangerie* and I bought a baguette. Joe refused to let me buy one for him, but when I offered him some of mine he accepted and tore off a bite.

"So Joe, I was wondering. How long have you been living on the street? If you don't mind my asking." I was getting up my nerve.

He dropped his pace a bit so that we were in step. He didn't quite look me in the eye, but he was still smiling. "This time?" he chuckled. "Oh, only about eight months. Since I left my third wife. Before I married her, I spent about five years without being tied down, what you might call being a vagabond. Most of that was in America. Few years in New York, then a couple years crossing the country. Sometimes working, sometimes hitching." We were still side by side. I sensed that there was more to the story, but it wasn't the one I wanted.

"How long were you married?"

"To this wife? You mean how long have I been married? I'm still married, if you want to get technical about it. I've been married for about three years."

"Technical?" I advanced. "Correct me if I'm wrong, but you're either married or you're not, right?"

"Far as I'm concerned, that matrimony is over." He chopped a line in the air in front of him with flat hands, palms down. Finality. A lot of the white of his eyes was showing. I only allowed a second of berth. I still had my nerve up and moved closer to it.

"But when you were together, did you live on the street?"

"No," he smirked. "We had a happy little home in the Big Apple, and she had a great job. I was doing all right, but she really pulled in the big money in the family. I used to run a pizza joint. I can do everything: make the dough, toss it, bake. I made the sauce from scratch. Managed.

"Done a little of everything. Used to box a bit." He snapped into a boxing stance when he said it and showed off a little footwork. "Sang for a living. Sold hot dogs at Yankee Stadium. Ran a nightclub. You name it, I've probably done it."

Then abruptly, "We're here." We were in front of an alley between a hotel and an office building. It was full of sunlight and paved in the same bricks as the sidewalk we were on.

"In here?" I took a step into it.

"Wait, wait, wait," he growled, stopping me with a gesture. He was standing with his back to it, looking all around us. I examined my nails while a clump of pedestrians passed. "Okay," Joe decided and slipped into the passage. I jogged along after.

The alley crooked left and then right to accommodate the oddly shaped hotel. At the end it opened up into an almost square space, like a room without a ceiling. Up against the wall of the office building was a two story scaffold smattered with paint. That was it.

"Welcome to my estate." Joe folded his overcoat into a square, which he then placed under the scaffold next to his guitar. I had expected to see more possessions stashed in his den, but he was outfitted as ascetically as a monk. We stood quietly and surveyed. "It's all I need. I sleep under the stars. It's private." He nodded at the scaffolding. "Got a roof in case it starts to rain." Then in a snooty voice, "I've even got running water." He pointed to a spigot I hadn't noticed before, jutting from a wall.

"Not bad. Hot and cold?"

He squeezed his lips and squinted his eyes at me. "Let's not get carried away, kid. Come on." He led us back out the alley. He repeated the same show of caution exiting as he had entering. He didn't explain this hesitation, as though the logic was obvious. The most obvious reasoning I could conceive of was that he was protecting his home by not drawing attention to it.

"I'm meeting a friend to talk to him about joining Pete's band. You want to come along? You got anything going on?"

"No, that's cool." We walked along the main drag.

I was almost ready to ask him. Joe always deflected my flattery, but I knew that somewhere inside he was responding to it.

"I was wondering. You're one of the smartest guys I've ever met. I was here in the city, whining that I was so miserable and I wanted to leave. But I've got George's roof over my head, plus a nice warm college to go back to with a guaranteed hot meal a day, plus my parents to fall back on. And I'm the one complaining.

"You don't rely on anyone for anything. You're the most totally independent person I've ever met. All the women at the store fall in love with you. You've got music, you're well fed, you know the city. *You're* the one helping *me* out. Don't take that the wrong way. No disrespect intended."

"None taken."

"What I wonder is, with all your talent, you could probably have a job doing whatever you wanted to do. I mean, if I had a business and I needed help, I'd hire you in a heartbeat."

"Well thanks, Jake."

I fired past that to not lose where I was going. "So where I'm confused is, why don't you have a job?" The words were carefully selected.

"You could have a great apartment here in the city if you had a little income, you know?"

"It's not about that, Jake. It's not about money and having things. That was what Elias could never get through his head—"

"I'm not Elias, Joe." It was the first time I'd ever interrupted him, and I was very conscious of his reaction. He stayed in step with me. "I'm not asking you from a materialistic point of view. I just see so much talent when I look at you, Joe. I guess what I'm getting at is, with all you've got going for you, why do you choose to live on the street?"

We came around a corner and stopped. He faced me.

"I'm on the street because I'm running away from my wife. It was the only way to get away from her."

Far below each of his eyes were crescent shaped creases. The flesh between the creases and his eyes was whiter than the rest of his face. There were straight, vertical ruts on either side of his mouth, from nose to chin, deep enough to hold coins.

I decided against saying I was sorry for hitting a nerve.

"I still don't get it. Why did you choose the street? I mean this is a little extreme, don't you think? Couldn't you just have gotten a divorce?"

"No, it isn't that simple. Things had gone too far. We used to get into some fights. I'm talking battles of Olympic proportion. One time she threw a hot frying pan full of eggs and hit me in the jaw, almost knocked me out. Dishes? She'd throw them like it was nothing." We started walking again.

"Part of it was, I think deep down she liked it when I smacked her around. She used to get me so mad, but she knew what she was doing. I think she was just pushing my buttons to see what would happen, and the only way to stop her was to punch her lamps out. Then we'd make up; sometimes it would take a few days and I'd have to hit the street, but we'd make up, and it was like when we first met, when we first fell in love."

"I don't know, Joe. I'd never hit a woman."

"Well, good. Don't be surprised if it happens someday, though."

"No. If I even thought I was going to, I'd walk away. That's just not what I'm made of." It was one of the things Dad had taught me. He'd imbued the directive into me at a very early age. I was old enough now, though, that the value was my own. We were slowing down to a halt in front of a café.

"You'll see. Anyhow I found out she was cheating on me with my best friend. Don't ask me how I found out." There was a tint of savagery in it when he said it. "And I threw her down a flight of stairs."

"Jesus."

"I knew that if I stuck around, sooner or later I was going to kill her. I was afraid that I would literally kill her. So I got out of there, got on the plane to Rome, and I've been on my own ever since. I honestly do not foresee the day I stop living this way.

"The thing is, I still love her. But I know I can't come near her. Listen, Jake. I don't ever claim to be the smartest man in the world, but I have some knowledge of these things. You want to know what love is? I'll tell you what love is. Love is a lot of hard work.

"Well, here comes Kevin."

A man about twice my age came out of the café and reached out to shake hands with Joe. He was dressed in cheap new clothes that were styled after expensive trendy clothes. He brought a miasma of cloying pine cologne with him. I immediately felt like, young as I was, I could dominate him, and I felt embarrassed to be near him. I stepped aside while Joe talked to him.

I still knew that I would never hit a woman. I thought back through my childhood and couldn't even come up with a time that I'd hit my sister, even when we were kids, and even though she'd punched me a couple of times.

Joe's gestures while talking to Kevin were mostly open-handed push-ing motions, reinforcing the space between them. Joe's relationship to Kevin was different than ours. He hadn't befriended me because I had any money, because I hadn't, nor as a bodyguard, nor as a sidekick. Joe had unloaded a burden of confession on me. Everything he'd done for me had been like a down payment for it. I was there to judge him, to tell him he was wrong. He wanted me to reinforce his guilt.

"Listen Kevin, Jake and I have got to meet someone, so I'll see you later, all right?" I'd heard enough of their conversation to know that Joe was letting him down easy, that he wasn't getting let into the band. Joe hustled us away from Kevin and around a corner. After checking back over his shoulder, he said, "That's the key to being a good friend, Jake. Always have someplace else to go." It made me think back to all the times he'd done the same thing to me.

We were crossing the *ile de la cite*.

"Here's where my wife and I spent our honeymoon." We were in front of an extravagant hotel.

"You brought her to Paris?"

"I wonder if they still have the fountain. Come here."

We passed under an arch into a courtyard. I saw through the glass doors into the well-appointed, marble-floored vestibule, where a concierge eyed us. Joe paid no heed to the scrutiny. He was looking at the dry fountain.

"Must still have it off for winter. That's a shame."

We exited the courtyard and continued towards the bookstore. There was a Galois box on the sidewalk, which I picked up and looked inside.

"What are you doing?"

"Checking to see if someone dropped a full pack." I tossed it back on the ground.

"That's not how you do it. Here." Joe gave it a kick with his toe. "You judge by the weight of the pack when you kick it if it's full or not. That way you don't always have to be stooping over."

When we got back to the store he told me what the plan was for the burger run. He drew me a map of where to meet him before he left.

"I'll see you tonight, Jake. I've some things to take care of."

CHAPTER 22

This was how Joe managed to keep himself fed while he was in Paris:

Le Quick, the ersatz McDonalds, closed at eleven PM. Joe would show up fifteen minutes later and wait for the final load of green plastic trash bags to be brought out to the curb. Le Quick kept a certain amount of food prepared and warm at all times, as did most fast food operations. Whatever hadn't sold during the last shift would end up in one of the bags, untouched, wrapped, and often still warm.

A couple of other men converged on the pile of bags while Joe and I were still searching for the right one.

"Hey, hey, ho, ho. Don't tear them open," he commanded. "If we make a mess, they'll stop throwing away the food," and with that, Joe was in control of the situation. Then I found the right bag.

"Let me in, kid." Joe took over the bag and began doling out sandwiches to the others. "What do you want, hamburger? Here you go. Fish? You want fish? You got it." I experienced a primal moment of resentment when he took the bag out of my hands, but I recognized it as an aspect of my hunger and kept my mouth shut. I was criminally hungry.

When he'd filled their hands with food, the others left. There was still plenty: hamburgers and cheeseburgers wrapped in logo printed wax paper; bacon cheeseburgers, fish sandwiches, and chicken sandwiches housed in cardboard containers; garden, Caesar, and shrimp salads in clear plastic boxes. There were also cold fries, which were too disgusting to eat. Joe twisted the bag shut and slung it over his shoulder.

"Come on. We've got a few stops to make before we eat."

Administrating my hunger required most of my concentration, and I had to follow in a quiet daze. We were in a business district, just beyond the nightlife. He led us to a doorway where a couple of men were huddled in a cardboard box. It had gotten cold again. Joe greeted them by name and handed them each a burger and a salad.

He took us around the corner to another doorway where a man was sitting. Joe gave him a chicken sandwich. Joe didn't know him by name, but they spoke to one another as familiars before we moved along.

There was a man lying on the sidewalk on a corner, and Joe approached him slowly.

"Franz. Hey Franz, are you hungry?"

There was no response from the man. He was curled fetally atop large Metro grate. Steam was rising from it. Joe was moving delicately, so I stayed a few steps back. White hair showed from under the man's wool cap. I looked to see that he was breathing.

"I think he's awake," Joe told me in a hushed voice. "Hold this. Hold it open for me." He rummaged around in the green plastic bag. He found one of the paper bags used for carryout orders and filled it with one of everything.

"He got beaten up pretty badly a few nights ago in his usual spot, so he's taken to sleeping out on the grates."

"At least it's warm."

"He's doing it the hard way." Franz still wasn't acknowledging us. Joe stepped closer and gently put the bag down in front of Franz. He patted it once when it was down. "Some food for you, Franz. You eat this now, okay?" Then to me, "I just hope nobody takes it from him. All right, let's go eat."

We walked a couple blocks away and sat on the curb of a side street. I ate a bacon cheeseburger, and then another one while Joe was working on a fish sandwich. Then I ate a fish sandwich and one of the shrimp salads. I used my fingers. There were croutons on the salad, but I skipped them because they took too long to chew, and they scuffed my gums. Then I ate a cheeseburger.

"I guess you were hungry," Joe told me, finishing his salad.

I still had some room, so I took another cheeseburger and started working on it. I had a stupid smile of content on my face. Joe was fastidious about our rubbish. I heard music coming from somewhere.

"Are you playing with Riverboat Pete tonight?"

"No. My guitar was stolen."

"I'm sorry. What happened?"

"The bastards found me." He sat with his forearms on his knees, and he looked at his hands.

"Who found you?" I was almost done with the cheeseburger.

"The Mafia, that's who. They caught up with me."

"Are you serious?" I breathed out something like a laugh. "What makes you think the mob took your guitar?"

"You think it's funny?" Joe looked at me with hard eyes. I thought that he was about to hit me. I figured that I could take a punch from him. I wouldn't hit him back. I never expected that I'd have to think these thoughts with regard to Joe. "It was the *mob*. I know it was. This is just like them." I kept quiet. "They must have found my place while I was out, and stole my guitar. Once you cross the mob, they never leave you alone. They never forget! Caught up to me in Rome, then Greece, and now they found me again. They're everywhere, and once you cross them, they never leave you alone! That's why I'm on the street. It was the only way I could get away from them."

I focussed on my cheeseburger until it was done.

"It could have been some kids or something, too, Joe. You know? You might still be safe."

Joe stood up and took up the bag. I brushed the crumbs off of my clothes and whiskers and stood up as well.

"It was them. It was the Mafia. I know."

He walked me back to the store in silence. He stayed a couple of steps ahead of me most of the way there, but slowed when we reached block. At the corner he piled my arms with a salad and a burger each for the girls. I had promised food to them to make sure they'd let me back into the store.

"Maybe I will check out the band, see what's going on. I'll see you later kid."

Beata let me in, and after I gave out the food, I went to bed.

I thought about the mob story from every angle to try to make it true, but even late at night in the dark I couldn't believe it. Maybe he had crossed the mob in New York, and he was holding onto the idea so he wouldn't have to think about his wife. It could have been some minor thug he'd pissed off, or just some Italian whom Joe had assumed was in the mob, and the idea had ballooned in his head.

Or maybe something really terrible had occurred with his wife, and he was blocking it out of his head with the mob story. Maybe he had killed his wife, and that was what he was running away from. Or he had beaten her so badly that he was running away from the police. And living on the street, helping me out, was all part of his penance.

Maybe he was making up the mob story, trying to make me believe that he was crazy to scare me away from him. It was almost time for me to go back, and he was insuring that I would go, that I wouldn't fall into street life. It was Joe's way of saying goodbye to me.

I chose that idea, because it was the best one. I didn't want the legend to be crazy.

George still wasn't back Sunday night, the night before I was scheduled to leave. I bought a thank you card from the store and wrote it out to him. I was worried that he would think I was being lazy because the card came from his own store. I was more worried that if I'd bought the card somewhere other than Shakespeare and Company he would have been offended. It was a gamble.

I took Cami to the refectory for dinner that night. I'd been eating Le Quick with Joe the since the night he showed me, so I could afford one dinner out. I felt like I'd put on some of the weight I'd lost. It was the best I'd eaten the whole time I'd been abroad.

After dinner we played poker with my cards. I was beating her so harshly that I had to throw a couple of hands just to feel decent about it. Every time I won I'd say, "We said we were playing ten francs a hand, didn't we?"

"No. Said that last time, didn't you?"

"Oh, sorry. I got carried away. Sometimes I have to repeat things to you several times just to make sure you get it."

She smiled. "Oh shut up." She punched me in the shoulder.

"Hey, hey, ho, ho, don't touch the merchandise. I'm a very attractive individual, and I don't want you spoiling my beauty." Actually I hadn't had a shower in a week, and I was badly in need of a shave, and I was wearing the clothes I'd spent the last three days in, waking and sleeping.

"Can't think of anything more interesting to play for than money?"

"I just don't want to fry your little brain with any new ideas."

We played a few more hands until I got bored of it. Cami sat there and looked expectantly at me, so I told her I'd show her where to get a five-franc beer. The way she was eating up my abuse I knew she was in the mood for me to entertain her. She'd go wherever I wanted to take her and like what I told her to, so she was easy company.

I would have liked to go to the Mazet and hear Magrite sing one last time, but I was leaving very early in the morning and didn't want to be too tired. Along the way I pointed out a sign to Cami on a fast food joint.

"See that? That's too expensive for a serving of French fries. I'll show you where to find the cheapest ones in the city on the way back."

I took her into *Chez Chien,* and we each ordered Krönenbergs since it was the cheapest beer they had. I thought about paying for hers, but I didn't. It was a dingy, smoky little bar that I felt comfortable in, and standing there on the bar top was a Zippo lighter, the same model as the one that had been stolen from me. I picked it up and examined it. I could tell that it wasn't the same one; it had a different set of nicks and dents, the Braille of unfamiliarity. I left it on the bar for a while to see if anyone was going to claim it, then pocketed it.

"Let's get you good and drunk tonight," Cami proposed.

"No, I can't. I've got to be up nice and early tomorrow. If I miss the boat, I'm a dead man."

"Don't be silly. Your last night in Paris. Make the most."

"If I wanted to be silly, I'd just try to be more like you." I waited for her to laugh. "That reminds me, do me a favor. Come downstairs in the morning and make sure I'm awake by seven. I paranoid about missing the boat."

"Why don't you sleep upstairs tonight?"

"There's another bedroom up there?"

"There's room."

I thought it through. It would be harder to get to sleep in an unfamiliar apartment. "No. Besides, what if George comes home in the morning? Won't he be a little upset?"

"You'll be leaving anyhow, won't you?"

"Thanks anyway. I think I should stay in the studio. Come on, let's go."

The evening manager had closed up Shakespeare and Company, but he was outside in front of the store talking with the residents. There was a new guy as of that morning who was going to inherit the floor washing duties. Joe was with them.

"Kid. We're going to the Mazet tonight for some music. Are you in?"

"I can't. I've got to be up early in the morning to catch my boat."

"That's right. You're leaving tomorrow. Let's go for a walk."

We left the company of the others and headed around the block, and he asked me about my school. As we were coming down the boulevard towards the river, a man rushed past some cars at us.

"You speak English! I am hungry. Give me some money!" He went on like that in an eastern European accent.

"I'm street," Joe cut him off with and kept walking.

The beggar decided that he didn't understand and got in front of us again. "Come on, I'm hungry. I haven't eaten in—"

"I'm **street**," Joe insisted, and this time the bum got it. Even I felt intimidated. "You understand? I'm **street**. I don't have anything for you." The beggar was so turned around by it that I thought he would cry. "Listen, you want to learn how to eat? I'm going to score some food tonight. At eleven fifteen. You want in?"

"Yes," the guy stammered. There was no way not to answer Joe.

Joe told him where to go. "You know where that is?"

"Yes," but I wasn't convinced. The beggar took off in the other direction, and Joe and I finished our walk.

"He'll never show," I predicted.

"Anything can happen."

It was time to say goodbye. We kept it short, and I shook hands with him, and he started to walk away. I called out to him.

"Hey Joe. Tell me something."

"Tell you what?"

"I don't know, something. Anything. You decide."

"Kid," he told me. "You're going to be all right."

I was almost asleep when I heard the knock on the door.

"Come in." It was unlocked, and I was too sleepy to get up and see who was there.

"You'd let just anyone in your room? Are you insane?" Cami asked. She came in and left the lights out.

"If I'd have known it was going to be you, I'd have locked the door." I tried to remember where my tobacco pouch was. She started tampering with the bedcovers at the side of the bed to make a seat for herself.

"Christ, early boat, remember? I don't have time to be yapping to you."

"Don't have to do any talking." She wasn't making herself a seat on the bed after all; she slid her body under the covers.

"Excuse me young lady, what do you think you're doing?" I could be so slow sometimes. Calling her "young lady" was weak; she was only a year younger than I was. She was just wearing a tee shirt. I could tell by sense of touch.

"What's the matter Mr. Attractive Individual? Afraid I'll spoil your beauty?" She moved her face very close to mine.

"Hey, you don't want to come too close. I haven't brushed my teeth in about two days. I haven't showered in a week, either."

"What's the matter? You don't want to be with a virgin, is that it?" Oh Jesus. I had an answer for her, but I knew better than to use it. She was confessing.

I put a hand on her back. "Cami, any man who wouldn't want to be with an attractive woman like you would be an idiot." Not exactly true. "You're a wonderful woman. But I have a girlfriend, Cami. A girlfriend I love, who I'm sailing home tomorrow to see. Believe me, I would love for you to stay the night with me," liar, "But I can't."

"Liar," she said, but I could hear that she believed me.

"Oh great, now you're going to insult me by calling me a liar. After I've just shown myself to be such a nice guy."

"She'd never find out."

"It's not the point. It just wouldn't be right."

"I think it would." She put a knee over mine. I wondered what the movement did to the hem of the tee shirt. I put my hand on her leg and gently slid it off.

"No you don't. I know you better than that, Cami. You're a better person than that."

We were quiet for a few seconds. "Sometimes it's so hard to do the right thing."

"Believe me, I know. Now get the hell out of my bed so I can get some sleep, you brat," I ordered, and slapped her naked ass.

"Hey! You'd better not do that, else you'll make me change my mind."

I deserved a cigarette after she'd gone, so I had one. I had to laugh. Kurt's voice was in my mind telling me I was an idiot. She was right, Tabi, you'd have never found out. I probably stank, and even the socks I had on were the ones I'd worn all week. And then there was my face.

Sometimes the world tries to tell you that you're beautiful, even if you don't have the ears to hear it.

My travel alarm clock did the trick in the morning, and I was packed and ready by the time she came down to check on me. She found me downstairs in the shop, waiting for her to let me out. I gave her a hug goodbye and an appropriate kiss on the forehead.

"You're a classy fellow, Jake," was the last thing she said to me.

"Nah. You're the one with the class. Make sure George gets that card."

She'd change her mind about me, in time. That morning I was in control of her self-esteem, but time would tear me down in her memory. Time, and the next crush.

The trip back to England was by hovercraft rather than ferry, and I got there in forty-five minutes rather than in hours. It was a lot of time I hadn't counted on. That was good, because I had to hitch from London to Birmingham to get to Kurt's house. Kurt's parents were going to put me up overnight, then Kurt was driving us back to campus.

I looked at my luggage while I was waiting at the seaport for the hovercraft, just to make sure it was all there. I unzipped my jacket and made sure that my passport hadn't gone anywhere in the two minutes since I'd last checked. I also took out my money stash and counted it. That morning when I'd been waiting for Cami to come down, I'd opened the cash drawer and looked inside. Not only are the different denominations of francs different colors, they're different sizes. French money is really beautiful. I stole as much out of the drawer that morning as five grams of hash cost.

End of Part Two

PART THREE

CHAPTER 23

Kurt blared his favorite rap CD on the stereo of his little red Ford as we sped over the flat gray highway from Birmingham to Harlan.

"You know, Kurt, you might as well be an American."

"How do you reckon?"

"You drive a Ford. You wear Nikes. You're the only one in England beside myself who drinks coffee instead of tea. You listen to rap music. You're practically a citizen on those merits alone. It's a compliment in the highest order, trust me." Sitting on the left side of the car, which to my American way of thinking was the driver's side, might also have contributed to this judgement. It made me feel like I was back in the States behind the wheel of my own car, driving.

"If you say so." He suddenly halved our speed down to the legal limit and made pig noises, meaning he'd seen a cop. Kurt's constant smile was very young. He had such a tough looking body that, if it weren't for that smile, he'd have been pretty frightening. His arms were an avalanche of muscle. "So tell me really, did you go to any of the prostitutes when you were in Amsterdam?"

"No, I told you already. I'm being faithful to Tabi. Besides, I don't have to pay for sex."

"What about the lass in the bookstore you told me about? You shagged her really, didn't you? You can tell me."

Now that we were out from under his parents' roof, free from the net of their influence, he was starting to loosen up.

"Kurt, if there was anything to tell, believe me, you'd be the first to know." I wondered why he was pushing the issue. "So you were faithful to Rachael over break, naturally."

He did his trademark maniacal laugh accompanied by furtive glances left and right as though to see if anyone was watching him.

"I'll take that as a 'no.'" He'd asked the question more as an excuse to make this admission than to hear my answer. I felt badly for Rachael because I was protective of her. I was protective of her because she was the girlfriend of my best friend. Kurt's friendship was primary to Rachael's, so it wasn't for me to direct his behavior towards her; I stuck to my role as a confidant.

Leaning against the "driver's side" door I assumed a new facial expression I'd taken on, one I'd borrowed from Joe: mouth smirked to the left side, right eyebrow cocked. It was an attitude I'd assumed when I used the Turkish style toilet at the store, and for other moments when I was thinking, "Just another experience that seems mundane to me now, that would have shocked me just a short while ago."

"There's something I feel badly about," he confessed in a solemn tone. "It was a mate's ex-girlfriend that I had a little snog-fest with." A snog-fest was making out. "He'd split up with her a while ago, like. She was the one who started it, anyhow. I had no idea that she liked me. She just suddenly jumped on me. She had the greatest knockers I've ever seen, a good sight bigger than Rachael's. You could have landed a helicopter on each one of them." He ran his sentences together as if to get all of the evidence out in the open before judgement was passed. "I wouldn't have done it if I'd thought there was any chance they'd get back together. I wouldn't get off with a mate's woman."

"I'm with you on that one. Mates' girlfriends are off-limits," I agreed, maintaining Joe's expression.

Kurt conversed like an American. He'd say everything on his mind in a little story rather than in the tennis match method of the English, and it was one of the roots of our friendship.

So was weed. Ostensibly we'd met through his hallmate Albert when I was looking for weed first semester. In truth I'd known Kurt by sight before that because of Rachael. One of the first weekends of the school year Kurt's friends and my friends were at the same table at the pub, and I'd picked out Rachael as the one I was going to hit on. Rachael had pale English skin, small English bones, and an abbreviated English nose. She wore her dark hair long in the front and cropped in the back, very short at her neck and gradually longer further up her head. It made you want to run your hand along the back of her head to see how it felt. She never swore and she had a dignified carriage, but she had naughty eyes. Dusky, brown, bedroom eyes that told half a secret when she smiled.

I'd been staring at her from down the table, searching for an excuse to talk to her, when a pair of shoulders the width of a condor's wingspan swooped in, placed a drink in front of her, and sat next to her. It was Kurt. I'd put her on hold for the time being, but after I'd met Kurt and we became good friends, I turned my desire for her off completely. I still recognized her as attractive, but I wouldn't let it mean anything to me. She was a sister in my mind.

I wanted to tell Kurt about this to show him that I was a good friend, but I doubted that I'd get the desired result. It seemed likelier that once I told him, he would feel threatened, and his trust in me would be poisoned. A younger me, even one just a little younger would have blundered along without thinking this through. It struck me that I'd just witnessed myself become a little more mature. Sometimes you do something for someone without having to let them know about it.

When we left the highway and entered Harlan, the roads changed from straight to twisted. Kurt barely slowed down. Every time Kurt drove through town he'd take the roundabouts a little bit faster, the corners a little bit tighter, sharpening the edge because the thrill from the last drive had already worn off. Because he wanted that high that comes from being close to disaster.

My favorite part of the route was a tight curve on Cotterly Road dissected by train tracks. The corrugation of the tracks at that speed made the tires lose their grip so that the car vibrated and the ass end of it swung along the arc of the curve.

"Bumpies!" Kurt purred as we rattled over the tracks. He said it every time. We went over it five kilometers per hour faster than the last trip.

"Kurt, you are without a doubt the best driver I know. The most exciting, anyway."

"Thank you."

"I'd better just make note of your next of kin."

We survived the trip through town. Kurt parked his Ford in the student lot and we headed for the dorms.

"No offense Jake, but I'm going up to my room for a nap. Bloody knackered. Been working ten hour days at dad's factory over break. School's a vacation after that. Tell you what. Are you up for a weed later on? I'm planning on visiting Mouse Boy tonight. Your presence is mandatory." Mouse Boy was our dealer.

I sucked air in through my teeth. "I don't know, Kurt. I'd better pass."

"What's the matter?"

"Money issue. I've got to have enough money for food this semester."

"What about that loan you told me about? Should be coming in soon, shouldn't it?"

"Yeah. Well I spoke to my dad about that over break, and he said that there were some complications with it. Problems with the paperwork. I'm not really sure when it's gong to come."

"Listen. Don't worry about it. Remember, one must never let a silly little thing like money get in the way of one's priorities. Like hash. We'll just do a buy like usual and you can pay me back when you get the chance."

"Kurt, I'm starting to feel bad about that. I hate to leave you hanging like this."

"Nah. Like I said, that's what friends are for. We've all been a little short before. I know that if things were the other way around you'd do the same for me, right?"

"No. Frankly I'd tell you to piss off."

He laughed. "Punch it." The routine went like this: we shook hands with an overhand grip, then, without letting go, switched to an underhand grip. As we were releasing we'd hook our fingers to catch one another momentarily. One of us would swing a fist downwards to punch the top of the other's upward swinging hand, then we'd repeat the motion the other way around.

Kurt had never made me feel like a beggar in any of my transactions with the Bank of Kurt. I wondered when he'd ever been short on cash and had to lean on a friend. I doubted that he really had. His parents' house was huge.

With the ritual complete, we split up and walked to our respective dorms. Mine was at the top of the hill, the absolute furthest one from the campus.

I could hear voices somewhere in Frank Hall, but it wasn't anyone I knew. I walked up to the second floor and opened the door to my single-occupancy room. It still had that smell to it, like cardboard, dust and carpet cleaner, that I'd forgotten about until I was immersed in it again. I put my rucksack down. It could stay packed for a little while longer. I was glad enough to be free of its burdensome weight.

I opened the sliding glass door at the end of the room and stepped onto my balcony. The skin of my scalp and the muscles of my neck were loosening. I was getting used to hearing my name in my best friend's accent again, and somehow this room had become my home. There was one thing to take care of.

The back of my wardrobe was a corkboard. At the top of the cork-board were the words "I wank off every day because I am an American" written in highlighter marker. I knelt on the bed and lifted the lower half of one of my earlier paintings, which was tacked to the board. Reaching under it I removed he photograph of Yvonne. This I took to my desk. In the top middle drawer was an envelope of photos from home, and I looked at Yvonne one time before putting the photo in the back of the envelope and replacing it in the drawer. I did not allow the task to take up much room in my mind. When it was done I took a walk into town to get some things.

Rachael was back on campus and in Kurt's room when I came by again that night. Kurt and Rachael usually refrained from public dis-plays of affection, but they were sitting tightly together on his bed hold-ing hands. They were glad to be back together again, glad enough to dissolve their regular composure.

"Hello Cedric. Good haircut," I said to Kurt's roommate, the Ubergeek.

He made a display of being surprised that I was in the room, but I knew that he listened to everything that went on. "What? Oh, me? Um. Yes. Hello, Jacob. Yes. Thank you. Yes, I did get it cut. Thanks for noticing."

"Looks less like a crew member from Star Trek now," Kurt jibed. Kurt really did not like his roommate, because Cedric was so socially under-developed. I was the only one out of the three of us who even said hello to him.

"You did have an uncanny resemblance to a Star Trek character before, kid," I told him. "That there is one good-looking haircut, though. An improvement." I held my gaze until we locked eyes and he felt my eye contact. The thing was, he was probably *trying* to look like a Star Trek character, which in Kurt's value system was synonymous with geek.

Ubergeek was a title I'd bestowed upon him behind his back for Kurt's amusement, and now I felt badly about it.

"Make sure you recommend your barber to Kurt so he can avoid another mishap like that one," I said, indicating Kurt's head.

"Hey!" Kurt had gotten a new haircut as well.

"Hey," cooed Rachael, and stroked his hair. I really didn't like Kurt's new cut, but Rachael did, and wasn't that what mattered?

After tea, which is what the English called supper, Kurt drove Rachael and I to the Student Union to seek out Mouse Boy. Rachael didn't partake in our habit, so we weren't about to bring her along for the actual buy. Kurt didn't want to abandon her at the Union. We elected that she and I would stay at the Union Pub. Kurt was always the one who dealt with Mouse Boy and knew better where he might be found.

After I brought us a round, Rachael and I sat in a corner in a booth that was too large for us.

"So why is this fellow called Mouse Boy?" she inquired.

"Kurt started that one. He just looks like a mouse. If you saw him, I think you'd agree." I sipped my Newcastle Brown Ale. "I was going to try to tell you that it's because he has a penchant for cheese, but I figured you're too smart for that."

It got me a laugh, a real laugh, not just a polite one. This was the first time we'd ever been alone together.

"You and Kurt make a nice couple," I confessed to her. "My friend Jamie, the one from home, never had a girlfriend I got along with. I'm sure it wasn't *my* fault," I said with mock arrogance.

"Oh, I'm sure," she played along. "So you must be excited about seeing Tabi again. You should have asked her to come along so it'd be the four of us."

"She's not back till tomorrow."

"We should all go out together soon."

The girl I'd slept with after I'd split up with Tabi, Camilla, was Rachael's best friend from home. Rachael hadn't hidden that she was trying to fix us up at the time. Kurt pushed us together as well, but Kurt had a thing for Camilla, so I figured that he wanted the vicarious pleasure of sleeping with her. Maybe Rachael had just wanted me to be part of a couple that was compatible with her and Kurt.

"I'm getting comfortable spending time with you and Kurt," she admitted. "I wasn't going to tell you this," she smiled, "But I used to be jealous of you, because Kurt spent all his time with you."

"Really? But we always ask you to hang out with us."

"Right, for your hash parties." She put a funny emphasis on the word "hash." "Do you know what I used to call you?" she asked, and her eyes picked up that naughty glint.

"What?"

"'The other woman.'"

"Ow." Then, in a soap opera-serious tone, "So you've found out my secret." It got her laughing again. She had run the risk of offending me by saying something like that, since she didn't know me so well. I looked at her and decided that it wasn't just a gaffe, that she hadn't ignorantly done it. She had known of the risk but figured that I was hard enough to take it.

"So are you in love with him?" I asked her. I saw the flicker in her eyes for a sliver of a moment. I'd decided to test our new bond.

"With Kurt? Am I in love with him?"

"Well I didn't mean Cedric."

"I suppose I am. Yes, I love Kurt."

I waded out into deeper waters. "Is it the first time you've ever been in love?"

It turned out that it wasn't, and I asked her about it. It turned out that her previous relationship had lasted three years.

"It's funny you should ask about him. I actually bumped into my ex-when I was home over break, and we ended up snogging like we'd never broken up. Isn't that strange? Both of us were surprised. After it was over we just went our separate ways and that was the end of it. I can't believe I'm telling you this," she said as she wrapped her fingers around her pint. Her expression changed to one belonging to the old Rachael, the one who was a stranger.

"Well I'm glad that you trust me," I soothed, trying to retrieve the new Rachael. "That's happened to me before. Sometimes once you're outside of the relationship and all of its problems you look at the person and remember that you were attracted to them."

"Maybe that's what will happen with you and Yvonne when you go home."

"I doubt that," I laughed. "I don't know if Kurt told you what happened, but after she dumped me, I put my hand through the window of my car." I assumed that Kurt had told her, but I didn't press her to divulge this. "Word got back to her about it, so now she probably thinks I'm some kind of lunatic. I think we can pretty much write off any chances I had with her." Rachael settled back into the padded seat and met my eyes again.

"Please don't tell Kurt what I told you. I know he's your mate, but I don't think he could take it."

"I promise I won't." I raised my right hand when I said it, and I wondered if the gesture of taking an oath would make any sense to an Englander.

After that I turned the topic to her family, and then to the city she was from. By the time Kurt returned with the hash, Rachael had evolved in my mind from being just the role of Kurt's girlfriend into a whole personality.

"Sorry to keep you waiting. Mouse wasn't at the Union at all, so I had to track him down at his flat. Shall we go?"

"Oh, let's stay for another pint, Kurt. I was just starting to enjoy myself."

"We shouldn't keep Jake waiting for his hash." He did his maniacal laugh.

"No, that's a good idea, Kurt," I concurred. "Let's stay for a drink. I'll get us a round."

He shrugged. "All right."

"And wasn't it nice of Jake to invite Cedric to come with us?" she asked him.

"He doesn't drink!" he chortled.

"That boy needs a few bad habits. We'll get him one of these times."

"Excuse me. I'm just going to go do the necessary," Rachael told us discretely as she shimmied out of the booth with her handbag.

"That means she's going to take a shit or a pee, Kurt," I instructed.

"Oh Jake!" she scolded.

"Uncalled for!" Kurt agreed. I laughed. It was a great joke: it insulted Kurt's intelligence and ruined Rachael's discretion at the same time.

CHAPTER 24

I checked at her hall in the morning, but Tabi wasn't back yet. In the afternoon I went for a run around Ellison, the neighborhood that the halls were tucked into. On the way back I was seized with the ungrounded certainty that Tabi had arrived in my absence. I urged my unpracticed lungs to keep the pace on the run back, but at her hall I learned that I had been wrong. She wasn't there yet.

Her best mate, Christine, stopped me on my way back down the stairs.

"Hello you sweaty Yank. Are you all right?"

"Christine! How was your break? You look great. You lost some weight, I can tell." A lie; a suck-up.

"Tabi won't be here till after tea, but she will stop by your room as soon as she's back, or she'll meet you at the pub." She recited the words in a way that made me suspect she'd been instructed to tell me this.

"Talk to her?"

"Spoke to her on the phone this morning before my Mum drove me up."

Most of the residents were already back, and I could hear stereos playing through the windows of the various buildings.

"Thanks Christine. Am I going to see you there?"

"Naturally. If I don't make an appearance, the lads will all feel cheated." Christine was a kick, and she always made an effort with me.

I managed not to have to deal with Tabi's ex-boyfriend on the way out. Back in Frank Hall the lads were hanging out in Alex's room, so I decided to make an appearance. I knocked, and three voices called out, "Come in!"

I got hellos from them, except for Alex, who greeted me with, "Fucking hell, they let this Yank back in here? Whatever happened to standards?" Alex was big and tall with ginger hair. He spoke with a thick cockney accent, so it sounded like, "Kinell, they let iss Yank bok inere? Tever oppen to stonduds?" The rest of them laughed a derisive laugh.

"I was invited by the university administration to raise the I.Q. level. Just in time, I tell you." Devlin and Grahame were smoking rolled cigarettes, but I could smell that it was just tobacco.

"Kinell," Alex continued. "Smells like you've been exercising. We're about to go to tea, and you're likely to spoil it."

"At least an American knows the difference between the word 'tea' and the word 'supper.' Tea is that stuff you drink from a cup. What's the matter, afraid you'd run out of words?"

"Watch it, Jake," Grahame warned. "You're in a room full of English you know."

"Three English versus one American? In America, that's what we call 'fair.'"

"So how was Amsterdam?" Alex asked. That was the standard chain of events in Alex's kingdom; anyone who joins an existing group has to take a ration of shit from him until he's satisfied, then it's back to normal.

"I can't really remember most of it, so it must have been pretty good." I sat myself on the floor with the others and listened to everyone's holiday tales for a while.

Alex had been the King of Frank Hall all year, and the room he shared with Devlin was the default post-pub smoking room. I would have liked for us to hang out in my room once in a while, but it had only happened one time when they had a serious dope shortage and I was in possession. I'd lost my chance at leadership at the year's start. Alex had defined himself in the role while I was still struggling at being a foreigner.

I went to take a shower; I'd been taking two a day since I'd returned. After Paris, a shower left me feeling especially naked. Back in my room I opened up a Dickens novel which I was supposed to have finished before the break for my Victorian Literature class. I didn't recognize any of the characters anymore and had no idea what was going on. The work I'd need to do in order to catch up was towering. I let it ruin my spirits until it was time for tea, then I walked over to collect Kurt and that lot.

I had the urge to check Tabi's dorm one last time on the way to the dining hall, but I decided not to. I had been by plenty of times already, which Christine would report, and I didn't want to appear too eager.

Cedric and Rachael ate with us, as did Albert and Dark Ray.

"So Rachael," Albert said. "Remember that old Jaguar I told you about? Did I mention that I finally got it running?"

"Did you really?" she smiled.

"Yes, for about a day."

"Isn't that the one that you had to fill the oil tank on every time you ran it?" Kurt began. "It was like, one liter of petrol to every two liters oil. That old Frankenstein Jaguar with the green—"

"Right, the one with the ten cylinder engine," Albert interrupted. "How many cylinders does your Ford have again?"

Kurt shut up.

"It has four, I believe," I said. "Let's see, that's, oh, I think approximately four more functioning cylinders than your Jag, am I correct?"

"What's that you say?" he asked, cocking his head and turning an ear towards me. "Oh right. Well, you got me there," and he finished his story to Rachael.

At one time it had seemed like Albert was going to be the leader of Kurt's block. He was tall and came from money and had a decent wit, but he fizzled out as a leader. Girls pursued him, but he failed to capitalize on the opportunities. At first he'd confide to us that a girl in question wasn't really his type, or that there was someone else he was more interested in, but as time went on and he was still alone, the excuses weren't enough.

I think that deep down he was happier having these little failures to sulk about. He had a few girls who were his friends whom he confided in, and I think he was more comfortable in that role than he was in the role of a pursuer. Rachael was his frequent confidant.

Albert was Rachael's target for Camilla before I was, but after a promising start nothing happened between them. When I asked Camilla what had gone wrong, she pronounced him as having one of the worst maladies a guy can have:

"Albert's nice. *Too* nice."

Dark Ray was his best mate. Dark Ray was the kind of guy who wore a crusty, ancient, leather motorcycle jacket, black of course, and silver tipped leather cowboy boots everyday. He perpetually had three days growth of whiskers on his face. I suspected he owned one of those electric trimmers with a setting that let him keep it that length. He drank a pint of Jack Daniels almost daily.

On the walk back to the dorm, Kurt sneaked up behind Rachael and stepped on her heels as she walked. He did it over and over until she turned around and chased him, and I knew enough to give them some space. Walking astride the Ubergeek, *Cedric,* I said, "So kid, when are you coming to the gym with us?"

"Um. Me?" His face labored as he picked out words. "Yes, well, I've never been much for weight training. You see, I'm not so strong, like. I'm a bit of a weakling, like, sort of—"

"Cedric, that's why people lift weights, right?" I clapped him on the shoulder.

"I suppose there's some logic in that," he answered, nested in his usual array of "um"s and "yes, well"s.

I kept walking when we reached Kurt's block, and he called to me, "Aren't you coming up for a puff?"

"Oh, I suppose."

"What's all this then, Kurt? Are you lads partaking of the herb?" Albert asked.

"Might be," Kurt replied.

"Oh, well, don't worry about your good mate Albert. Old friend. You know what they say: a friend in weed is a friend indeed."

Rachael giggled a bit, so Kurt acquiesced quietly.

"Haven't smoked with you in a while, Albert," I piped up. "Isn't it your turn to supply the hash?"

"What's that?" He was fair haired and fair skinned so he blushed easily. "Oh, I wish I knew where to get some. I'd buy some if I did. How about you, Cedric?" he asked, turning towards him. "Do you know where I can buy a brick?"

"Who, um, me?"

"You smoking with us?"

He knew that Cedric didn't. Albert liked to trade barbs with Kurt because he could win, but he never locked horns with me. His favorite response to me was to say, "What's that?" like he couldn't understand me because of my accent, then deflect the focus onto someone else. Albert was all right, though. I just didn't like to let him pick on Kurt. I think Albert might have been a jealous over Rachael.

"You lot come up in a minute," Kurt instructed. "Come on up, Jake. I want to show you something."

When we were in his room he complained, "I just wanted to have a real smoke before those cheap bastards come up here. Always around when we smoke, but never around when I'm going to organize a buy. Tell you what. We'll smoke a killer fat joint before they show up, then I'll roll another crap one for them." He did the maniacal laugh.

We usually smoked hash by chipping little bits off of the brick and mixing them with tobacco, then rolling up a cigarette. I'd brought my pipe along with me, the marble one I'd picked up in Amsterdam, and without rehearsal I found myself saying, "I got you something in Amsterdam."

"You didn't have to do that."

"Too late. It's made of marble, so it should last forever. I say we should break it in. What do you think?"

"All right. Let me just finish rolling this one, like, for the others. I'm putting most of the hash at the tip of it, so make sure you get one of the first drags."

When he was done, he called across the room, "Cedric, do you want to try a puff with us? It'll be good for you."

"Oh, um, no thank you, Kurt."

"It's quite healthy, like. It contains vitamin C and such, and I hear that it makes you smarter as well."

"I don't do anything that involves smoke entering my lungs," he said more firmly, and I knew that there was no point in asking further.

"I mean it must make you smarter; look at Jake and I here. Right. And research shows that it's actually good for your lungs. Plus it causes your penis to grow. Sure you won't have a go?" Once Kurt had a thread of humor going he had to let the whole thing out to the end. Cedric stayed on his side of the room, and Kurt and I went out onto the balcony and smoked our first round on the pipe.

Rachael came downstairs in a bit and joined us on the balcony, smoking a Silk Cut cigarette instead of hash, then Albert and Dark Ray joined as well. Those two left us to go to the Ellison pub as soon as the joint was gone.

After a while, Rachael said, "I'm not going to stay out here all night, boys. I'll be upstairs."

"Come on, Rachael. Don't suck," Kurt reproved. You could see on her face that he hadn't said the right thing, and she left.

"Better follow that," he said. "Tell you what, stay put and I'll be back in a jiffy."

I stayed on his balcony and smoked a cigarette while Kurt did some maintenance on his relationship. He returned, masking a grin.

"I hate to leave you like this, but I think I'm going to skip the Ellison tonight. Rachael and I need some time alone, know what I mean. Sorry to do that to you."

"Don't be sorry. You haven't seen each other for a while. Believe me, if it were the other way around, I'd abandon you in a heartbeat."

"Thanks, Jake." He carved the remainder of hash in half and let me pick my piece. I added its cost to what I already owed him. All was quiet when I went back to Frank Hall to stash the brick, so I figured the lads had already gone down to the pub. On my door was taped a note, written on robin's egg blue paper in Tabi's distinctive script.

"Dearest Jake,

Came by at 7:30 to see you. Where the hell are you?!?

Went to the Ellison with Christine. Come down as soon as you can. Miss you like crazy, and I can't wait to see you.

Love,

Tabi"

I laughed at "Where the hell are you?!?" She was on campus. She had signed the note with love.

I went in my room and brushed my teeth at my sink and then shaved. I'd waited all day so my shave would be fresh when I saw her. I looked at my face in the mirror. I stepped three steps backward to the wall behind me, then approached the mirror, checking how I looked. I adjusted my hair, retracted to the wall, and approached the mirror again. I did it again and, satisfied, I pocketed some money, my student ID, a fresh pack of Marlboros, my Zippo lighter and my room key, and left for the bar alone.

It was early and it was only Wednesday, but I could hear a crowd. Three freshmen looking lads coming down the stairs looked at me and parted to let me through. When I reached the top step and came around the corner, I saw her sitting with Christine at one of the tall tables just beyond the door. That was just like her to sit in front of the door so she could see everything that was going on.

I discarded all of the things I had rehearsed saying while I was at the mirror. Tabi wore blue.

She looked up just before I reached the threshold of the door. I know that she saw me. She had been talking to Christine, and she looked back away from me to finish what she was saying. I felt the way that only she made me feel, and I knew exactly then how much I needed her. She had painted her lips burgundy. Her hair was down, and she wore nothing in it.

When I reached the table, Christine said, "Well fancy that, it's my new American friend, Jake," in a tone that was more familiar than she usually used with me. Tabi still wasn't looking.

"And it's that hot babe from Miller Hall, Christine. Fancy that." I paused, then sarcastically said, "Oh, hello to you *too,* Tabi. Yes, it's nice to see you as well." She had the smallest freckle on her left eyelid. Her ears were small and, I knew, sensitive.

"Oh, hello Jacob. Is that you? Did you get my note?" She asked it much too casually, and then added an impish giggle to make sure I knew it was a joke.

"Yes, I got your note. 'Where the hell are you,' she writes me," I directed to Christine. Then back to Tabi, "I was at Kurt's for a minute. You look gorgeous." She was wearing her blue Levi's that did things to her hips, that did things to me.

"I know," she chimed, still in character. "Are you still wearing those awful white socks?" she observed, aghast. White socks with pants had been okay to wear in the States when I'd left, but I was the only one I knew in Harlan who wore them. They were all I had. It was the source of her favorite torment. "Christine, do you fancy another Tanqueray and tonic?"

"Wouldn't mind at that. Cheers, Tabs."

"Newkie Brown Ale?" she asked me.

"I'll get this round."

"Sit down," she commanded. She was already off of her stool with her money in hand.

"Whoops," I said to Christine. "I got in trouble." When Tabi took a step away from me towards the bar, I said, "Hey!" and it stopped her. "What about my hello kiss?"

"Oh God!" She rolled her eyes and stepped towards me, pulling me down by the shoulder. I moved in to kiss her lips, but she turned away at the last second so that we kissed cheeks instead. She slipped into the crowd at the bar.

She turned around and looked at me when she was in the crowd, tracing the angles of my body with her eyes and raising her eyebrows before turning her attention back to the bartender.

"So Jake, Tabi's been telling me that you called her from Paris. I want to hear all about Paris," Christine urged.

"I was living in a bookstore." I started to tell her about it, but the story was suddenly more than I could manage. It felt like something heavy at the end of a long pole that I was trying to lift. "We would sneak into the *Universite Politecnique* and get breakfast by pretending we were students."

Tabi returned with the three drinks held together between her long, straight fingers and sat with us again. I offered her a cigarette and she shook her head.

"Got my own." She took one from her pack and lit it. She never accepted one from me if she had her own.

"So what's with the cheek kiss? I haven't seen you in three weeks and that's the best you can do?"

"Jacob, not in front of the children," she hissed through tight lips, motioning to Christine by jerking her head in that direction. "I'll kiss you properly later on."

"Yes, Jacob, not in front of the children," Christine said. "Remember, my virgin eyes."

"No need to inform me about your virgin parts."

"Jacob, behave," Tabi warned. "Isn't that the man I want, I mean your friend Ray over there? I'd better go say hello," and with that she was off the stool again. I forced myself not to follow with my eyes.

"Thank God you're here," Christine flattered.

"Why is that?"

"Maybe she'll shut up now. She's been talking about nothing but 'Jake, Jake, Jake.' I'm getting sick of you, no offense."

"You could have fooled me." I glanced and saw her laughing hard at something Dark Ray had said, or more likely something she herself had said. She was giving him her smile with her wide mouth, bending at the waist, touching his arm.

"Oh, you know how Tabi is," Christine reassured.

"I guess maybe I don't," I said to her, but then I dropped it. Tabi toyed with me sometimes by using Dark Ray. I knew that she really did find him attractive, or at least the image he conveyed. The rule of the game was, if I let it get to me, I lost. Tabi wouldn't have treated me this way if she didn't think I could take it. That's what she wanted: a man who could take it.

I saw Alex and the lads at one of the center tables. Devlin was talking to Alex, who was nodding his head and responding without looking directly back. I followed Alex's gaze to a corner table, where it was being returned unambiguously by a vampy brunette in brown velour. Alex had the power to draw women to his room for the night. "Pulling power" we called it. As a guy I couldn't help but envy this talent. He didn't maintain relationships like Kurt did. Kurt and Rachael had been together since the first week of the school year.

When Tabi came back, I said to her, "Will you do me one small favor?"

She leaned over and put her hands on my forearm. "What's that?"

"Sit your ass down for a minute. I waited a long time to see you." Her lips parted. Her eyes widened, but deep down in their brown I could see a flash of pleasure that let me know I'd done the right thing.

"Sorry," she said to me in a little girl's voice. Then to Christine in a stage whisper, "He's got a very violent temper."

"It gives me shivers."

"So where are Rachael and Kurt?"

"They decided at the last moment to stay in. I think the joy of being reunited came over them, if you know what I mean."

"I don't know what you mean," Christine joked coyly.

"Oh, isn't that sweet," Tabi gushed. "That's so romantic. How come you're not like that?"

When I started to respond, she said, "Got you." I shook my head but couldn't stop smiling; she liked my smile. She put a hand on my knee.

"All right, I'm going to sit with the gang," Christine said.

"Don't leave us," Tabi begged.

"We like you," I told her.

"You two go find a room or something. I've got to get closer to my man." She had a famous crush on a lad from another dorm. Tabi wove one of her hands into mine and pulled at me.

"Come on. Let's just say hello to the gang before we head out for a shag."

"If you're lucky."

Christine squeezed into the last bit of room at the booth, so Tabi and I stood in front of the table holding hands. I said hello to all of them one by one, even to Gil, her ex-. He muttered back to me without looking. Gil had been the one to end it with Tabi, so I wasn't sure why he was always such an ass to me. Maybe he had ended it because he couldn't get sex from her. Gil's room was the one beneath Tabi's.

I wasn't going to let the attitude of a punk named after the breathing apparatus of a fish get to me.

Alex was at the adjacent corner table, chatting up the velour girl, smiling boyishly. I caught the words "…later for a smoke," and she looked at him agreeably. Tabi squeezed my hand and led us away, out of the bar, down the stairs.

On the path, she said, "I couldn't wait to see you."

"Is that why you ignored me when I showed up?"

"I did not."

"I hate it when you do that. You argue that you didn't do something that you know you did." We were still holding hands, but it felt different than in the bar.

"Well then just agree with me from now on." We kept on walking for a bit, and then she said, "I just didn't want to act too clingy was all, bastard." She let go of my hand and jogged ahead a pace so I was looking at her back. I was supposed to run after her.

"Hey, don't be that way," I said.

"Piss off," she sobbed without looking back.

"Hey." I ran the two steps it took to reach her and grabbed her by her upper arm, gently. "Hey!" I said again, and she spun to face me with fearful eyes and parted, tremulous lips, and I said, "Come here."

"Stupid," she laughed, "I wasn't really cry—"and I reached behind her and pulled her lower back to me and held her tightly with the other hand behind her shoulder, thumb in her armpit, and I crushed our lips together.

You weren't really running away from me, I kissed her, *You already walked past your hall!*

You won't hide from me, I kissed her. *I **see** you, even though you spin and thrash around the bar like a wild animal in tight jeans,* my hands moved up and dug deep into her black hair, tangled, *Moving between Gil or Dark Ray or your group of friends. I see the woman you're afraid to show*

"What are you doing?"

"Remember-you were supposed to kiss me proper."

"You stupid bastard," her fingernails through the back of my shirt, her teeth on my lip, her tongue in my mouth.

To the heart of you, where the woman you really are lives, not the one you pretend to be for these people, I kissed. *Not the Brazilian caricature they assume you are when they look at you.* My arms around her tightly. *I know you don't really want Dark Ray. You know he's just playing a character, something he saw on telly or in a movie, and the hardness you want is in me. At the bottom. You bring it to the surface of me. You test me and test me; you want to know how much I can take?* I kissed, *Come and find out! I don't love you with the love that's between Alex and the girls who chase him into bed; not the comfortable, familiar love between Kurt and Rachael.*

I love you the way that only you can summon, with the love that only comes from me.

"Jacob." She let me hold her up with my arms. "Was that for me?"

"It's a special imported kiss I brought back from Paris."

"I really missed you."

"I thought about you once or twice too. I thought, 'What was that girl's name again?'"

"Oh shut up. Bastard."

"Come to my room. I got something for you."

Upstairs, the girls on my hall were still getting ready to go out clubbing. It was going to be a late night for them. Tabi and I went into my room and I gave her the flower I'd gotten from a florist in Ellison the other day, a single orchid.

"Haven't you heard of a dozen roses before?" she asked me.

"A dozen roses is a cliché. I wanted to get you something special."

She put it back down on my desk. I'd been hoping for maybe a couple of tears from her at least. Maybe she'd look back on it later and think of me fondly.

"I didn't get you anything," she told me.

"Come here."

It was dark and hot in the room.

Then, in a long while, "Just rape me."

"No. Like this."

"Do it!" Her fingers were sharp. "Coward!" I held her wrists, but gently. "Rape me!"

What she was asking for wasn't what she really wanted. Her passion was a thrashing thing. I held on. We were up until very late.

CHAPTER 25

Kurt and I were in the middle of our shoulder workout at the campus gym, when Cedric peered around the corner.

"Ubergeek alert," Kurt muttered. "Oy Cedric, where're your gym clothes?" Cedric had come in the same jeans he always wore and a polo shirt. The jeans were three or four centimeters too short, exposing a pair of white socks. I guessed that in his mind, white socks made it a work-out outfit.

"Are these not suitable? Um. Out of uniform, am I? That is, I had some shorts, but I didn't bring them. They're too small anyhow, and I don't know why I even brought them to university, seeing as I've grown so much since school. That is, in the last few years—"

"Hey, hey, ho, ho, Cedric. Life story later, weight lifting now, okay?"

Kurt had told me that one of the things that frustrated him about Cedric was Cedric's conversational greed. Once Cedric found a willing audience, he'd say everything on his mind, chasing each digression to its end. He'd hold his turn with a protracted "Um" or some similar syllable, like placing a conversational bookmark.

My trick was to cut Cedric off by talking over him. I did so in an overly obnoxious manner, so that it was funny but still got the point across. Cedric was a work in progress. That was one of the other things about Kurt; he had no patience for people who weren't as mature as he was.

Cedric was there at the gym by my invitation. He'd been asking me questions about weightlifting the night before, so I told him to meet us there. I could tell that he'd rather have me take him there than rendezvous, but it was important that he showed at least that much independence.

I wasn't having a good workout. I'd skipped lunch that day to save money, and shoulders weren't my best body part anyway. I'd rather have had him there on a bench pressing day, an easier workout for me, but that's really not the point of lifting weights. If it wasn't hard to do, it wouldn't be worth doing.

When we were done, Kurt proposed running back to Ellison instead of taking the bus.

"No way. I'd die on the way there," I protested. I could do the distance, but I'd never tried it after a workout.

"Come on. Don't suck," Kurt urged.

"I'll do it," Cedric offered, so I had to do it.

Cedric put us both to shame, breaking ahead in the first kilometer and staying out of sight the rest of the way there. I caught up to Kurt on the path back to our dorms.

"I'm knackered. I'm going back to my room for a nap. What time did you want to go to tea?"

"Let's go do some sit-ups."

"Piss off. I'm dead."

"That's because you smoke those fags. Don't suck." Fags meant cigarettes in England. Back in his room we did sets of sit-ups and stomach crunches until our abdomens burned. Cedric wasn't there. I guessed he'd gone to the television lounge; he wouldn't have assumed we'd ask him to go to tea with us. Cedric had had a big day already, socially.

I walked the up the remainder of the hill to my block on shaking legs and got into the shower. The water blasted what felt like a pound of sweat off of me. I changed into jeans and a white tee shirt. In the mirror my skin was red and still hot from the workout. My muscles were tight and hard all over.

I fetched Kurt from his room and we walked to the dining hall.

"We have lifter's tan," I told him. His skin was as red as mine was. As we walked through the doors a group of five guys was coming the other way, and they parted to let us through. We'd known they would. After we'd gotten our trays and picked out a table, I stepped ahead of him to side on the side that had a view of a table full of women.

"Tosser," he said, but then sat on the same side.

"I feel brilliant."

"I bet we're the fittest men in Ellison."

"You only think that because we lifted against Cedric."

"He did all right, didn't he? Maybe there's hope for him yet."

"He can outrun us, that's for sure."

"I don't know who it's meant for," he said discretely, "But one of us is getting some serious fuck-me eyes from two tables up."

"I had noticed that."

Three girls at the table we were facing kept staring at us with wide, flashing eyes, holding the gaze even when we looked back.

"I think they can sense how brilliant we feel."

And Kurt said, "Confidence is the key."

Right there he had carved down to the bones of truth. He'd put into words that certain *something* which some guys had, but I'd never been able to define.

I hadn't known I could run all the way from the gym to the dorms until I was on the other side of the task. Every step had brought me further into new territory of my abilities. My boundaries were wider now, and it showed in the way I carried myself through the crowd in the dining hall.

I got up to get another glass of orange juice, which would bring me past the table of girls. It didn't matter what my face looked like.

This was one of the keys to Alex's charisma: he was very, very nice the first time he met someone. It left a soft spot in one's heart for Alex, allowing him to dole out as much abuse as he wanted to ever after. Alex was the one who came over to my room to invite me out drinking the first weekend of school, and he had shown patience for my trouble with everyone's accents. "You're all right for an American," he had pronounced. Every night thereafter I was "the fucking Yank," to him.

I went down to the Ellison the second weekend after break with him and the lads, Devlin, Grahame, and Angela. Angela, the girl who lived across the hall from me, was one of the lads by default since she had screwed around with each of us at one point or another during the school year while still remaining our friend. Our turn had been while I was still with Yvonne.

"Where's your mate Kurt tonight?" Alex asked. "He's not smoking without you, is he?"

"No. He's still on his honeymoon. That reminds me, you know those little handheld scales you use to measure out hash with?" I had the table's attention. "Well Kurt had this plan for how he'd get a better deal with his. He drilled little holes into it so the measurement wouldn't be accurate, and our dealer would be screwed."

"That's not too stupid," Alex admired.

"Right, except I looked at it when he was done, and he'd drilled holes into the wrong side of it. He drilled the weights, so that the dealer was screwing us without even knowing it."

I scored a laugh out of all of them.

"So I was like, 'What's your major, Kurt? Accounting? Well I suppose that math isn't too important in your field anyhow.'" Kurt and Rachael had retired to her room soon after that. It was nice that they liked to spend so much time together.

"Here comes your woman," Angela announced. Tabi and her mates had just stepped up to the bar. When she saw me she came over to our table and sat down on my lap.

"Hello love. Oh my!" She hopped a bit and reached underneath herself to my crotch. "Someone's happy to see me," she said to the others. I didn't play into it; it was in poor form. "I'm going up to the bar. What are you drinking?" she asked me. I couldn't afford to decline the offer.

"What's this, are you only offering Jake?" Alex asked her.

"Oh I'll make him pay me back before the night's over." Tabi was wearing white. She went up to the bar, and when she returned she brought a round for the whole table.

"Cheers Tabi."

"Yes, cheers. I was only kidding you," Alex told her. "Now Jake is going to be mad that I tapped his girlfriend's purse."

"You were kidding?" she gaped. "Now you tell me." She offered me her cigarettes and I accepted one. "Come visit me before you leave," she said, kissed me, and joined her friends at their booth.

"Is she not sitting with us?" Alex asked, sipping his pint of Burtons.

"No. I'll meet up with her when she's ready to leave."

"Let me get this straight," he said for the benefit of everyone. "She comes over, sits in your lap, buys you and your mates a round, then leaves? And you meet up for a shag later on?" To Devlin he said, "Fucking *ideal*, isn't it?"

I didn't bother to disagree. Alex's latest conquest was at another table. She would show up for the post-pub smoke at his room, then one by one everyone else would make an exit. Velour Girl was sitting at a booth somewhere behind our table; her week was up.

I was a master in the art of nursing a pint. I could make one drink last as long as it took the others to drink two each. Taking the time to roll cigarettes helped me stall. When Alex got up to make an appearance at his new girl's table, I knew the lads would be heading back to the dorm soon. The new girl was tall with short curly hair, and she could roll a joint masterfully which impressed all of us. Angela went to sit with the inseparable Erin and Sheila, and I ambled over to Tabi's table.

"About time you got here," she said. "I was beginning to think that you forgot about me. You'll never get any sex that way." It was a joke for the benefit of the rest of the group, Christine, Gil, Tabi's roommate Kay, and some of the others from her dorm. I slipped into the booth, and she moved to sit on my lap again.

"Sit on the seat like an adult."

"Now Tabi, what did we tell you about how to act in public with your lovers?" Gil added, to the amusement of the rest. There were a lot of empty glasses stacked in front of them, so he scored a good laugh. Gil grinned in my direction, but the disrespect intended when he chose the word "lovers" wasn't lost on me.

"There're your friends Ray and Albert," Tabi noticed. "You didn't tell me they were here. I'm going to see if they want to join us." She shoved at me to let her out of the booth.

"So Jake, you're an American, right?" Gil asked. He was the king of his block, so everyone listened to him. I could tell by the inflection as he said "American" that he was gearing up to try to put me down.

"I'm an American. What gave me away?" I answered in my heaviest accent, and it scored a laugh from the table.

He tried to recover. "So you're here from your American university, right? Are you an American Studies major?"

"No, I think I already know enough about America, Gil." An even bigger group laugh. I could see he knew the error he'd committed, but I wasn't gong to let him off that easily. "Wouldn't make much sense for an *American* to go to England to study *America*, would it? No, I'm an English major. Makes more sense, right?" It culminated in a big laugh.

"Decided to go to the source, right?" one of his mates chipped in.

"Anyway, where were we," Gil continued, picking up the conversation he had been having before I showed up. Albert was making Tabi laugh over at his table; Alex's joint rolling girl was leaving the bar on her long, denim-wrapped legs. The lads had already left.

"Have you seen my special man tonight?" Christine asked me, ostracizing herself from the conversation to keep me company. "He's got a mad crush on me you know, only he just doesn't realize it yet."

"He must be pretty thick then."

"Hey! Don't be picking on my man."

"Don't get your knickers in a twist. I haven't seen him."

Albert and Dark Ray didn't end up joining us. Tabi was ready to head out when she got back, and we walked Christine back to Miller Hall.

Tabi's roommate was still at the bar, but I knew I would have to leave once she returned. Tabi and I had a routine of spending Friday and Saturday nights together at my place, but that night she wanted to pay some attention to Kay. She felt like she had to baby-sit her.

I tried to make sure we spent one weeknight together as well. I wanted us to spend time together on a regular basis rather than live the whole relationship like it was one pick-up at the bar after another. I craved some stability. Even though I'd been in the country since September, I was still a foreigner, the one who didn't have a parental cushion nearby or even simple familiarity with the customs of the region.

It was this same desperation, this same lack of sophistication that had lost Yvonne. Why was it that guys like Alex never had to do the chasing? Maybe I was the fool, maybe demonstrating my needs was my downfall. All year I'd felt superior because I believed that I knew what love was, and that guys like Alex would never experience it. Maybe he had one up on me with his "Treat them mean and keep them keen" philosophy.

I was lying across Tabi's bed while she changed her clothes behind her bureau, in the niche in front of her sink and mirror.

"One of these nights we should go out with Kurt and Rachael," I called over to her.

"We will." She stepped out from behind the bureau with her hairbrush in her hand. She was wearing a set of white cotton pajamas with little panda bears printed on them. There was a drawstring at the waist of the pants. She put her naked right foot on top of the left so that one knee bent in front of the other. The movement made the cotton whisper of the shape of her hips. Her foot was dark, and I thought of the rest of her dark skin.

Tabi turned away from me, back to the mirror, and duplicated the movement to show herself what my eyes had followed.

"One of these nights we'll all do something," she continued, stepping back out of sight. "I'm shy."

"You weren't shy about going over to Ray and Albert's table."

"Oh but that's different. That's *Albert*," she dismissed.

"Yeah, well you abandoned me with your friends."

"I did not."

I took one breath. "I'm not going to argue with you. You did so. You left me there with my good buddy Gil."

"Isn't Christine the best?"

"Yeah. Can I have another of your Silk Cuts?"

"Not in the room." She stepped out from behind the bureau again, and this time she was wearing just a white silk nightshirt that exposed her legs. She was still brushing out her hair. "Kay doesn't smoke." One black lock drifted down across her face. She smiled that smile, then turned back to the mirror to see what her hair looked like. She smiled to the mirror.

"You about done yet?"

"In a minute. Impatient bastard. I have to finish brushing my hair."

"Well do it over here. You've had your whole life to look at yourself. Now it's my turn."

She came around the bureau to me with a fragile looking walk, holding the brush.

"Do that again," she told me.

"Do what?"

"That look you just did. The way you looked at me."

I hadn't been aware that I was doing anything. Sometimes it was best that way. "Give me the brush. I want to brush your hair."

I sat up on the edge of the bed and Tabi sat in my lap. She knew she wasn't too heavy for me. She showed me how to brush her hair without tangling it by starting with just the end of a lock and gradually working my way up. Her hair was like handfuls of warm water.

I sank my fingers into it and moved it away from her neck. I brought my lips there so she could feel my breath, in that spot that was hidden all day just below her hair.

"You're driving me crazy," she said, took the brush away from me, and turned around.

Her roommate came home much too soon.

"Sorry. I'll be right back."

"That's okay," Tabi called, hopping off of my lap.

"You don't have to go, Kay. It's your room."

"I'm going to the loo," she said in a voice that didn't convince me.

"He's leaving now anyway." Then in a fake whisper, "Thank God you're here! He's a bloody rapist!"

When Kay returned, Tabi suggested I go out into the lounge with her for a cigarette. I sat in one of the straight-backed chairs and she sat on my lap facing me. She lit one of her Silk Cuts, took the first drag, and passed it to me.

"I wish you wouldn't—"

"You don't like it when I sit in your lap at the pub, do you?"

I exhaled smoke. "It's not appropriate. I don't want everyone to feel uncomfortable around us. That's not what I was going to say."

She bit my lip.

We kissed until the cigarette went out. The feeling was taking over, and I wanted to let it wash over me, to forget about words. But I had to tell her, or the feeling wouldn't work.

"Don't call me a rapist."

"I wish you were." She moved her body a certain way.

"No. I told you what happened to my sister. Anything else, but not that."

She was still holding onto her smile, which meant she was not taking me seriously, but I didn't want her to stop looking at me that way. "I thought a real man was supposed to respond when a woman came onto him."

"Hey." I sat up straighter and lifted my chin at her, frowning. Her nostrils flared. She watched my lips. The tips of her fingers bit the back of my neck.

I let my hands into the nightshirt. "When are you going to spend some time with my friends?"

"Is that all you can think about."

"No." I moved my hands.

"Who wants to spend time with your stupid friends?"

"I'm serious. It's not fair that I'm always the one making the effort." Silk touched the backs of my hands; her skin was in the palms.

"I'm serious too. Honestly, these people you spend time with." She made a noise because of a way I touched her.

"I don't always want to baby-sit Kay with you."

"Hey! Don't you dare pick on Kay. I mean it."

"But it's okay for you—"

"Yes it is."

All my muscles were tight, like they would be during a workout. She closed her eyes and took a hard tug on the cigarette, then I moved my hands and she opened her eyes.

"Rape me now."

"No."

"Do it. Ray would do it."

The tension in my muscles left. I stopped kissing her.

She put her face close to mine and she was all red lips and hot breath and I could smell her. "Quitter."

I kissed her. Hard.

"What if someone comes in here?" She said it small voiced, fearfully, like the thing she'd asked me to do was really asked by someone else.

"What if they do?"

We made up in our usual fashion.

Forest surprised me the third week of break by showing up at my room. Forest lived in Alan Moore House, a student house about halfway between Ellison and the university. He'd only been to my room once before, at the beginning of the year.

"Jake! So you *are* alive. I was starting to wonder if you got hit by a bus or something."

"Still alive," was all I said, and I let him in the room. I sat back down at my desk chair, the only chair in the room, so he sat on the bed and had to turn sideways to look at me. "You're the one who gets hit crossing the street." I let him be the only one to laugh at it. I figured that he was looking for hash. I had some, and I would have shared it if he wanted.

"Jake buddy. Rex was asking about you. He's wondering if you dropped out." Rex was the professor of our Victorian Literature class. I hadn't gone since break ended. There had been a major paper due before break, which I hadn't done yet.

"Tell him I had some things to take care of."

"I think he just wants you to show up, buddy."

I didn't have to answer to Forest about anything, so I let it hang there.

"Is everything all right?" he asked me. He was being very sincere, but I could still remember that I wasn't his close friend.

"Sure. So whatever happened with you and Kara?"

"We split up in Germany. She took an early flight back. I met these really cool blokes in Germany, though. We went hitching all over."

When he figured out that I wasn't in the mood to talk to him he went back to Alan Moore. He'd left me distracted with worries about Victorian Literature, and I had trouble getting back into my reading.

I'd been missing class because of the hunger. In the morning I'd wake up knowing that I only could only budget a little bread and some milk for breakfast and nothing again until tea. The thought made it hard to get out of bed. Victorian Literature was my earliest class: 8 AM, Tuesday and Thursday.

The meal plan at Ellison only covered tea. Sometimes someone would skip dinner and let me use their meal card for a second meal, but I was still losing weight. I'd quit going to the gym as well. I hadn't wanted to give it up after all the improvements I'd made during the year, but I had to admit that it was only making me hungrier.

I had an idea why Forest had told me we'd never be close friends. At the very beginning of the school year he was the first of us to score some hash, and he invited me to Alan Moore for a smoke. We killed off about half a joint together, and we were hanging out in his room when his roommate walked in. While they were talking I palmed the other half of the joint out of the ashtray and slipped it into my pocket. That night I got a call from him.

"Jake, you stole my roach."

"Yeah. I forgot all about it. It's right here in my room. I haven't smoked it."

"That wasn't cool."

"No, I wasn't stealing it from you. I was hiding it when your roommate came in the room. I didn't know if he was cool about it or not, and I didn't want you to get into any trouble."

"You're lying, Jake."

"No, really. I just didn't want you to get into any trouble. Remember that information package we got for travelling abroad, that said if we were arrested we'd get kicked out of school and deported?"

"My roommate doesn't care, Jake."

"Well I know that *now*, but I didn't know it when he walked in, and then I forgot all about it. I'll bring it over right now if you want. I haven't smoked it."

"No. Just keep it." The way he said it I knew he didn't believe me.

Later that night the hunger was dueling with *Henry IV, Part One.* I kept having to reread verses because the words weren't making it past my food fantasies into my head. When the hunger began to prevail I went into the kitchen. Someone had left a jar with some spaghetti sauce on the counter, not enough to make spaghetti with, but enough for some fuckwit with too much food to leave out to spoil. I put the sauce between two bread crusts and toasted it in Alex's sandwich toaster.

The crusts had been swiped from the refrigerator on the ground floor of Kurt's dorm as I returned from our evening smoke. If someone had caught me I would have claimed that it was my own food that I'd left on an earlier visit. I would have acted all indignant about it when I said it. The sandwich was warm and pizza-like and good, and I washed it down with an entire half-pint of milk I knicked from the fridge.

It succeeded in waking the rampaging hunger up completely. I scanned the cupboards and found that Devlin had some pasta. I took some because he's a fat pig who didn't need it as much as I did, and I cut off a chunk of Erin's cheese. I liberated a scoop of Sheila's margarine but dropped it on the floor, so I replaced it with some of Erin's. While the pasta was cooking I discovered another box of noodles in Grahame's cupboard, so I added some of that, and when it was all tender enough I drained it and put it on a plate and took the good chunk of margarine and melted it into the noodles. I shredded the cheese onto the pasta while it was hot and washed the cheese grater of the evidence. Then I took the chili powder that was in somebody's cupboard, I didn't know whose, it was starting not to matter, and I sprinkled it on top.

It was good and warm and I ate it quickly. I went back to my homework but wanted more, and I recalled a bouillon cube that I'd seen in the same cupboard with the chili powder, so I went out and boiled some water. It was one AM by then, and I wasn't worried about someone coming out and catching me, so I went through every cupboard to see what I wouldn't feel too badly about taking. There were eight or so pieces of bread in one of them, but I thought that it was Erin's cupboard, and I didn't want to rip her off too badly, so I left it. I ate the broth after adding some flour from an anonymous flour bag to it to give it some body.

Then I went up to the third floor and checked their kitchen. Most of their cupboards were locked except for Chui Peng's. No one ever talked to her, so I figured her life is tough enough and left her stuff alone. I took a yogurt out of the fridge and put it in my pocket and carried down a milk container with about ¼ pint left in it.

I went back up when it was done because I really wanted a banana that I'd seen there, and I took the other yogurt container, from which I'd separated the first one. The banana was small and I hardly noticed eating it. The yogurt was incredible. It had these tropical fruits in it. The first one had mandarins in it, and the second one had litchis and something called golden berries in it. I figured that these must have been Chui Peng's after all, but I guess that that's just life, Chui.

Then I saw the can of chili with about 1/3 left. I cooked it right in the can on the stovetop. I added a bunch of flour in lieu of Erin's bread, and some more chili powder, and it was so good that I used the spoon to scrape out every bit I could from between the metal corrugations on the bottom and the sides of the can.

I could hear Grahame and his girlfriend fucking in the room next to mine. Earlier in the night I had heard her through the wall crying loudly.

All part of the package, Grahame my boy.

Lastly I knicked one of Devlin's frozen fish sticks and I cooked it in the oven. A few nights prior I had asked him if he would spare a can of beans so I could make beans on toast, and he'd said no. I reminded him of the time first semester when he'd been broke, and Alex and I had had pizzas delivered after a smoke, and I'd given Devlin a quarter of mine without him even asking, but he still refused me the beans.

That would piss me off for a long time. He was just a boy, but that kind of thing just stays in your mind.

For my birthday I received a little money in the mail from my parents. Kurt drove me into town to a bank to exchange it. I couldn't use my own bank, because my account was overdrawn, and they would have kept the whole thing.

There was a birthday party on my floor, but it was really in honor of Erin's birthday, which was a few days before mine. When I started dropping hints that mine was coming up as well it morphed into a joint birthday party. There was a cake, and a big bowl of fruit punch and cheap vodka with indeterminate chunks of fruit floating around in it, and Alex turned his stereo up loud.

The party flowed in and out of the landing and people's rooms. Kurt, Rachael, Albert, Dark Ray, and some others from Kurt's hall came over, even Cedric. It made me proud to be bringing the two groups together. I knew a lot of good people. I guilt-tripped Cedric into having a cup of punch, his first drink ever.

"Where's Tabi, Jake?" he asked me after his second cup. It was the question of the night for me.

"She had to meet with some classmates from her Accountancy class to work on a group project. I'm going to see her after."

"Is she not coming over to the party when she's done? It is your birthday party," Kurt said.

"No, she's shy."

"Come on." He and Rachael laughed at that.

"Just in certain social situations, like when I know everyone in the room and she doesn't."

"Do you suppose I'm drunk yet?" Cedric asked.

"She should have come," Rachael said.

"That's silly," Kurt continued.

"One of the keys to a good relationship is respecting the other person's boundaries, even if you don't understand them. No Cedric, you're not drunk yet. Next drink should be your last drink, though."

"Maybe I'm immune to alcohol," he said with the slightest of slurs.

It was about then that someone decided that we should put Erin in the shower because of her birthday. Grahame and Devlin were forcing her into the bathroom while Sheila and Angela screamed and pretended to come to her rescue.

"I reckon you'll be going in next, since it's your birthday as well," Kurt said, and did the maniacal laugh.

"No, I don't think that will be necessary."

Cedric was smiling but undecided.

"Perhaps I should tell Alex," Kurt said.

I sat up straighter, puffed out my chest, and showed him a fist. "Say hello to your doctor and your dentist for me. You'll be seeing them shortly."

Cedric and Albert both laughed. Albert might have been laughing at the prospect of me taking on a guy of Kurt's physique. It would have been a pretty close fight in my estimation.

"Well we've definitely got to help out with Erin," Kurt recovered. "We can't let two perfectly good cans of whipped cream go to waste."

And there they were, two perfectly good cans of whipped cream someone had bought for the cake, sitting on the table behind us. Kurt and I armed ourselves and rushed the bathroom, spraying Angela and Sheila. They both started screaming and calling us bastards and chasing us around the hall. I kept stopping, letting Angela catch up to me, squirting her with whipped cream when she did, and then running away again; I did it over and over again until I was laughing so hard I could barely breathe.

Kurt came over to join me, and Angela turned to him and said, "Don't you dare, or you're a dead man."

"Hey. Nobody talks to my friend that way except for me."

"I think she needs a shower to cool her off," Kurt said.

"Oh most definitely." She was standing between the two of us. "Very cold water."

She started squealing and calling us names, but we knew she loved it. Once we got her into the shower stall I held her arms, and Kurt directed the shower nozzle.

"A little in the face…now tits, right one…left one. Now fanny…down the pants…" He'd move the spray just when the shock wore off.

When we finally let her go we stalked back into the hallway. There was a tap on my shoulder, and when I turned around it was Rachael. She threw a pint of cold water in my face and grinned. I menaced her for the benefit of the audience looking through Alex's door, then laughed along with her. Everyone headed into Alex's room during the drunken, stoned, orgiastic blur. I went to my room. I peeled off my wet shirt and started to towel my hair dry. Rachael opened the door and let herself into my room.

"You're not leaving already, are you Jake?"

"Yeah, I have to put on some dry clothes and go." I started towards the bureau behind her to get the shirt I wanted.

"You can't leave. The fun's just starting." She kept in front of me and pushed me back, just her fingertips against my wrists.

"I've got to head out."

"No, stay here." She said it in a certain way and my eyes locked with hers and we were alone in my room and suddenly the moment was there. The whole world was the inches between us.

I looked at the floor and said, "I have to head out now," I looked back up, "Or else I'll never get any from Tabi tonight."

She nodded. "Got a little birthday present for you? You mustn't miss that. Gor I'm rat-arsed." She walked back out of my room towards Alex's, and I put on my shirt, walked down the stairs and out the door.

CHAPTER 26

Not a lot of work got done when Kurt and I studied together, but it was better than the madness of sitting alone in my room, unshowered, talking to myself. There were two weeks left until the assessment period, what I would call final exams.

"What's that?" Kurt gestured to *Henry IV Part One* as I entered the room. He was sitting at his desk.

"It's a *book* Kurt. Remember, I told you about these things? Pages, words…"

Rachael was sitting on his bed. "Oh good, someone to have a fag with," she said, which meant "Oh good, someone with a fag to give me," for me. Hand rolled were never as good as the ones out of the package.

"Greetings, Captain," Cedric said from his desk, bowing his head slightly. He was wearing a tee shirt I had given him to work out in, one that I'd gotten too big for. Although considering the weight I was losing I probably could have fit into it again.

"Hey kid. You behaving?" When he started to reply, I said, "Rhetorical question, kid. Not meant to be answered."

I was wearing a new shirt I'd bought the other day. I hoped that Kurt wouldn't notice the purchase. I had needed the ego boost that came with consumption. Besides, it was my birthday money.

"Say Rachael," Kurt began. "Did you know that today is a holiday?" She looked. "It's Make Fun of Americans Day."

"Is it really?"

I ignored him. There would be more coming; that was the way Kurt's humor worked: he'd save up a stash of little quips and spend them all in one go.

"We'll be going out later for *cheeseburgers and fries*." He said it in what I knew he thought was an American accent.

"That's right, Kurt. It's all we ever eat."

"*We'll charge it on American Express.*"

I pretended not to hear it. Rachael was laughing, but it was at the whole exchange, not at me.

"*Let's go down to the bar in our trucks and drink Budweiser,*" he continued.

"Okay Kurt. You're being funny, right?"

"*Then we'll watch one of the 487 channels on our TV.*"

I left just the right amount of pause, then said, "Kurt, don't make me humiliate you."

When Rachael said, "Oooo Kurt," I knew I'd gotten him good.

"Oy, that's me breakfast," he complained. I'd been helping myself to handfuls of his mueslix.

"Look what I got in the mail this morning." I pulled the letter out of my pocket and handed it to him. It said:

"Jacob,

"Enclosed please find the phone bill for your collect calls." The word "your" was underlined three times. There was the beginning of another sentence crossed out, then: "Please send remittance, or an explanation of how you intend to pay for these. I cannot afford all this.

"Hope your hand is better.

"Yvonne"

Kurt looked up at me. Rachael asked to see it, so he handed it to her.

"She sent you a bloody phone bill?"

"I feel great. It's the nicest thing she's ever done."

"I don't get you sometimes, Jake. You're in shock, aren't you? I think you need some hash."

"I wouldn't say no," I said hopefully. "Don't you see? She's set me free. If there was even the slightest lingering question that we'd ever get back together, it's gone now."

In the mail that same day was a notice of account closure from the bank, along with a demand for payment on my overdraft. There was a letter from the university as well, informing me that if I didn't make payment on my accommodations, they wouldn't give me credit for my coursework.

"So, um Jake," Cedric announced. "I wanted to ask you something. About Erin. The one in your hall? The one who had the birthday party with you? With the blonde hair?"

"Right, right. I know her."

"What I wanted to ask you was…First I should tell you that I've been down to the pub a few times since your party to have a pint. Because I followed your lead and started to drink, just socially, like. And so I've seen her down there, at the pub. And I said hello to her and such, but I'm not really sure how to find out if…that is…"

"She doesn't have a boyfriend, Cedric. That's what you're getting at, isn't it?"

"Sort of. That is, essentially yes."

"She's nice. I approve." Kurt and Rachael stayed out of it. They were warming up to him, but Cedric was more or less my personal project.

We were surprised with the arrival of Tabi. She'd never been to Kurt's room before. She rushed in, said hello to everyone, sat herself in my lap, then stood back up again.

"Oh my, I forgot. He doesn't want me sitting in his lap. Totally unromantic, don't you think?"

From where she sat on the bed, Rachael said, "And she's such an attractive girl, Jake. I'm starting to wonder about you." I don't respond to gay jokes, but I didn't give Rachael any grief.

"Did you hear what he gave me when he came home from Paris? One bleeding flower, and it was some kind of weird flower to boot. What's the matter, you've never heard of a dozen roses before? Cheap bastard." It fell into the category of Jokes About Jake She Doesn't Really Mean and Are Just For Group Amusement, and so I laughed along with them to stay in good form.

"You should hang out with us more often," Rachael said.

"I figured that this one," Tabi said, indicating me, "Would be here, since he's never in his room. I stopped by Albert's room on my way up. He's a nice boy, isn't he?"

"Nice is a word," Rachael replied.

"He's nice compared to some people, say, an axe murderer," Kurt quipped.

Cedric wasn't conversational yet.

"We like Albert," I concluded.

"What's this, you have on normal socks?" she asked me.

"I had to do something to make up for my abnormal girlfriend." They were black socks. I hadn't bought them. They were in the lost and found box in the laundry room, and I had decided to find them. I was hoping that she wouldn't mention the shirt.

"You're cheating on me, and your other woman got you these socks, didn't she? You over-sexed bastard. Well come on back to my room. I'd better shag you to win you back." I was still sitting down. "Come on, then."

"And that, ladies and gentlemen, is how it's done," I said as I got up to follow her out.

"That's how what is done?" Cedric asked. "Showing us that Tabi's the one in charge?"

Tabi laughed, but I just said, "Cedric! Good man!" He flinched a little when I reached over to shake his hand. I was genuinely proud that he'd taken a parting shot.

Tabi and I walked back to her room holding hands. She told me to lie down on her bed, then she went behind her bureau to work on herself in front of the mirror. Being prone made me drowsy. The hunger contributed. I knew she had a box of these excellent little cheese-filled toaster pastries in the fridge. She'd made them for me the last few times I was over, but I didn't suggest it this time. I didn't want her to think that they were the reason I came over.

"In case you were looking for me, I'm over here on the bed. You won't find me in the mirror."

When she came around the bureau she was wearing different outfit.

"You'd better hurry, or you'll miss your quota for changing your clothes twenty times a day."

"You don't like my new dress, do you?"

It was a little white number that was too short. It ended above the knee, beyond the range of enticing into the range of distracting.

"I like it just fine."

"Then why are you giving me grief? This is what I get for trying to look nice for you."

She put a different CD in the stereo and sat on the edge of the bed. Every sentence I uttered was preceded by the vision of a little cheese toaster pastry; I put it out of my mind.

"Stop it," she said and took my hand off of her. Then, "Are you mad about something?"

"No, I'm not mad about anything. Is the guy in this picture your brother?"

"Which one, him?"

"This one." The back of her bureau and the wall next to her bed were sheeted with photographs, all of them of people, many of them of herself. Every time I was in her room I superimposed what I'd learned of her over the collage of pictures to try to understand her better.

"No, the one next to him is Timothy. The one you pointed at is Reggie. That's Timothy's friend. That's his very, very good friend."

"Do you mean, more than just his friend-friend?"

"I mean his *boy*friend. And if you say one obnoxious word you're a dead—"

"It sounds like he has the same allergy to the opposite sex that my sister has."

"What's that supposed to mean? I mean it, don't you dare make fun of my brother."

"Easy, easy. I'm not." I soothed her as best as I could from my prone position. "My sister is gay. Isn't that a bizarre coincidence? How long have you known?"

"I don't want to talk about it."

"Are you two very close?"

"Sort of. I haven't called him in a long time. I really ought to."

"Does he live with his boyfriend?"

"Do you understand when I say I don't want to talk about it?"

"Okay. You don't have to snap at me." She got up to manipulate the CD player. "Are *you* mad about something?"

"No." She sat down again. I tried something. "Stop it. Just behave. Kay could be home any minute."

I put my hands down at my sides, like I was lying in a hospital bed. "Fine, I'll deny myself for the sake of Kay. You don't have to sit in my lap whenever we're in public—"

"I didn't!"

"-and you don't have to yell at me."

"I did not yell at you."

"I'm not going to argue that you yelled. You know, you're always on me about not doing anything in case Kay might—"

"It's different, it's *Kay*."

"Just forget it. It obviously doesn't really matter to you what I have to say."

"But it's *Kay*. Give the girl a break."

I kept quiet for too many moments, and she got up and went out of the room. I stayed right where I was while her CD played, and she returned empty handed.

She sat on the edge of the bed and the song ended. The next song began. She put her hand on my thigh.

"So you're not going to talk to me now?"

"What's the point?"

She grinned and taunted, "Quitter."

"It's just that whenever you're in front of my friends—"

"I thought you wanted me to come over and spend time with you and Kurt! I'm sorry I came over now."

"It's not the point. Will you just *shut up* for a minute? You never listen. Will you just listen—"

"I'm listening—"

"Stop it! That's what I mean. I'm trying to say something and you always cut me off. It's like you don't care what I have to say, or like you think you already know what I'm going to say, and it really pisses me off. Will you just…Can't you just listen to me?" She just looked at me. "Thank you." She kept looking. "It's just that whenever we're with my friends you sit on my lap and say all make all those sex jokes, and I think it makes them uncomfortable. Can't we just hang out with them? That's all I'm asking. It's only fair. I always try to listen to your wishes when it comes to Kay."

She just sat there quietly. I had been yelling. I raised my brows.

"So you're through? I'm afraid to interrupt you."

"Yes. That's all I wanted to say."

"Well I didn't know you felt that way," she told me formally. "Why didn't you mention it sooner?"

"This was the first time it occurred to me to say something."

"I'll try to be more considerate in the future, Jacob. Can I just say one thing?"

"Anything."

"You're supposed to listen to my wishes. I'm a *girl*."

"I know you are, Tabi. I'm sorry I yelled at you. I didn't mean to."

"You should be."

"I am. I'm sorry I told you to shut up. I shouldn't have. I'm way behind in all of my classes, and I'm worried about it. And I'm about to run out of money. I've been ignoring that fact all semester, but I can't afford to eat anymore so it looks like I've got to face it. I'm sorry."

"It's okay. Stay there. I'll make you something."

I followed her too short dress out the door with my eyes. It felt bad to see her dressed for seduction after we'd been fighting. By then I knew that we weren't about to make love. We hadn't done so in a few days. No, it had been even longer than that.

She came back in the room with a plate of toaster pastries and fed them to me while I was still lying down. She liked to talk to me when I was lying down. I was getting sleepy. Having that kind of argument with her took a lot of energy.

The lads asked me if I wanted to go with them to the Olympia on Friday, but I couldn't face another night of trying to bum drinks off of everyone. Short Redheaded Girl was in Alex's room by six PM and out by eight, then everyone left for the club. When the hall was essentially empty, I went through the ashtrays on each floor and in the television room to look for any cigarette butts. I'd crush them open and collect the remaining tobacco out of them, so I could roll some cigarettes out of it later.

Every once in a while I could hear people talking as they walked up the path outside, returning from wherever, probably out having fun. I tried to read for Victorian Literature, and when that failed I'd switch to Shakespeare or to something else. Around midnight when the Olympia closed I became anxious and couldn't read. I paced and smoked until I heard my hallmates return. They sat out on the landing talking drunkenly for a while, then dispersed to their rooms. Hours passed.

At two AM I walked down the hall in socked feet to Alex and Devlin's door and listened for any noises that would tell me that they were awake. If anyone stepped into the hall and saw me I would tell them that I was pulling a prank on the lads. The doorknob made the slightest click when I turned it. I eased the door open just enough to admit myself. The most dangerous element of the maneuver was letting the light from the hallway into the room. Light could have jarred them out of sleep. I slowly allowed the knob to return to its original position without letting it click again. I moved the door back so that it was almost touching the jamb. I was inside the room.

I listened to the rhythms of their breathing until I was certain that I hadn't woken them. I lowered myself to the floor as slowly as I could so that my joints didn't crack. I made sure that my sweatpants didn't hiss against my leg hair as I crouched. On the floor any sounds I made or disturbances I created in the air were less likely to reach them.

My breaths flowed gently in and out of my open mouth. The floors of the dorms were carpeted with low, industrial carpeting. I stalked across the floor one limb at a time, plucking my limbs straight up so that I wouldn't disturb the nap of the carpet. I could tell that Devlin was asleep because that overfed fuck snored. Each time I made a noise I held myself in position so that it would camouflage itself with the sounds of the building settling.

Alex didn't snore. He might have been feigning sleep. I slunk another pace closer to his desk. The desk was next to his bed. If he woke up, I would laugh and tell him that I was trying to pull a prank on him. I hadn't thought out what the prank would be. I would tell him that I was going to write something on his face in marker. If he asked me where the marker was, I'd act like I had stupidly forgotten it. He smacked his lips in a manner that seemed like he was asleep.

The corner of his desk was only a fraction of a meter away from his pillow. My arm bent through the darkness towards it. I was cautious that the shadow of my arm didn't cross his eyes and that my movement didn't stir up a draft.

Alex didn't just carry his wallet, he wore his wallet. It was a big fat mouth of leather which he kept full of bills so he didn't need to go to the bank. When he shoved it in his pocket it made an obvious bulge. Each of his jeans had a faded spot in its shape. He had pocketed it before going out to the Olympia, then asked me if I was going with them. When I said no he had called me a "Sorry Yank" who was going to "sit in his room like a tosser on a Friday night all alone." Alex got away with saying whatever he wanted to and we all still tried to be his friends. Tabi had gone out to the Ellison, and if I'd had some money I could have seen her. Alex got laid before he even went out because his women went chasing after him.

When my fingers were locked onto it I lifted it off of the desk and began to retract my arm. It took many seconds. Alex cleared his throat and smacked his lips. The lips of the wallet opened wide so that bills could have been slipped out without making noise. There were many of them, and Alex didn't count them very often, so that he wouldn't notice the absence of a few of them right away. Then there were all the other little insults one had to suffer whenever you entered in Alex's company. Behind every joke there was a truth. We were a circle of friends Alex maintained only to improve his pulling power. It wasn't the kind of leader I would have been.

I was poised on the floor of my friend's room with his open wallet in my hand. I was in the middle of doing the worst thing I had ever done.

I took just as long to replace the wallet as I had to retrieve it. The instinct was to escape quickly, but I fought it in order to maintain my stealth. I crept back across the room. I stood back up and peeled the door away from the frame. There was no one in the hallway.

It was two thirty. In my room I rolled one of my recycled cigarettes and took it out onto the balcony. It tasted like ashtray, but it had nicotine in it. I hadn't taken any money from the wallet after all. I'm sorry

Dad. Dad, I'm so, so sorry. "Just do the thing I'd want you to do, son, and you'll be all right. You'll know what the right thing is." I'm trying, Dad, I really am. I understand that you aren't making life hard on me. Life was that way already.

Not taking the money did not change the fact that I'd done something wrong. Leaving the money was still the right thing to do. It was the small good thing in the middle of the big bad one.

I guess no one knew I was in my room when they were out on the landing talking Sunday night. Erin had just gone into the refrigerator and said, "Oh no, someone's taken my yogurt!"

"That's the second time this week. This is getting ridiculous." That was Angela. Angela's the type of girl who knows the world won't go on if she doesn't give her opinion about it. She never says anything that isn't a complaint.

Erin and her inseparable roommate chirped up, sounding like they were sitting together in a corner. Together they're as strong as Angela. "It must have been Jake..."

"...been Jake," they chorused.

"It must have been. Everyone else has money." Then they concocted this little scheme the housekeeper to go through people's rubbish bins when she emptied them to see if there was a yogurt pot in one. Ooo, you clever little detectives.

I decided to rush out of my room, rubbish bin in hand, and while they were riding on the wave of shock that I was home and I could hear every word they said, shake it under their noses. "Here, here's my bin. Have a look. It's all my garbage. I'm wasting away on one meal a day and I've got to listen to you accusing me of stealing?" I wasn't afraid of them.

I didn't do it, though. Should have done.

I got the knock on my door I'd been waiting for. Tabi came in and purred, "Hello," in her sweet little way that I always look forward to. Kay walked in behind her. That was a little odd-Kay had never come over before. I figured she was feeling depressed after the Ellison. She should either get her ass to the gym and get rid of some of that extra body or stop battering her ego at the Ellison night after night, but that's the sort of stuff that's easier to say when it's someone else and not you.

"Hey, baby. Hiya, Kay-Kay. How was the Ellison? You didn't get picked up or anything, did you?"

"Wanker American," chimed Tabi as they curled up together on my bed. The words written at the top of my corkboard were in her handwriting. "Jacob thinks he's getting a threesome tonight, don't you, darling?"

"I hope so. Kay, did she warn you about our proclivities?"

"Oh lovely, Jacob. And how was your night?"

We talked our silly little shit for a while. I tried to make meaningful eye contact with Tabi so I could silently ask her if Kay was okay, but I couldn't reach her.

There came a knock at the door. It was Angela.

"All right?"

"Yeah, what's up, Angela?"

She closed the door and hovered around the entrance of my shoe box capacity room.

"I saw you tonight, Kay. Too good to come to our table and say hello?" She kept sneaking glances underneath my sink to where my bin was. "God, I got pissed tonight!"

"It's right there, Angela. Have a look."

"Sorry?"

I opened up my eyes really wide and leaned forward like I was talking to a little kid. "My bin, Angela. It's right there under my sink. If you want to have a look."

"What? That's not what I came in here for."

"Go on, get it over with."

"What, do you want me to go knocking on people's doors and look through their bins?"

I smiled. "I don't care what you do Angela."

"Do you want to look through my bin?"

"I don't want to go through anyone's garbage." I used garbage, the American word, instead of the British.

She leaned forward to use a new tactic. "Oh, the yogurt pot theory!" she whispered conspiratorially.

"Oh yeah, that!" I intoned, slapping my hand on the side of my face in mock surprise. Oh, the yogurt pot theory. Way too fucking late, honey.

I let her babble her way around it for a few seconds until I took her off the cross. "So did you meet anyone interesting at the Ellison tonight?" I didn't listen for the answer, though. I focused back on Tabi again.

"Well, see you later," said Angela when she finally bounced out of the room. Kay and Tabi looked at me so I leaned towards the bed and whispered them the whole story.

"'I didn't come in here for that.' She hasn't been by for months. Here I am starving to death and they're going to accuse me of stealing from them. Bitches. And I have to listen to them right outside my room. Fuck you, Angela," and I waved an obscene salute to the closed door. I was having a good laugh. Kay just sort of sat there, not knowing how to react to me. Tabi was quiet too, which wasn't right.

"Your friend Cedric went tonight," she finally offered.

"My man." Cedric was to me as Kay was to Tabi.

"Jake, will you walk Kay home now?"

I leered. "Of course I will. I might just end up staying with her though," and we laughed. On my way out the door I glanced back and she finally looked right at me. She made sure I saw her peel her black stretch pants off before sliding under my covers.

I chatted with Kay the fifty yards back to her dorm, but my mind was on another planet. Planet Guilt. I was having this paranoid fantasy of Tabi sorting through my garbage, opening up my empty milk container, and finding the crushed empty yogurt pot.

Yeah, I took it, but I was still mad about being accused. My hall-mates had no valid reason to suspect me. It was just that I was a for-eigner, and I never hung out with them anymore. It's easier to blame a stranger.

I wasn't going to accept accusations from a bunch of well fed girls who live off of Mommy and Daddy's money, and throw away heels of bread and leave milk and cheese out all night to spoil. Not after I'd eaten garbage to survive.

Still, I had this lingering bother about Tabi finding out, and on the way back I crafted what I'd say if she greeted me with a little plastic yogurt pot in hand.

When I came back in the room, she was sitting up in bed with her back to the wall, a bag of Noble's Crinkle Cut potato crisps in hand. She handed me another bag wordlessly as I sat down and wove my Levis-clad legs in with her bare ones.

I didn't know if it was paranoia or her quiet, but I asked, "What's the matter?"

"Nothing." Which really means, "Everything."

She opened a can of 7-Up that she'd brought with her and sipped, and put it down, and didn't light a cigarette, didn't even take one out, didn't make fun of my white socks.

"What's on your mind?" My mind raced to think of what I could have done to upset her in the last week.

"I have something to tell you." Nothing good ever followed that sentence. "You have to promise that you won't get mad." Her face changed expression. "I mean not that you won't get mad, but that you'll just listen to what I have to say. You probably already know what I'm going to tell you, don't you?"

"No idea." I tried to make it sound funny, but it came out kind of gray. I moved my hand off of where it was holding her strong, naked calf muscle.

"Albert tried to have sex with me," and before she could leave it, she topped it off with honesty, "He did have sex with me. We had sex. He was really, really drunk."

I thought for a few seconds, discarding a lot of the things that I was going to say but shouldn't. I unwound myself from her and laid back. "When did this happen?"

"Friday night when you didn't go out with us." While I was breaking into Alex's room. "Remember how I told you I was over at his hall and we had that shaving cream fight? I was so drunk." She tried to predict my train of thoughts with, "And you can't blame Albert, he was so drunk he could hardly walk."

"Yeah, but he could have sex," I said.

Silence. I filled it with, "I'm not surprised that this happened."

"What, with Albert?"

"Yeah."

"You didn't think I was going to say Ray?"

"No. Why, did you fuck him too?"

"No." She sounded like I'd just knocked her down. I wished I hadn't asked, but if ever there was a time, it was then.

Tabi put her hand on mine and I didn't respond at all, so she moved it back. We suffered through a few more aftermath seconds and I finally decided to say, "I'm not surprised. But I am very disappointed." I kept almost looking at her and then not.

She stood up and said, "I'm going to go back," and she put a hand on my shoulder, and I looked right at her and this was the moment I was supposed to ask her to stay, but I only said, "Okay."

I heard her slide her pants back up, and she tried again. "It didn't mean anything, Jake. It started with a little kiss, like this." She leaned forward and touched those Tabi lips to mine, and I kissed her back a very little bit. I felt like throwing her out of my room. I also felt like pulling her to me and holding her tightly.

"See you tomorrow."

"Okay." The word fell out of me like a dead butterfly.

"Bye," she said at the door. It was like a question.

"Bye."She closed the door and I followed the sound of her footsteps downstairs and out the door. She had left her 7-Up and the two bags of crisps, the opened one and my unopened one. I picked up the opened one instinctively and said out loud, "No. Thinking about eating these makes me sick."

I laid down for a few minutes and wished she'd left a cigarette. My thoughts bubbled over and I let out, "You fucking bitch," about Angela, though. I was glad I'd nailed her. The only money I had in my pocket was the sixty pence I'd found in the washing machine, and she was out to get me.

I decided that the next time I saw Albert I'd punch him. Then I decided that I should at least ask him, "Albert, is there anything you want to tell me?" to give him a fair chance, and if he wasn't a man about it, *then* punch him.

Saturday, the night before, I had stopped by his room to say hi, and while we talking I noticed some dried up shaving cream all over his wardrobe. "I see you have a reminder of the night Tabi was over." He looked at me and all the expression dribbled out of his face. I thought I'd confused him.

"Your shaving cream fight?" I thought that would jog his memory. She had told me that much.

"I don't have any idea what you're talking about." He talked really quickly, like he had to get the words out of himself. He always talked that way though. He was a nervous guy.

"Tabi said you two had a shaving cream fight, remember?"

"Oh yeah, right, that!" he laughed, and I laughed too, because he thought that I thought something went on. Albert was a pretty big guy, but he was soft and he didn't want to tangle with me. And there I was, right in his room where something actually did happen, bringing it up,

giving him every chance in the world without even knowing it, and he
didn't say a thing.

There were three differences between Albert and I. One, he had
blonde hair, and I didn't. Two, he had a lot of money, and I didn't.
Three, I had balls, and he didn't.

My mind almost went back to her, and I scrambled back to Angela
and I gloated over my little victory and smirked. And I ran out of places
to run and I pictured Tabi and replayed the whole thing and I even went
over the parts that hurt. Tomorrow she'd come over to my room again,
I just knew, and I'd tell her that it hurt because it was with my friend,
but that wouldn't change what was going to happen, it just had to be
said. I remembered when I called her in Paris, and she said, "Stop it,
you're making me cry," just because I was being me. Then something
happened, that *something* where my spell on a woman just went away,
and I became just another guy. It was a something I hadn't figured how
to get around yet.

And I wanted to believe that when two people said, "I love you," it
meant the same thing; I did believe it for a few weeks but now it would
go away again, it goes away a little further each time. She'd be over the
next day and one of us would have to say, "I think we should break up."

I looked at the opened package of crisps on my desk and still felt sick.
I picked them up and ate them, and drank the 7-UP.

CHAPTER 27

She was the one who broke it off the following afternoon. She came over to my room and told me, "I think we should break up," but "not because of Albert," he was "something that shouldn't have happened." She told me that "we haven't been happy together for a while now anyway," and that "I'm trying to understand you, but I just can't," but "it's my fault, not yours." She said some other things. I didn't have much to say. Before she left she asked me for a hug, and I refused her, and then I was alone in my room again. That was the end of it. It was over quickly, like going to get a shot, and I went back to studying.

And then there was the hunger. On and on it was with me. It wasn't like the sound of dripping water, or the radio in a neighbor's room, something that slipped unobtrusively into my subconscious. It was a pair of glasses coloring everything I did and thought and looked at. It was there the next day when I was in the shop with Alex and there was a packet of biscuits on a hip-level shelf and the shopkeeper was looking the other way. It asserted itself in every step of my walk to campus in the morning. It was the hatred I felt towards some blubbery school kid shouting in his annoying little English accent to one of his mates. It made me eat the strands of pasta stuck to the colander in the sink with the other dirty dishes.

Hunger.

The hunger complained to me the day I sat in the campus library try-ing to complete an overdue essay on **Hamlet**, complained and com-plained as I threw my mind at the work again and again. Then it moved my legs down the stairs of the library, across campus past the brick Student Union, past the gym that I no longer went to, and in the direc-tion of Ellison because tea started at half-four.

A man walked by me drinking a Coca-Cola. Maybe if I'd had enough money to go out with her more often it wouldn't have hap-pened. I had four pounds, sixty-three pence for the next three weeks; there wasn't even a fast food joint in town that I could camp out behind. The amount of money I owed Kurt was almost two pay-checks from the car wash.

It felt like everything in my life was held together with string. It would take half an hour to walk to Ellison and I wanted to be there *right now* but I wasn't, I was so far away I wasn't even in view of my goal, and the hunger finally did it. Just one stupid-faced sob, then another, weaker one, no tears, and it was done. It did not make me feel any better or get me any closer to Ellison, so I resumed walking.

Cedric had told me his trick for running long distances: break it up into shorter distances. He'd pick something close, a tree, a house, an intersection, and focus on reaching that goal. When he made it that far he'd pick something else. His method got me down the long straight stretch of Cotterly Road, past the elementary school and the cookie cut-ter row of houses, around the curve with the train tracks that I loved to pass over in Kurt's car, past the little shops in Ellison common, around the back of the Ellison dining hall and up the path to the dorms.

I would go up to Kurt's room and tell him that I couldn't pay him back until I got home to the States, and we would have tea. That would be one thing set right. It would be hard to break it to him, but I could imagine the feeling of relief I would have once I was on the other side of it. The meal that night was chicken. The stairs took me past Albert's room on the first floor. There were no sounds coming through the door. I hadn't seen him at all since I'd found out. It had been two days.

Kurt was leaving his room as I reached his floor. Rachael was putting on makeup in his mirror.

"Ready to go?" Kurt asked me.

"I thought I was going to pass out from hunger on my way back from the library."

Cedric was looking at me and lurching with his head like he had something to tell me. I didn't meet his eyes.

"I decided that I'm going to catch the next flight home I can get," I said to Kurt. "I can't take it anymore."

"What's the matter?" Kurt asked. Dark Ray showed up. He was without Albert, meaning that he wouldn't talk to anyone.

"I just can't take being broke all the time. I can't go out, I'm always hungry. I've got to get out of here."

"What ever happened to that third loan you promised you'd get?"

"It fell through."

He was hot on the trail of my words. "Fell through? What does that mean?"

"It means I'm not going to get it. Which reminds me, I'm going to have to mail you that money I owe you once I get home. I'm just not going to have it before I leave." Done.

"Could you not ask your parents for the money? I need money too, Jake."

"I'll pay you back, Kurt. Don't worry. My parents are not an option, though." He folded his arms in front of his chest. "I'm sorry to leave you hanging like this."

"Don't worry? I know what happens now. You go home and I never see the money again. I should have seen this coming. I've been screwed by my friends before."

"What?"

He unfolded his arms and dropped his right hand to his side. He pointed at me with his left forefinger. "You could come up with the money somehow. Have you not heard of a job?"

"I haven't got a work permit for this country, Kurt."

"I'll just bet."

"I…Are you calling me a liar?"

His right hand folded into a quivering fist by his side. I'd never noticed how big the veins in his arms were before. The things he was saying were coming out quickly and articulately like he'd talked it all out previously. Rachael was standing next to him, turned away from me, looking at his face. His cheeks were red.

"You know, I would have like to go trotting around Europe for my Easter break, but I was working ten hour days instead. I knew this was going to happen."

Albert came out of his room and started climbing the stairs behind me.

My voice started to match the pitch and volume of Kurt's. "Listen, I'm not going to screw you, Kurt. I don't know what your other friends might have done to you, but I'm going to pay you back."

"Is everyone going to tea soon?" Albert asked Dark Ray. He had made it past me and onto the landing. Lucky.

"Yeah right. I should have known this was going to happen."

"I don't know what else to tell you Kurt. I can't help it if you won't believe me. I don't like to be called a liar. I thought that we were friends. I guess not." I turned around and started back down the stairs.

"I guess we both found something out."

It filled me with fire. I heard Rachael's voice, but I couldn't make out the words. I left Kurt's hall and walked the remainder of the hill to mine. Some of the lads were about, but I ignored them and went straight to my room.

I replayed the scene in my mind and thought of the things I should have said. I was filled with pre-fight adrenaline. Okay, so maybe I shouldn't have tried to talk to him with such a large audience.

I'd have to wait for tea, because I couldn't go to the dining hall with Kurt there. Albert would be there too, protected. If I allowed them half an hour then it would be the time when Tabi usually went. If I allowed her half an hour, say forty minutes to leave a margin of safety, then I could get there just before they stopped serving. The feeling in my stomach wasn't hunger anymore.

I sat down at my desk and took out the draft of my *Hamlet* paper and my copy of the play. I closed my eyes tightly so that I was seeing lightning behind the lids, rubbed my forehead, and when I opened my eyes the *Hamlet* paper was still there, still needing to be finished before the exam. So I started working on it where I'd left off at the library.

I went to the sink to get a glass of water just to have something to put in my stomach, and I saw myself in the mirror. I took off my tee shirt and looked for any muscle I still had left and flexed it. I retracted to the wall behind me and approached the mirror again, watching myself. *Can you do it?* I asked myself, and did it again: approach, retract. Approach, retract.

I had planned on waking up early to edit the paper before going to the exam, but I couldn't get myself out of bed until it was time to leave. On the sidewalk outside the examination room there were a lot of discarded cigarettes which had hardly been smoked, the detritus of nervous students with only enough time for one drag before an exam. I coveted all of that good tobacco, but I didn't want anyone to see me picking it up.

The exam lasted two hours. I'd read most of the plays that the questions referenced, and those I hadn't read I'd attended the lectures on. I left feeling like I had probably passed the exam. When I realized that I'd never have to go to the class again, I started to really feel like my year in England was almost over. I forgot about collecting the cigarettes until I had walked halfway back to the dorms. When I reached Ellison I approached the dorms the back way to avoid running into any of my friends.

The telephone operator had a northern English accent so thick it could have stopped a bus. "I have a collect call from the UK from Jake Archer, will you accept the charges?"

"Say yes, Julie," I interjected.

"I'll accept the charges."

"Go ahead, dear," the operator signed off.

"Jacob? How's it going, honey?"

"Julie, Julie, Julie," I answered. "You go first."

"Uh oh. That doesn't sound good. Do you need me to come there and kick some butt for you?"

I exhaled something like a laugh. "Actually, I might need that."

"What's the matter, Jake?"

"Nothing that about a thousand dollars wouldn't fix."

"A thousand? That's a pretty tall order. I tell you what. I bet if you tell Dad that you can cure me of lesbianism, he'd pony up twice that much.

"I knew that'd get you to laugh."

"How's Pamela?"

"Pamela? She's wonderful."

"I like the sound of that. How's living with each other? Everything it's cracked up to be?"

"You know. It's got its ups and its downs. So far more ups than downs. How's your love life? Find someone with a sexy accent yet?"

I exhaled the sound again. "Well, that there's another subject I'd rather drop. Let's just say it hasn't been a good week."

"Jake, Jake, Jake. Listen. Is there anything I can do for you? Seriously."

"Yeah. There's one thing. Can you just tell me that you love me? That'd be nice to hear."

"Oh Jake. Of course I love you, honey. I love you, dear, sweet Jake."

"Thanks, sis. I've spent enough of your long distance bill, I'd better let you go. I'll be home in a few weeks."

"You'd better come see me as soon as you're back. Jake, you don't have to talk about it if you don't want to, but whatever it is, I know you'll get through it. You always do, somehow. Sometimes you even surprise me. All right?"

Back in my room I rehearsed the fight again. We'd sparred a few times at the gym, and he wasn't as quick as I was, and he didn't know how to handle a combination of high and low punches. He was so strong, though. He had better lungs than I had, too. I'd better try to knock the wind out of him right away.

First I'd tell him that I didn't like to be slandered in front of all our friends. And that he'd get his money back. After all the time we'd been friends, didn't he have more faith in me? Every time I went over the words in my mind it ended in a fight.

There was a knock on my door at tea time. A flood of prepared reactions washed through my mind as I anticipated whom I would find, but it was Cedric.

"Come on in. Visiting the enemy camp?"

"So this is what your room looks like."

I sat at my desk, and he sat on the edge of my bed with his elbows on his knees. He was starting to put on a bit of meat on his arms.

"Still going to the gym, aren't you. It shows."

"Isn't this the time you normally go to tea?"

"I was going to wait a while so that I don't run into everybody who hates me."

"Um, why do you say that? That is, nobody hates you, Jake. And, um." He closed his eyes and shook his head back and forth. "I'm trying to stop saying 'um' before every sentence. Bear with me. If you mean Kurt, he's already gone and come back."

"Then let's go." I was glad he'd thought of me. It's pretty bad when you have to eat alone at the end of the semester. We walked to the dining hall together, and when we got our trays, I steered him over to a table. "Here. This way we have a good view of that table," I said, nodding to a table full of girls.

"Well actually, there was something I wanted to ask you about. Do you remember that girl I mentioned to you? The one from your birth-day party?"

"Erin. The one you fancy."

"Well, sort of. I mean, she's the one I meant. Anyhow. So I saw her down at the pub with her friends the other night. With some other girls from your hall and such." He was speaking in a rush. "And so I started talking to her again."

I gave him a look to let him know that I was still listening, but he was stuck. "I'm with you. Go on."

He looked at his hands. "And anyway to make a long story short, I sort of, like, sort of, asked her out on a date and she said that she does-n't like me that way." He looked away from his hands and into my eyes, and when he did his cheeks boiled to a red color. Tears were poised on his eyelids.

"Hey, hey, ho, ho. You did good, kid."

"But she doesn't like me." His lower lip curled up under his upper teeth, and he coughed it back out. One tear got free. I didn't think any-one around us saw it.

"Hey, you're looking at this the wrong way. This is a triumph. Asking her was the hardest part. You're more than halfway there."

He swiped away the moisture. "Sorry."

I disregarded it. "It's the guy who hears the most 'no's that hears the most 'yes's. I couldn't even count the number of times I've been shot down. If a guy with my ugly mug can get a girlfriend then you're going to have no problem, mate. Confidence is the key. If it wasn't hard to do it wouldn't be worth doing, right?"

"I suppose."

"Damn straight I'm right. This is Erin's loss. She just missed her chance to be with a great guy. Don't let anything make you forget that. You're right where I was when I was your age. Just think, in a couple of years you could be just like me. Lucky, lucky you."

He laughed at me, but it worked. I had broken his blues.

When I was about eight years old, Dad took me to the backyard and taught me how to hit a baseball. He told me to concentrate on my stance, and on my grip on the bat, and on keeping my eye on the ball, and on judging the pitch, and I'd try to hold it all together in my mind, but I still couldn't hit the ball. If I started to get frustrated, he'd say, "If it wasn't hard to do, it wouldn't be worth doing."

My father had prepared me better than I had given him credit for. The only way to pay him back was to be the best man I could be. The issue Cedric was contending with was every bit as imposing within the context of his life as any of my problems were within mine. Cedric did not possess the currency necessary for paying me back for my father's advice, but the act paid for itself. Cedric looked up to me like I was a wise and beneficent friend. You give and you take. Sometimes it's the same thing.

The meal that night was fish and chips, and it was pretty good.

"You know a whole lot about relationships, don't you."

"I wouldn't go that far. I know a thing or two about a thing or two. I don't know anything that you won't figure out on your own." I was tempted to accept his compliment, but someday he'd realize that I was just a guy who had a little more experience than he did. I didn't want him look back and remember me as being arrogant. Is that why, Joe?

"Besides, if I knew so much about relationships, my best friend wouldn't hate me right now."

"Nobody hates you, Jake. I just think, I mean, um, it isn't my place to really say anything, but. But Kurt was talking to Rachael, and, well, um…"

"You're doing the um thing again."

"Oh right." He laughed it off and concentrated on not doing it. It distracted him from realizing that I was using him as an informant. I knew what I was doing.

"Well, he seems to think that you always treat him like he's stupid." When he got the words out, a nervous laugh escaped with them.

"I never treat him like he's stupid."

"Well, um, I, um, that is…"

"Okay, okay, forget it. I won't put you in the middle." I finished eating and sat there with the plate for a while. This was the time I would usually spend joking around with Kurt, before going back to my room and getting ready to go down to the pub to see her.

There were a couple of days until my next exam. There was one more the day after that one, and the last one, Victorian literature, the following Monday. The assessment period lasted another week after that, and I had the option of staying at the dorm through the end of it. I wasn't planning on it. I had to get home.

It was quiet in my dorm during assessment period. In the evening I could hear every scuff from every foot along the hall. Finally I heard the sound of steps come up the stairs to my floor and travel down the hallway to my door. I answered the knock and let Tabi in.

She turned off the ceiling light leaving only the desk lamp on, because my room was always too bright for her. I sat on the bed. She stood with her toes just inside the gap between my feet.

"So, do you hate me now?"

"No, Tabi. I don't hate you."

"Find yourself a new girl yet? Get back with Camilla?"

"No." Sort of a laugh. "I think I'm going to be alone for a while."

"I heard you had some trouble with Kurt."

"Yeah. We had a falling out." She took out her cigarettes and gave one to me without asking. I lit us up with my Zippo.

"Are you all right?"

"I'm fine. What about you?"

"You've lost a lot of weight. I'm really worried about you."

I shrugged my shoulders. "I'll be okay. I'm out of money, so I'm not eating right. I just need to get home, that's all."

"Do you want me to loan you some money?"

"No, thank you. That's the last thing I need. That's what happened between Kurt and I. I owe him money."

We each took a drag of our cigarettes. She had a really pretty way of French inhaling. Enough time passed.

"So will you take me back?" she asked me. She stepped closer.

"Why do you want to be with me again?"

"Because you're good in bed. Because I miss you. Because I love you."

"Why'd you do it?"

"Why'd I…"

"Albert."

"Please don't ask me about that. I feel bad enough about it already. I told you, it was something that never should have happened. It wasn't…Please don't do this. I made a mistake. It'll never happen again, just believe me, okay?"

"So you think I should just forget about the whole thing? You sleeping with my friend?"

"Jacob. Please." It was making her face look lined and pained. It made me feel bad to see her that way. I took another drag of my cigarette. Tabi was wearing red.

"Okay. I'll take you back."

"Do you mean it?"

"I mean it." She hugged me, burning me a little on the back of my neck with the cigarette, but that was okay. "Every night since you broke up with me," I said into her hair, "whenever I heard footsteps coming up the stairs I would hope that it was you, and every time that it wasn't it hurt me."

"I know. Stop it. Just shut up." She pulled away enough to look me in the eye. "Stay just like that."

"Okay."

"Aren't you going to kiss me?"

I corrected the situation. She still smelled the same way, and her lips felt the same, and when I put my hands on her they moved down to hold her hip bones just like before. All of the feelings that I had the very first time I kissed her, all of those feelings were there again. I tried very hard to memorize exactly the way it felt. I kissed her the best I possibly could.

"Will you stay?"

"We have to go to sleep though. I have an exam tomorrow."

"Okay."

"I mean it. Horny bastard."

"Okay."

"Let me just get some things from my room and tell Kay what I'm doing. Otherwise she'll think you kidnapped me."

"Okay. Kiss me again."

She kissed me again and left. I listened to the sound of her feet going down the stairs and out the door, and I kept sitting there on the bed for another minute.

I got up and brushed my teeth. I combed my hair. I got fresh sheets out of my wardrobe. I changed the bed.

I started to worry that she wasn't coming back. My mind built a story about her changing her mind, realizing that she'd made a mistake.

Then her footsteps came back up the stairs, and she walked into my room with her overnight bag and said, "Hello," and it was all right again. She said it in the sweet little way she always did, but it meant something different now. "I brought you some pasta. Keep me company in the kitchen."

I took a chair into the kitchen and watched her boil the water and prepare the pasta. She sat in my lap while she was waiting for the water to boil, and again while she was waiting for the pasta to get tender. She put it in a bowl when it was ready and added some cheese and watched me eat it.

"Do you want to tell me what happened with Kurt?"

I told her about the Bank of Kurt, and how he'd humiliated me in front of everyone.

She told me what she thought I should do about it.

"I know I should," I told her. "You're right."

"You stopped eating. Isn't it good?"

"It's perfect." I ate the rest. "So Cedric's been my best friend through this whole thing. He's really a good kid."

She took the bowl to the sink and started to wash it.

"If I ask you something, will you answer me honestly?"

"Of course I will," she told me. She rinsed the bowl and put it in the drying rack.

"Do you think I treat Kurt like he's stupid?"

"Don't be mad." She sat down in my lap. "Jacob, you treat everyone like they're stupid, myself included. I know how to take you, but not everyone does."

"I don't mean to."

"I know you don't. I just laugh at you when you do it to me," she smiled, "But Kurt might take it to heart. You look tired."

"It's the pasta. I'm not used to having a full stomach."

"Come on then. Let's go to bed."

"You go ahead. I'm going to take care of this right now."

"Now? It can wait until morning, can't it?"

"Now is a good time."

Tabi went ahead to my room. I went down the hall to the phone booth and did what I had to do. It only took a little while. When I was done I went to my room and rinsed my face at the sink, then got into bed with her.

"Are you all right?" she asked me.

"Yeah. Thank you for the pasta."

"You don't have to thank me."

"Thanks for being honest with me about Kurt. It was important to me."

"I know, Jacob. Go to sleep, dear."

"I'm glad you're my girlfriend again."

"Me too. Go to sleep."

We slept facing each other, so that my left shoulder was underneath me. It was uncomfortable, but I would keep it that way so I could face her. She fell asleep before I did, with her little hands in front of her, touching my chest, and her hair on the pillow. My other arm was around her, protective. She came back to me. When I was with her I felt like I was ten feet tall and invulnerable. I felt like I could do anything, even dig a hole in the sun for her.

We woke up before the alarm clock the next day. She opened her eyes right after I did, and we just lay there looking at each other. Sleep and dreams hadn't taken her away. There were three more exams to take. I tried very hard to memorize what she looked like at that moment. Then she got up and went back to her room.

She left me a toaster pastry for breakfast, which I had with instant coffee. It was enough to fill me up. It was easier to get full; my body wasn't expecting as much. I stayed in my room studying until the afternoon, then got ready to walk into town.

After I was finished at the bank I bought food and a couple of packs of Marlboros. I splurged on a taxi to take me back to Ellison. After I'd put all my food away I walked over to Kurt's hall and knocked on Kurt and Cedric's door.

"Is Kurt around?"

Cedric opened the door all the way, and I saw Kurt sitting at his desk. Rachael was lying on the bed with a notebook opened in front of her. Kurt's face was a locked door.

"What is it?" he asked me.

"Do you think I could talk to you in private?"

"Shall I leave?" Rachael asked.

Kurt's face was caught between reactions.

"Why don't we step outside?"

Kurt agreed to this and stepped away from his desk, smiling nervously. I caught Rachael stealing a glance at my face when she thought I wasn't looking. I led the way downstairs and out into the sun. Some of the lads from my block were lying out on the lawn, ignoring their books. I handed Kurt the envelope.

"This is the money I owe you. Plus a little extra. Consider it interest for the loan."

He peeked inside the envelope long enough to see the notes. He kept it in his hands instead of pocketing it right away, like he wasn't certain it was his yet. "How'd you get it? If you don't mind my asking. Did you rob some little old ladies or something?" Kurt grinned.

I didn't laugh yet. "I took your advice and asked my dad."

"Really? I know you two aren't getting along too well."

"I just don't want you to think that I was lying when I said that my parents weren't an option. I really didn't think that Dad would agree to it, but he surprised me. We had a good talk. This actually ended up improving my relationship with my father."

"I believe you."

"There's a couple of things I need to say to you."

"What's that?" He shifted reluctantly from elation to concern.

"First I need to thank you for lending me all that money—"

"Oh hell, you don't have to thank me, Jake." He patted my right shoulder.

"No, I do. You've always been a gentleman about it. You're best friend I've got in this country, and I felt bad when I thought that I ruined our friendship. If I had the chance to do it all over, I wouldn't borrow the money from you."

"Nonsense." He was smiling widely, and I could see he was ready to friends again. "If you ever need anything, then what's mine is yours. That hasn't changed. That's what mates are for, right?"

"Well, there's one last thing that I need to get off of my chest." He corralled his high spirits. "Remember when we had the argument? When I first told you that I couldn't pay you back right away?"

"Yes. That was a bad time, wasn't it?"

"What I wanted to say is that I didn't think it was right of you to slander me like that in front of all of our friends."

"Slander you?"

"In the heat of the argument you inferred that I was trying to rip you off. You said as much in front of everybody, so now I feel like everybody looks at me like some kind of a villain."

"No one thinks that about you, Jake." He cleared his throat. "I don't think that I slandered you, but I'm sorry if I made you feel that way." A complicated series of emotions played over his features. Whatever it was that I was looking for from him must have been there in the mix.

"No, don't be sorry. I'm the one who was wrong. I can't blame you for thinking that I was going to rip you off. I wouldn't ever do that to you, but I can't blame you for thinking it. We were both angry. I just needed to say that out loud to you, that's all."

"You're too complicated for your own good, Jake."

We punched it.

"I feel much better now," he beamed. "That was horrible. It was hard staying mad at you. Tell you what. We should celebrate with a weed. Have you any left?"

"I'm smoked dry."

"Likewise. Well we deserve a celebration. Let's take a drive to see Mouse Boy and pick up a brick." He led us back up the stairs. I felt welcome in his block again.

"I'll go with you, but I'll pass on the weed. I'm still broke."

"Never mind. This one's on me."

"Kurt, after all we've been through the last thing I'm going to do is owe you more money."

"This is a present."

"Absolutely not. I mean it."

"Well at least come along with me and give me the chance to talk you into it."

When we went back to the room it was obvious that we'd made up. Kurt left to go to the loo.

"Did I hear that you and Tabi are back together?" Rachael asked me.

I hadn't meant to let Cedric know just then. "She took me back," I smiled. "So are you still my friend?"

"Come outside and have a fag with me." She got up and opened the balcony door, and we lit up our cigarettes. "I never stopped being your friend. It was a strange couple of days, though, wasn't it?"

I didn't have a better way of putting it, so we changed the subject.

This is how I got the money:

I called my father at the office the night Tabi and I made up. It's seven hours earlier on the East Coast than in Harlan, so I knew that he would still be at the office. There was no telling what kind of mood he would be in at the end of a workday.

"Son, how's everything?" It came out softly. He was tired.

"Not so good, Dad. I'm in a bit of trouble."

"What's the matter, son?"

I took a deep breath. I was still holding it together. I hadn't brought a cigarette with me to the phone.

"I borrowed some money from a friend, and now he wants it all back. I don't have anything to give him. He's convinced all our friends that I'm going to skip the country and screw him."

He put on his business voice. "How much money is it?"

I told him the figure. "And I still owe the school some money too. If I don't pay them, they won't give me my credits."

"How much do you owe the school?"

I told him the figure.

"That's not so bad. When are you coming home?"

I told him the date. "I can't afford a plane ticket."

He wasn't done yet, but he paused, calculating. "Okay, forget about the school for now. An organization like that can live without your money until you're ready to pay them. They'll send you your credits later. Now. How long can this friend wait for his money?" He enunciated "this friend" hostilely.

"I really ought to pay him back right away." My words sounded weak to me.

"Tell this friend to relax. He'll get his money. And don't worry about the plane ticket. I'll have your mother send it to you. Where do you want me to wire the money to?"

"I'm sorry about all this, Dad. I know that you didn't want to have to send me more money."

"Have I ever not come through for you when you needed it?"

Right then was when I stopped holding it all together. "I just...I feel like I'm letting you *down*, Dad."

"It's okay. I know, son."

"I wanted to show you I could do this, and now I'm borrowing money from you again."

"It's okay. I know, son."

"I don't want you to think of me as a failure, Dad."

"Listen. I know you care about what your old man thinks about you. What's important to you right now is that you finish school. Don't worry about all that other stuff, okay? You've come this far; don't give up when you're so close. I don't think you're a failure, Jake." I could hear that it was hard for him to say it, although I didn't know why. We worked out the details of the wire while I wiped my face and pulled myself back together.

Kurt drove us into Harlan the usual way.

"Bumpies," he purred, right on schedule.

"Confession for you."

"Go on."

"Did you think we'd end up getting in a fistfight over this?"

"The thought crossed my mind," he grinned.

"I was actually kind of looking forward to it. I've wondered since the day we met which one of us could take the other one. It would have been an incredible fight."

"Of course I'd kick your ass."

"Sounds like an interesting dream. What happened when you woke up?"

Kurt only bought a couple of grams off of Mouse Boy. He wanted to buy a bigger brick and tried to talk me into taking half, but I wouldn't let him. When the transaction was complete Mouse Boy rolled up a joint from his personal stash, and I watched the two of them share it.

Back in Ellison I went to Kurt's room for a study session. Kurt was having a hash-induced fit of fastidiousness on his side of the room. At one point I heard Kurt's stereo click on and off many times in rapid succession. I looked up and saw that he was wiping the dust off of the stereo's remote control while it was pointed at the stereo. I held down the urge to make a joke about it at his expense. It was a really good joke, too.

The last time I saw Albert he was sitting at the table in Kurt's hallway. I knocked on Kurt's door to see if he was ready for tea, and he told me that he'd be right out. The only other place to sit was the chair across the table from Albert.

"Hello Jacob. I haven't seen you in a while."

"Isn't that strange."

"Are you going home soon?"

"I'm leaving Monday. You?"

"I haven't decided yet."

"Oh." *Why do you ask; so you can try to get at Tabi again?* I thought. *Albert, do you have something you want to tell me?*

"He takes forever to get ready for tea," he said.

That's nice, but don't we have something to discuss?

"Do you have any exams left?" he asked me. He smiled the smile of fear. I told him that I had one left. I asked him if he had any to take. He had three left, and two of them were on the same day. He didn't think he was going to pass one of them, but he was beyond caring, he said. There was a long lull in the conversation when I could have said something. I left it alone. So, he was attracted to the woman I loved. I knew that she was attractive. So, he took advantage of the weakness in our relationship.

She told me that he was awful at it. Even considering the drunkenness, she said it was pathetic. I didn't want to hear about it, but if I had to, at least that was what she had to tell. It was a shitty little victory, but I would take it.

When Kurt came out of the room I caught sight of Cedric sitting on the edge of his bed next to someone I knew. They were sitting closely.

"Did you see that Cedric has himself a woman?" Kurt cackled as we walked down the stairs. "I know her from somewhere, but I can't quite place her."

"That's Christine. Tabi's best friend."

"They couldn't get me out of the room fast enough. In a hurry to make out again, I reckon. Like they were when I got home. Cedric!" He was laughing. "I can't believe it."

"I can."

Kay took the train home for the weekend, so I stayed at Tabi's. Victorian Literature was the only exam I had left to take. Christine came by for a study break Saturday afternoon, and I was all over her.

"Well, hello temptress."

"Leave my friend alone, Jacob," I was instructed.

"She knows I'm only kidding her. I approve. Cedric's a great guy."

"Well of course he's a great guy," she retorted. "He likes *me*, doesn't he? Obviously he's got great taste."

"Oh my," I answered.

"I just feel bad for my other special man," she continued. "I hope he doesn't do something desperate now that he knows he's lost me."

"Oh God. Listen to this. She gets one boyfriend and now she thinks she's the hottest girl in town."

"Well, now that you've set me straight, I think I'll go back to my room and finish studying," she joked. "See you later Tabs."

"Don't leave, Christine," Tabi told her. "Oh Jacob, look what you did," she scolded. Christine closed the door behind her. "You really hurt her feelings." She was still using her scolding tone.

"She's just playing. She knows I'm just kidding her. Hell, I introduced the two of them."

"Jacob! Jacob...Jacob." She enunciated my name differently each time, like a car gearing down. I was lying on her bed, and she sat down next to me and looked me in the eye. "She's my best friend. You really hurt her feelings."

"I did?"

"Remember what happened with Kurt."

"Do you really think I hurt her feelings?"

"I think you ought to apologize to her."

"Okay."

"You have to pay attention to a girl's feelings, Jacob."

"I know."

"I'm going to go get her. You be nice to her."

Tabi left the room. It was another unannounced left turn. I felt nervous while I was alone waiting for them. She came right back in with Christine, and they sat together on Kay's bed.

"Just opened my book," Christine was saying, "And you go and interrupt me. If I do poorly on this exam it'll be your fault." Against the backdrop of Tabi's insight I could see that she was putting up a front.

"Jacob has something to say to you."

"Well get it over with, I haven't got all day." She didn't look at me until after she had started the sentence.

"I'm sorry if what I said hurt your feelings." The words pained the back of my throat, like they just barely fit.

"Oh is that all? Never mind."

"He's not finished yet." Tabi pressed her arm down to stop her from leaving. My voice sounded very young.

"I really owe you an apology. I didn't mean what I said." She was looking at me. I forced myself not to look away. Obnoxious things kept jumping into my head to say to her, and I batted them down. "Sometimes I say mean things to people to try to be funny. I hurt other people so they won't hurt me first. I really think you're great, and that Cedric's a lucky guy. I'm sorry."

"You *were* mean to me." It hurt me to hear it, but part of the apology was to allow her that opportunity. "But it's alright, Jacob. I still love you."

"Isn't he sweet, when he tries?" Tabi said.

Christine was leaving. "When he tries very, very hard."

When she was gone again, Tabi sat down next to me on the bed.

"You did so good," she chided me.

"I feel like such an ass."

"Stop it. You're not an ass. You're the man I love."

"You're taming me." I pulled her across my body and down onto the bed, so that she was between the wall and myself. We made our little adjustments so that our bodies were puzzled together. The sun came in through the sliding glass door along with the breeze.

"So tell me about your brother," I said.

She looked at me from up close. "Okay," she answered, and she did.

Sunday night instead of studying I packed up everything in my room while she watched me. Packing is a lousy job, and it took a lot of cigarettes. When I was done the room had a bit of an echo in it. It was the same echo it had had the first day of school, and I had forgotten about it until I heard it again.

"Going to study for your Victorian Literature class now?"

"No. It's too late now. Let's just go to bed."

"Our last night together," she said. It was in a voice she hardly ever used.

"Don't," I said. "Not yet. I don't want to miss you yet. Be here with me now."

"When did you get so smart?" she asked, as if I knew what I was talking about.

"If I was so smart, I wouldn't have that stupid thing written at the top of my cork board. If they charge me for that, I'm going to send you the bill."

"I'll take care of it."

"You'd better."

There was some more talking.

Then we didn't say anything for a long time.

And then there was an argument. She asked me why I had cheated on her with Camilla, I countered with Albert, and it got very bad. She told me that she was sorry, that it was just because it was our last night together, and it was done. We were on the other side of it and it was all better again, and I thought, *At least this one wasn't my fault as well.*

There were some other things,

And then we were together in a way where there is nothing else in the world and you notice every detail like you would in an emergency, and we said things to each other while we reached for it, reached for it, reached.

After the quiet time, she said, "So what do you think will happen with us when you go home?"

I lit us each a cigarette.

"What do I think will happen? I think I'll cry on the plane back. The nights at home will be bad for a while. We'll write each other a lot of letters. Maybe a phone call or two, maybe we'll plan on a visit.

"Then our lives will take over, and one of us will meet someone. Some great guy will come along and you'll fall in love with him and forget about me."

It was easy to say it. For some reason it was as if I was talking about two other people, some characters in a movie or something. Maybe it was like that because it was half-three in the morning.

"So one day you'll forget about me."

It made me very angry. "I didn't say that. I will *never* forget about you. You will *always* be with me." I said it with perfect certainty. "Don't ever make that mistake again. You will never be forgotten." It was the right thing to say. I knew it in the way that sometimes you just know things.

After a while the light came in through the sliding glass door. It was almost the time I'd set my alarm for. I shut it off.

"You'll be in rough shape at your exam."

"I'm not going. I would have failed it anyway."

She fell asleep in my arms. There was a very bad feeling that I almost let out, but I put it away for later. I fell asleep too.

I woke up again at the time when the exam ended.

I took a shower and brushed my teeth and did some last minute things. I went to Alex's room and said goodbye to the lads, and when I came back she was awake.

"I thought you'd left me."

"I'm still here."

"I have to go back to my room. We're taking the cab together to the train station, right?"

"Yes."

"Make sure you come to my room first."

"I will."

Well, I could make up the credits lost from Victorian Literature somehow. I had some bread, some milk, and some cereal left, so I made myself a meal and ate it in my room. After I bathed I packed my towels, razor, and toothbrush. I took one thing out of my big duffel bag, then tied the bag closed again. With everything packed I felt like I was already travelling. The plane tickets, which had arrived days ago in the post as promised, were in my jacket pocket.

I left the room unlocked with all of my possessions in it and walked to the housing office to drop off my key. I walked back up the path and journeyed up the stairs to Kurt and Cedric's room.

"Beautiful weather we got today," Kurt observed. He'd just gotten back from an exam.

"Summer's almost here," Rachael added.

"Happens every year," I quipped.

We talked generically like that while the goodbye squatted heavily in the room with us. Then Cedric stood up and said, "I've got to go to my Statistics exam now."

I stood up, approached him, and offered him my hand. We shook. "I hope I see you later. Thanks for everything."

"Don't know that I did everything. Um, before you go, there was one thing I wanted to ask you to show me. There's something I wanted you to teach me, that you do, that I think looks cool."

"What is it?"

"I was wondering if you would show me how to smoke a cigarette. I haven't decided if I'm going to be a smoker or not, but I thought, like, that it looks kind of cool when you do it, and—"

"I tell you what. I'll do you an even better favor. I *refuse* to teach you how to smoke a cigarette. In fact, I forbid you to smoke a cigarette. If I find out that you've been smoking I will come back here and kick your ass."

He thought about it. "Okay. Thanks, I suppose."

"It's the least I could do. That's the kind of friend I am; one who does the least for you that he can do."

We shook hands again. As he was walking away I said, "And Cedric, remember."

"Um, remember what?"

"Just remember. Everything. In general."

Then Cedric left the room.

When I looked at Kurt and Rachael we all felt that the goodbye had already begun.

"I'll definitely see you later," I said to Kurt. He stood up and we did our ritual handshake.

"You'd better believe it. I'll miss you, Jake."

"I'll miss you too. I'm glad I met you, Kurt." I reached for him and gave him a hug.

"Oh, this is sad," I heard Rachael say. When Kurt and I let go, I looked at her. She was standing close behind me.

I looked into her naughty eyes.

"Goodbye Rachael. Thanks for being my friend. I'm going to miss you."

"You'd better write me," she said as I stepped closer. I put my left arm over her shoulder and around her upper back, and my right arm down around her lower back. She wrapped both arms around me and held me back. Our bodies were pressed together from waist to neck, and she was warm.

You were the only one I didn't mess up with, I hugged. *I could have told him a story to prove that I was trustworthy, one that you were in, but I didn't.* Aloud I said, "You two are my favorite couple ever. I expect an invitation to the wedding."

"Oh Jake," she said, but I think she knew what I meant.

We all said some more sloppy things, and then I had to go. I said goodbye, walked to the door, looked back at them one time, standing together, said goodbye again, then left. On the other side of the door was the incongruously mundane task of walking the twelve stairs down to the first floor.

I went and got Tabi at her dorm.

"Did you call the taxi yet?"

"Not yet. I was waiting for you to say goodbye to your friends."

"The whole idea was that you would call the taxi while I was doing that."

"You should have been more specific," she yelled. "I'm sorry. This is just making me a little bit emotional, okay? I can't help it." We walked down to the lobby where the phone was.

"Okay. At least you're telling me. You waited until my last day in the country to start warning me when you're in a bad mood? This is irony."

"I'll call the taxi. Just go away. No, don't." She grabbed my arm.

"Call the taxi and meet me in the parking lot. I have to get my luggage." I kissed her and went back to my hall.

It wasn't my room anymore. It was an empty room with my luggage in it. The mark of my occupation was her handwriting on the corkboard. I could finally laugh at it. The feeling that I was in motion, travelling, was almost physical now.

I lugged the duffel bag and the rucksack down the stairs and around the corner to the parking lot. I worried over the taxi. I could see all the way to the front door of her dorm. She came out, and I watched her cross over the path and cut across the lawn to where I was standing. She had changed her clothes. She was wearing the little white dress.

"I'm not going to wait for the train with you."

"Please?"

"I can't do it. I'll say goodbye to you there and take the taxi back. I can't do it."

The taxi came. The driver introduced himself as Nicholas but didn't help me put my things into the trunk. We both got in the back seat.

"You are an American, right?" he asked me.

"No, I'm Swedish. I make great meatballs."

"I knew you were an American. I have friends in Seattle. Bob and Audrey Hawthorne."

"Fascinating." Tabi and I were holding hands. She was holding me very tightly. My hand was getting tired.

"Going home then? Taking the train to the airport?"

"You mean I can't take the train all the way there? Tabi, why didn't you tell me I'd need a plane."

"Oh shut up, Jacob," she smiled.

When we arrived at the station we all got out of the car, and this time the driver helped me with the luggage. Then we were all standing there in front of the station with my luggage, so Tabi reached her hand out to me for a handshake.

"Well, so long and thanks for all the great sex."

Nicholas almost said something, but I said, "Walk with me to the platform. Then you can go."

I paid off the driver and picked up my things. She had a cigarette going. We walked to the platform and I bought a ticket for London while she called for another taxi.

"That driver was awful," I complained to her. "I thought he'd never shut up. Can't he see that we're trying to have a romantic moment here?"

"Oh leave him alone, Jacob. He was just trying to be nice."

She took a drag off of the cigarette.

"Give me that," I said, and took a drag too. We stood there facing each other, smoking it. I didn't want to stop looking at her.

"Do you really think we'll stop writing each other after a while?" she asked me. "Did you mean that?"

"No. I'll keep writing you."

"For how long?"

"Until we're together again."

She pitched the cigarette onto the tracks. "You're just saying that."

I asked her to light me another cigarette.

"I don't mind, though," she said. "It's what I want to hear. See, I trained you well."

"You just behave until I come back for you. If I hear that you're even in the same room with Albert, I'll fly back and give you the spanking your mother should have given you a long time ago."

I still thought that Tabi's English accent was the sexiest thing, even as she said "You *bastard*," to me one last time.

A taxi pulled up before my train arrived. She jogged over to it to find out if it was hers, then walked back.

"This is it," she said.

"Come here."

We hugged each other until I heard her crying.

"I promised myself that I wasn't going to do this," she said. "I've got to go."

"I have something for you." I reached into my pocket and pulled out a plastic bag. Inside of it were the things I had taken out of my luggage. "Don't open it until you get home."

"What is it? A pair of white socks?" She started to open the bag.

"It's a surprise. Don't look until you get back. I mean it." I knew she wouldn't wait that long.

"You got me something. That was so sweet. I didn't get you anything. I win." She smiled at me. "I'd better go before I get emotional again. Call me when the plane lands."

"I'll try. Tabi. I love you."

"Stop it. I love you too. Stop now. Good-…Talk to you soon."

I watched her walk back to the taxi. I tried to notice everything I could about her as she moved. When she got to the car she looked at me and waved, and mouthed some words. I mouthed them back.

As the car started to move I saw her look up from the open bag and laugh. She looked at me and said something, but I couldn't tell what. I pointed down to try to get her to look into the bag again, to make sure she got everything, but the taxi took her away.

The train wouldn't arrive for ten more minutes. Then there was a three-hour train ride, then time in the airport, then a long flight. I had much ahead of me. More people were coming out to wait on the platform.

I found myself narrating a conversation to Cedric in my mind, thinking of all the things I should have said to him, that I could have taught him. "When you're looking for a relationship, always be more afraid of selling yourself short than you are of being rejected." That was a good one. Maybe I would write that to him. I hoped he would learn it on his own. It's a hard concept to put into play when someone is so attractive they intimidate you.

"Just think about all of the tasks you've ever approached that appeared so daunting before you completed them, but looked so simple once you were on the other side." And all of the people you were so daunted by, so afraid to approach because they seemed so amazing, turned out to be so average once you got them into your life.

But not you, Tabi. You only got better.

Inside of the bag? A pair of my white socks. If she hadn't guessed it I could have gotten the last laugh. When she looked in the bag again she would also find my Zippo lighter. Take good care of it, Tabi. You've got to admire stuff like that. Stuff that lasts forever.

Edward Austin Staples
2/21/1999

ABOUT THE AUTHOR

Edward Staples was born 11/12/1970 in Rochester, NY, in the same hospital his mother was born in, though much later. Come to find out, he was born *exactly* one year *to the day* of his grandfather's death-you don't think that messed with his head? After that there were several non-productive years consisting mainly of doing nothing but eating, sleeping, reading comic books, and being a general source of worry for his hapless parents. They never asked for all this. Skip ahead to 1988, when he began attending the University of Massachusetts at Amherst, where he majored in English, with a concentration in creative writing. He attended the University of Hull, England on exchange his senior year. Yes, he did a lot of drugs, just like the main character. No, he doesn't do them anymore. Later he would also attend Clark University in Worcester, Massachusetts. His parents were no longer paying his way at this point, so we now move on to the career portion of our program. He has been a liquor store clerk, a commission salesman, a telephone customer service representative, an exotic dancer, and a web master. I made the dancer part up. Pay attention! His outside interests include computer programming, comic books, and competitive weight lifting. He would be happy to talk comics with you for hours at a time. The weight lifting thing is obviously an attempt to compensate for massive insecurities. *Digging a Hole in the Sun* is his first novel. The author would like to thank you for reading it, and he hopes you enjoyed it. Feedback is welcomed. Please remember to wash your hands.